WILL CHASE
THE SIOUX LANDS

Based on a True Story by

ROBERT PRIMEAUX, PHD

Will Chase: The Sioux Lands
Copyright ©2021 Robert Primeaux, PhD. All Rights Reserved

In consulatation with Elders of the Hunkpapa, Oglala, and Rosebud
Sioux Tribes

Published by:
Trine Day LLC
PO Box 577
Walterville, OR 97489
1-800-556-2012
www.TrineDay.com
trineday@icloud.com

Library of Congress Control Number: 2021940093

Primeaux, Robert,
Will Chase: The Sioux Lands—1st ed.
p. cm.
Epub (ISBN-13) 978-1-63424-344-5
Print (ISBN-13) 978-1-63424-343-8
1. Fiction. I. Title

First Edition
10 9 8 7 6 5 4 3 2 1

Printed in the USA
Distribution to the Trade by:
Independent Publishers Group (IPG)
814 North Franklin Street
Chicago, Illinois 60610
312.337.0747
www.ipgbook.com

This book is dedicated to:

My Dad and Mom: Arthur Roger Primeaux and Mary Harrsion Primeaux, Both of whom kept the American Indian Culture Alive in me.

My little brother Richard Arthur Primeaux, who died when I was in Vietnam 1970.

Especially to my wife: Dawn M. Primeaux, who helps me stand tall.

All members of the Standing Rock, Rosebud and Pine Ridge Sioux Tribes.

Gary Busey, My Big Brother who always was there for me.

Carol and Jim Demberg who helped me with these books.

My brothers, whom I served with in Vietnam in 1969-1970.

Delta Troop, 2nd/17th Cavalry, 101st Airborne Division

John "Spider" Oakley

Mike Fitzmaurice, Medal of Honor Recipient

Major General Raymond "Fred" Rees, Ret

Lt Col. Jon Jones, Ret

Lt Col. Blair Craig, Ret.

Lt. Col. Steven Rausch, Ret

Command Sergeant Major Jerry Trew, Ret

Paul Kremer

Judge Joe Vukovich, Ret

Robert "Mike" Lafever

And the rest of my buddies in my squad, platoon and all of Delta Troop who give me courage to keep moving forward.

And, the men of Delta Troop who paid the ultimate sacrifice in Vietnam.

To the family of Willie Burnette, my heartfelt gratitude.

THANK YOU!!!

Author's Notes:

Over a period of six years, seven Elders of the Sioux Nation told the author of the legend and history within the Sioux Nation of a man, half white and half Lakota (Sioux), so the Elders and this author committed this legend to paper.

There were nine manuscripts written, but tragically, all but two manuscripts were lost to a house fire on the Rosebud Sioux Indian Reservation in South Dakota in 1983.

These books are the story of the Sioux Legend, Will Chase.

The Elders

1) **Isaac Dog Eagle**: Eldest Great Grandson of Sitting Bull, Hunkpapa Lakota from the Standing Rock Sioux Indian Reservation.

2) **Joe Walker**: Eldest and only Grandson of Rain in the Face, Hunkpapa Lakota from die Standing Rock Sioux Indian Reservation.

3) **Felix Kidder**: Eldest Great Grandson of Little Soldier, youngest Warrior at the Battle of the Little Big Horn on June 25, 1876. Felix is from the Standing Rock Sioux Indian Reservation.

4) **Baxter Wolf Girts**: Great Grandson of Wolf Guts, saved his village by killing wolves and feeding his village in one of the worst winters in South Dakota history in the 1870's, Baxter is also a descendant of Crazy Horse. Baxter is from the Rosebud Sioux Indian Reservation.

5) **Willie Burnette**: Descendent of Crazy Horse, and a modem warrior from a long line of Warriors in Rosebud Sioux history.

6) **Oliver Red Cloud**: Grandson of the late and great Red Cloud. Oliver is from the Pine Ridge Sioux Indian Reservation.

7) **Robert L. Primeaux**. Ph.D.: Great, Great Grandson of Louis Primeau, interpreter for the Standing Rock Sioux Tribe and also Interpreter for Sitting Bull while Sitting Bull traveled with the Buffalo Bill's Wild West Show.

A special dedication goes to all families of the Elders named above who have passed on since these books were written. Thank you!

Map showing the location

OF THE

INDIAN TRIBES

WITHIN THE

UNITED STATES

Prepared to accompany the Manual of Missions

MAPS OF EVERY DESCRIPTION
PREPARED
and the
Largest Assortment
of ATLASES & MAPS etc.
in the Country at
Colton's Geographical Estabt.
G.W.& C.B. Colton & Co.
NEW YORK.

Scale 1/5,000,000.

STATUTE MILES
0   100   200   300   400

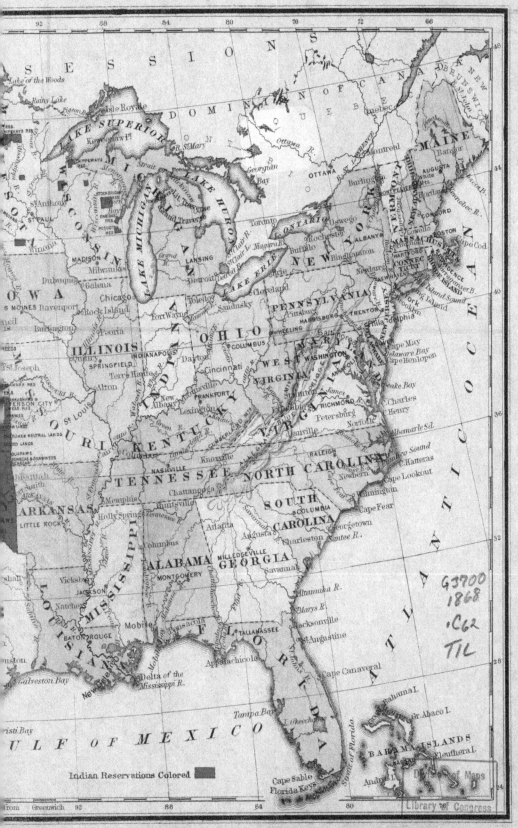

1868

Contents

Introduction

The year was 1840, the spring morning was fresh but had a good crisp feeling in the air, Jacob Chase was pacing around the teepee, because SunBird his wife was inside giving birth.

It was a difficult birth, the first baby was out but the second son got tangled in the umbilical cord and was strangled to death. Outside, Jacob was visiting with Buffalo Hump, while pacing. Buffalo Hump said, "Look over west." Jacob looked and saw a lone coyote chasing an injured Hawk. Jacob looked at Buffalo Hump and said, "That is the name of my son. Chasing Hawk!" Jacob was deeply saddened by the death of the other son.

Jacob goes inside the teepee to comfort SunBird and says to her, "We will not be sad over the death of our son, but. Chasing Hawk will live the lives of two men, he will be half white, but he will be all Sioux," SunBird looks at her husband with much love and respect and agrees with him. Then Jacob again looks to his wife, "Chasing Hawk will also learn the ways of the White Man, because I feel that will be the only way our people will survive in the future, for in the White World he will be called Will Chase after my father." SunBird feels that her husband has made a wise choice for their half-breed son. Because they know his life will be hard and he has to be hard and be ready for all the challenges that will confront him as he grows up.

Chasing Hawk grew quickly, he was light skinned with sandy hair, a half-breed by blood, but as his father said of him at his birth, he was all Sioux. When Chasing Hawk lived through 16 winters, his father sent him east to be educated. He went to school in Baltimore, Maryland and lived with relatives of his father. After finishing high school, he then attended Princeton University in New Jersey. But, after 12 years in the East and finishing with a Law degree from Princeton he longed to be with his Mother's people.

So, he caught the first train west upon graduation. He left his many friends in Baltimore and Washington where he had been studying Law while working on his degree from Princeton. After 10 years of living with the Sioux and his woman Swan, they go back East to see how it has changed since the war is over.

The year is 1875 and Will Chase is now very rich because of the gold he has found with help from the Sioux. Will and Swan are visiting friends who he went to school with. They are sitting together on the porch and look at each other

The story in Will's own words:

Chapter One

Chasin' Hawk

It was fall an' the trees were beautiful in their many colors. After settin' awhile she said, "At home all would be on the hunt now."

I grunted.

"Do you miss it," she asked?

"Very much Swan. I miss the Gap and all that country and the people. Do you?" I asked.

"Yes," she said. "Here comes the Browns, they are early Will."

I was still wearin' my buckskins as was Swan, she was in a doeskin beaded dress. It was too late to change now.

I met them at the gate an' helped Mrs. Brown step down, she turned as Veldon came around the buggy. He introduced his son Chester, his daughter Loraine, she was beautiful but cold. Chester was a big good-lookin' young man, about twenty four or five. He was smilin' and forward.

The women went to the porch. Swan was there to greet them. Veldon said, "Chester is huntin' a horse Will, let's go and show him your stock or we will never get to talk."

We walked out to the barn, Chester in the lead, eagerness in every step. Veldon was tellin' me of Chester havin' finished his law schoolin', comin' here to start a practice with the firm of Welk, Burges an' Welk.

Hank led out four horses, they were brushed to a shine. Slim was behind him with a matched pair of gray buggy-horses. I introduced them to Chester, they already knew Veldon.

"Chester is huntin' him a ridin' horse," I said. "See if you horse traders can sell him one he likes."

A smile came on both men's faces and the tradin' was on.

Veldon an' I walked toward the house, had coffee with the ladies. Loraine asked how I liked the civilized world here in the East. Before I could answer, she asked, what business I was in out West?

"I have a couple tradin' posts ma'm, also run a few cattle and horses."

On the second cup of coffee, Chester rode up to the front gate ridin' a stockin' legged sorrel horse, "What do you think Dad," he called.

"You're the one who's to ride him," he answered.

Loraine said, "He's beautiful Chester."

Chester rode back towards the barn, I knew the horse was the best one on the place, and would come high!

The ladies excused themselves, goin' into the house.

Veldon immediately turned to the problem I was facin'. "There is a man called Felter who is spendin' a lot of money tryin' to get the Act through Congress. He is campaignin', offerin' to buy a small tract of the Hills himself, at a high price, even tho' it hasn't been surveyed."

"How can he do this?" I asked.

"Well it's a show of good faith on his part. He's got some friends who will also do the same. Each has offered to pay three dollars an' acre for a thousand acres of land. They will go there now and start their ranches, pay up when it's been plotted an' surveyed. They are puttin' up the money now in good faith."

I started in on him then, "I know this man Felter. He was Army. He's killed white people as well as Indians. He kidnaped an' killed a young lady I was thinkin' of marryin'. I tracked them, found her body, Felter had shot her in the head after a horse fell on her an' broke her arm an' leg."

Veldon looked at me in shocked surprise. "Will Chasing do you realize what you are sayin'? Do you have any proof?"

"Not with me but her father, Henry Long has a note signed by him statin' this."

"Are you sure?"

"Yes, I read it myself."

"We better go talk to someone of authority about this. This would have a lot to do with the decision that Congress is goin' to make later on."

"We can tell no one, promise, at this time." He did.

"Morgan Fairchild is the one we need to see. He has a lot of pull in Congress. Felter is playin' up to him also. Lester Walters is a Senator who is against takin' the Black Hills from the Indians."

"I know both of them," I said. "I have talked with them about the Hills that the government wants for farmers. I have talked of how the Indians can live because they hunt for their food an' move around with the seasons. If they let people move in there to farm, it won't work."

Swan came out an' asked if there was anything we needed? I asked for some whiskey an' glasses. She seen the frown on my face an' knew there was something wrong.

"Mr. Brown do you think it would be possible for me to buy the land also?"

"Why yes," he said. "If they let him an' his friends do that, then it would be okay for anyone to do it."

"Could you set up a meetin' with yourself, Fairchild, Walters and myself to see what the chances are of stoppin' the take over of the Black Hills."

I poured us a drink while he was thinkin'. He was workin' it out in his mind. "It could be done at my house, I'll talk with Margret an' see when it can be set up."

We had our drink an' sat watchin' Chester ridin' his new horse. He came back to the gate. "Father is it okay if I leave you, I'd like to ride with these men. I'll be home early."

Veldon just waved an' Chester was gone.

"He will be wiser about horse tradin' when he returns," I told him. Veldon just smiled.

We had another drink, the women came out, Veldon joined them. Swan an' I walked them to their buggy. We waved as they drove away.

"I'm goin' to miss lunch," I said. Goin' into the house with her on my arm, I turned and kissed her.

When I changed into my clothes for town, I put on my thirty-two Ivory Johnson. I wore it on my left side, to be drawn with my right hand. Hank had shown me how he wore his. We had practiced together. I had become quite fast an' was dead accurate.

I reached into the vest pocket an' the ring from the outlaws in Fort Laramie was there. I looked at it for awhile, put it back into my pocket and went downstairs.

Swan was waitin' at the bottom of the stairs, she looked lovely in her beaded dress. I stopped an' took the ring an' put it in her hand. She looked from it to me, a question in her eyes.

"It is the white man's way for you to wear this. We haven't had the weddin' but they don't know."

She stood awhile, then handed it back to me, "I know," she said.

I kissed her cheek an' left, puttin' the ring back in my vest pocket.

I rode to the Fairchild Inn, sat at a table in the bar side. Almost all the men were well dressed, talkin' in a language hard for me to understand. They talked of prices of products from overseas, how there was investments to be made. The stock market, they talked of many things. I sat an' listened to it all.

The stock market was confusin' to me but interestin'.

I made up my mind to go look one day at the Stock House as they called it.

A young man came over an' introduced himself. I asked him to join me in a drink. We talked of many things, his name was Fredrick Goodnight. He had heard I was a Western man, was curious of the West. His uncle was in Texas, had land an' cattle. He was drivin' cattle to Kansas to the railhead, shippin' East. It seemed he was doin' rather well.

As I rode home that night I was pleased to have met Fred Goodnight.

A week later I had been to the Stock House with Fred. He had showed me how it worked in a small way. He had bought corn, two hours later he sold, had made one hundred fifty dollars. On the way home he said it was good at times, other times you lost. Six years ago, he had seen many men go broke. Some had taken their own lives, some had come back, others were still broke.

"If you are thinkin' of investin', land is better for it's always there. If the goin' gets bad, you can always live on it," he said.

A stop at the Fairchild Inn for a drink was enjoyable. A message was waitin' at the house when I got there. It was from Veldon Brown, the meetin' was set for the followin' week.

Chester was with Hank an' Slim when they came in, there was laughter, Chester was enjoyin' bein' around these two men.

"Say Will, I made my first horse trade today. I bought a team this morning, made eighty dollars on them two hours later," he was smilin'.

Swan brought us a drink, she was also smilin'. She liked this happy young man as well as the rest of us did.

We sat at the table on the porch an' I asked Chester if he would be interested in doin' some legal work for me.

"Sure," he said, "What do you have in mind?"

"I'm interested in some land here. I was thinkin' of buyin' a small farm or place with a nice stream an' meadows. Been thinkin' of raisin' some horses, some thoroughbreds."

By the first of the year, he had bought me almost two thousand acres along a nice creek of fast runnin' water. There were many meadows, trees on the hillsides. The land bein' put in Hank an' Slims names for business reasons.

Three places with houses and barns, the rest of the land undeveloped. It had cost twelve dollars an acre.

Slim an' Hank had traded for some older thoroughbred mares that were due to foal, we were in the business.

Felter was really pumpin' the men in Congress to open up the Black Hills for homesteaders.

The last of January Mr. Fairchild came to the house for supper. Later over brandy, he came right to the point. "Mr. Chasing, exactly what is your interest in the West? Mr. Felter's talkin' the very opposite of what you are."

"He was stationed out there, says it's beautiful country. Perfect for farmin', small ranches. The Indians could be easily talked into settlin' on a reservation with us to feed them."

I had a large glass of whiskey, finished it an' poured another for both of us.

"Mr. Fairchild, if I told you the whole story in complete honesty would you give me your word of honor to keep it in the strictest confidence?"

"By all means young man."

"You sure?"

"Yes, on my honor"

Checkin' my watch, I said, "In about ten minutes Veldon Brown and Lester Walters will meet us here. I took the liberty of arrangin' this beforehand."

"The reason is simple to me, I'm gettin' nothin' done at blockin' the bill for settlers to move into the Black Hills. In about thirty days I'm goin' back, it must be stopped here."

Brown and Walters joined us in the parlor. Swan brought more brandy an' joined us. I started with. "Gentlemen, I have asked Swan to join us. Feel free to ask her any questions you might have. I ask that you not judge either of us before you hear the complete story."

Swan rose an' poured their glasses full of brandy.

I, sippin' mine, started to talk. "My name is Will Chase, my father was Jacob Chase, now dead five-an'-a-half years. I run a tradin' post in Fort Laramie with Howard Jensen. I own the one in Buffalo Gap by myself. I have helped the Sioux people as my father had. For years we were happy without the whites. Some trappers passed through but never bothered us. They traded an' trapped an' lived with us. The Fort was built, called Fort Laramie. We traded with them as well as Scottsbluff. We sold horses to the cavalry an' picked up our supplies there.

"Cattle started comin' into our country around Laramie, stolen from the south and sold to a man named Birtchfield. Gold showed up now an' then. We traded for it an' bought our supplies from a man named Hatcher with it. He started bankin' some in St. Louis for my father, then me. Captain Felter seen some of this gold. He was convinced it was comin' from the Black Hills. He sent men up into our hills to hunt it. Some were killed after they had killed our braves an' took the women. Leavin' the little ones to starve in the Hills. The white men who returned were without gold.

"Felter still wasn't satisfied to leave us alone. He escorted a wagon train into our land. We stopped them, made them leave their guns an' shells, go back to the trail west. Again Felter was not satisfied, he sent out two hundred fifty cavalry to our country to cause more trouble."

I stopped an' had a drink. "Am I borin' you gentlemen?"

All three said, "No, please continue."

At this point I have gotten ahead of myself so I must back up. "There is a chief named Buffalo Hump who has traded with my father for years. He's east of the Black Hills, two full

days ridin'. Together they set up a magnificent horse opera-
tion. The Indians lived good and we made money. Birtchfield
moved cattle in there. His men stole the cattle from a man
named LaMonte of Texas. His men raped some girls pickin'
berries. All the men of Birtchfields were killed.

"Three men from the LaMonte ranch who had brought up
cattle, holed up in a box canyon for three months. The Indians fed them but made sure they stayed in that canyon.
Word was sent to me, I sent word back to 'let them go.' The
men came to me with the story of the cattle.

"The Indians put all the cattle off their range. Two of the
men went to Texas, talked to LaMonte, came back, sayin', 'sell
me the cattle.' I had the Indians gather the unbranded ones.
I registered the Sioux a brand, they now have an interest in
cattle. They have meat when all the buffalo are killed off.

"At this point, I met Swan. We have been together ever
since. Back to the two hundred fifty men."

"Wait," Swan said, rose an' filled our glasses again.

"Are you gentlemen sure you want me to go on with this?"

Again all said, "Yes."

"Let me back up a little again. Some of the braves, seein'
the white man pushin' for our land, advised me to arm an'
train them to fight, the white man's way. This I did.

"Now, the two hundred fifty men, they went to the basin
of Buffalo Hump, tried to run him out of his home. My father
had taught Buffalo Hump new ways to fight. He was way
too much for the cavalry. Fifty or so cavalry were killed, one
Indian died an' five wounded.

"The braves from the Gap showed up now, remember we
are better armed, mounted, trained an' far tougher than the
white men. I was sent for again. By the time I got there the
cavalry had lost all but ten of their horses, had been forced to
hold up. Again I talked them into leavin' their guns an' shells.
The Sioux escorted them afoot to Scottsbluff. Killin' game for
them, givin' them horses for their wounded.

"Felter got a warrant for my arrest. Word came to me of a
hearin' in Scottsbluff, we went. Captain Bush told me Felter
had been busted for his many blunders against the Sioux, that
I'd have 'my say also.'

"It wasn't that way, in fifteen minutes, I was guilty, sentenced to prison in Texas. As they were takin' me away. Swan shot an' killed four guards, also shot one of the generals. We started for the Hills, I changed my mind, we returned.

"With the help of six of my braves we stole the horses. Swan an' I walked into the saloon, shot all three generals. On the way out I shot another soldier. We got away with all the horses from the cavalry.

"There was one more incident with the soldiers. I'm not sure how many I killed but first I gave them the opportunity to walk home. Because I was alone they thought they could take me, they failed.

"Felter kidnapped an' shot a beautiful girl, whose father works for me. He thought she knew of gold in the Hills, she didn't but he used her, then shot her. Swan an' I got eleven of his men, he escaped an' came here."

We sat for what seemed a long time before anyone said anything. Walters spoke first.

"We all have heard an' read about the great 'Will Chase.' He has thousands of Indians, they outnumber the cavalry a hundred-to-one."

I rose an' refilled their glasses as well as poured one large one for Swan.

Fairchild raised his glass to Swan in a toast, they drank. "Will Chase, are you tellin' me this sweet gentle woman has rode beside you an' killed three or four men at a time."

"If it wasn't for this woman. I'd not be here today. In our last battle I was shot, badly wounded, she alone fought off twelve soldiers, killin' how many I don't know. Alone gettin' me seventy miles, eludin' two hundred or more cavalry, goin' into Kansas not knowin' if I would live or die, but knowin' if I lived I would help our people."

Walters asked if I was "still wanted out West."

"Yes sir, I'm wanted right here. I'd be hung within a week if any of you were to turn me in.

"If you can't stop the new bill from passin' then you will open up the greatest blood bath for both sides ever known to man. My men are so trained an' armed, we can whip ten thousand soldiers. Your war is just among yourselves. You don't have that many to spare."

They talked with Swan an' I for about an hour. I told them if they could do nothin' to stop Felter from gettin' the bill passed I would go back, get my people ready. I'd rather they took care of it here.

"If you decide to tell others of this, of Swan an' I, we will have to fight there, our way. We are gentle people wantin' to be left alone as our people do."

They all thanked Swan for the fine brandy and me, for tellin' the story of our country.

After they were gone, we stood awhile together, she asked, "Will they help us?"

"I hope so, they are but three people!"

CHAPTER TWO

Fool's Gold

The next day Chester was at the house, so I took all three men into the parlor. Swan poured brandy an' then sat down. I started with sayin', "Chester how much a year would it cost me to hire you full time?"

He sat, thought for awhile, then said, "I'm not too happy with the position I have right now, it's payin' four thousand a year, borin' as hell, what do you have in mind?"

"I want to break a man, his greed, a bad man, he has others kill for him. For your service I'll pay ten thousand a year. You must be crafty, take care of all the legal ends."

"Hell man, when do I start," he asked?

"You just did, this might get a bit fast; if you want out okay. I must have your word of silence until I'm finished."

"You got it Will Chase."

"The land you have bought is in the names of Turner an' Walker as we agreed, is that correct?"

"Yes sir."

I now had Slim an' Hank's full attention. Swan was also on the edge of her seat.

"I want you to get to know Felter, know who's into the land buyin' deal with him, how much money they have, each and all the people who will invest with him. You must win his confidence, get to know him well, pretend to be his friend, be in awe of him, flatter him."

"I can manage that, I already know him some, he's interested in my sister."

This stopped me cold. "I did not know this Chester, if this poses a family problem I can find another to do this, it will just take longer."

"No, no," he said. "Loraine is not interested in him, father is some upset with her seein' him."

"Chester if you go ahead with us, you can't mention this in your house, to anyone, your father, mother or sister." He was excited more by the mystery now than the money. This was good I thought, also on the good side was his interest in the Indians an' the West.

"Do you want to know the straight of what's goin' to happen or not," I asked.

He thought a minute, then said, "No, maybe later." He left so excited he was bouncin'.

Hank an' Slim sat back down after walkin' to the door with him. Swan was smilin', that evil smile. Hank an' Slim were on the edge of askin' for they knew I had a plan they would like.

I had another sip of whiskey an' started, "Here it is, I'm goin' to break Felter, here's how.

"I want you fellows to find two old timers that knew the West, like as they knew it, open an' free. I don't know if we can level with them or not at this time. We need to be sure of them first."

Hank said, "I know three already, they all stay together, talk of the past. They'd spot a few horse trades for us."

By dark they all three had moved to one of the houses we had. It was far better than the shack they had been livin' in. They had agreed to help Hank an' Slim with the horses for a small wage.

Slim had mentioned some beavers in the stream. They were excited about this.

That evenin' at supper we went over the plan to salt the stream with gold. The old timers could use the money they made findin' it. Word would get out – we'd see to that. The land would be worth a fortune, all Hank an' Slim had to do was get Chester to let Felter in on this.

I had brought ten pounds of gold with me. After we salted the stream with a couple pounds, we still had a reserve to resalt if necessary.

A week later the old timers had found three nuggets, with the help of their new bosses. They were workin' the stream hard, pannin' a little gold here an' there.

One day, settin' in the Fairchild Inn, I heard the word whispered about gold, the next day it was talked openly about.

Goodnight came to me with a story he had heard about three men comin' into the First State Bank nearly every day sellin' gold but they would tell no one where it came from.

A week later Chester came to the house, was very excited about gold bein' found in the stream he had bought for me.

"William do you know what that land is worth?" he asked.

"No Chester, it's now time for you to let your sister, or you, get the word to Felter. Look what I have," I said, layin' out three nuggets the size of fat peas. "If they come up with a few more I'm goin' to have a necklace made of them for Swan."

Chester had never seen raw gold, he was fascinated an' sat starin' at them. "May I take these home with me," he asked. "Felter is comin' for dinner tonight. I'd like to show these to my father also."

"Chester," I said, "Whatever you do don't mention my name; another thing, Felter must not know Turner an' Walker are in any way connected to me. Felter knows me on sight, would turn me in so fast, I'd never have a chance."

He scraped the three nuggets in his handkerchief an' headed for home. After dinner, over wine, he laid them out on the table in front of his father. They shimmered an' shinned. He told the story of buyin' the land for two stockman from Missouri, how their hired men had found gold on it.

Felter turned the three nuggets in his palm, his eyes showed greed and lust. "Do you think these men Turner an' Walker would sell that little parcel of land?" he asked.

"No, I'm sure they have plans for minin' the land. They have two thousand acres of it. This biggest nugget is the best so far. They seem to have a plan to bring in someone they know from St. Louis to look it over – develop it for them."

"Is there any more land on that same stream for sale?" Felter asked, his mind and eye for gold was tellin' him this gold hadn't rolled an' been washed for.

After the evenin' was over and he was ready to leave, he caught Chester alone an' said, "Chester I have some money I'd like to invest in land on that same stream. Could you handle it for me?"

"Yes," Chester said. "I'm sure I can but it's goin' to be quite high now that the people know there's gold in that stream."

"What do you call high," Felter asked.

"I talked to the man right below them an' he was talkin' two hundred an acre. He wants to sell all one hundred acres at once, not just the stream."

"Come by my office in the mornin' Chester, I'll have the money for you. I'd also like you to buy more of this raw gold from the men who have found it. I need to examine it closer so I can tell about how far it has traveled."

The next mornin' Chester was at Felter's office. Pickin' up the money. Later that day he was back with two ounces of dust and two large nuggets.

Felter was wild with greed, people were rushin' to the stream, payin' the people to let them pan for gold on their land. It was mushroomin' into a gold rush.

Turner an' Walker Livestock Co. ran an ad in the paper, warnin' that trespassers would be arrested.

Chester bought another twenty thousand dollars worth of land for Felter.

Hank an' Slim were celebrities in the town. Things were given to them by nearly everyone. They were now livin' in one of their houses. Guards were hired to protect the stream an' surroundin' hills.

A man had came an' verified this was a major strike, he had found nuggets himself. Land was changin' hands so fast the land office couldn't keep up.

That night three men had a fight over buyin' a farmers land down stream. One was killed, another wounded and one arrested.

Hank an' Slim hired more guards. There was shootin' that night all up an' down the stream. The army was moved in.

Felter came into Chester's office, he was out of breath, in a terrible hurry to talk. "Mr. Brown, I'm settin' up a corporation to buy Turner an' Walker out. There will be four of us. Can you get Turner an' Walker to come in an' talk with us?"

"Yes, I'm sure I can but they have men workin', it's hard to catch them. Maybe if I see them tonight, I can get them to meet with us tomorrow some time."

Chester came to our house that night. We had finished supper when he rode in. I had never seen him so happy an' excited. He started talkin' the minute he walked in. He had four men who wanted to buy out Hank an' Slim.

He was talkin' about what a great find they had made, what a great buy the land had been. He never seen so much money change hands.

"Chester, stop," I said. He rattled on. I walked over to him, put my hand on his shoulder, shook him a little, sayin', "Stop man, an' set down."

He looked at me, went an' sat down.

Swan poured brandy for all of us. When she was seated, I asked him to tell me, "Who wanted to buy the stream."

He started to rattle again but I stopped him.

"Have a drink Chester, have two drinks." We finished our drinks an' Swan rose an' poured again. When she was seated I said, "Go ahead now slowly."

"Felter has three other men goin' in with him, they are interested in gold. I'm sure they are the same three men who was goin' with him through the government to buy the land in the Black Hills. I'm to make up contracts, they are goin' to buy out the Livestock Company lock, stock an' barrel. Felter as much as said at any price. He had two men go to work for Hank an' Slim, both of them have found gold an' reported to Felter. They now know for sure about how much gold they can mine there." He started on again.

"Seven pounds," I said.

He paid no attention, went on to tell me what they figured by the ton, then he stopped an' looked at me.

I was sippin' my drink, lookin' at him.

He gulped his down, stared at me, then looked at Swan.

"I want you to go ahead with everything as planned by Felter. Hank an' Slim will be in your office at exactly one o'clock. They will ask five hundred thousand in cash. When your men balk they will lay out the biggest gold nugget you will ever see, the deal will be made, the papers will be signed at the bank. If they can't come up with that much cash, have them put their homes an' businesses up for the rest. Tie up everything they have so they can't use it again for collateral."

Chester sat lookin' at me, "Seven pounds," he said, "Don't tell me how you know." He raised his glass to Swan and I, "Seven pounds," he said again.

I would have loved to have been there, for later that night while talkin' the deal over with Hank an' Slim they nearly busted laughin'. I gave them the huge nugget Swan had found in the Black Hills.

Slim said that the sight of a nugget this size would "cause a preacher to throw out his sick mother."

At exactly one o'clock Hank an' Slim walked into Chester's office. They were introduced to the four men, Felter, Hinkel, Lestergood an' Moore. Moore was narrow eyed an' mean lookin' though very well dressed.

They asked many questions about the gold. Finally Moore asked the price of the two thousand acres.

Hank an' Slim asked if these men wanted "to buy a percentage or what?"

"No," they wanted it all, "You boys pick up your clothes and leave today," Moore said.

Hank said," I ain't leavin' my four old mares, they go with me as well as my two saddle horses."

"Hell, you can keep all the horses," Felter said. "We don't want them. Now how much?"

"Five hundred thousand," Hank said.

The four men looked from one to the other, half-a-million dollars was a staggerin' sum.

Lestergood said, "Why gentlemen, that's outrageous, you don't even know if the gold will stay good and strong."

"Maybe we don't but we blasted one spot this mornin', look what came out of this little blast." He dug into his pocket, his hand dumped out about fifteen pea sized nuggets. One shaped long an' narrow. Anyone could tell it had come from a crack in the rock. The four men were lookin', movin' them around, gold shinin' in their eyes as well as greed.

"We are prepared to go as high as three hundred thousand," Lestergood said. Felter gave him a sideways glance, this was higher than they had agreed before the two got there.

Well Slim said, "I guess were wastin' our time here. We have to watch them hired men awful close, if they can pick it up like we do, they can steal it also."

Hank pulled out the big nugget, laid it on the table, "They don't have to walk off with many of these to make it count."

One of the men choked, the other three gasped at the size of the nugget.

Hank swept up the smaller nuggets first, dropped them into his pocket. As he reached for the big one Felter said, "Wait." Everyone's eyes were glued to it, the sun was hittin' the nugget, it seemed to grow as it shined. The men looked at each other then nodded their heads.

All seven men went to the bank. Chester made all the arrangements. Two hundred fifty thousand cash, the rest was the homes an' farms of all four men, this two hundred thousand was to be paid in one year in cash to the bearer of this contract. It was in two papers, both must be presented at the same time. In case it could not be paid all homes an' farms on the contract were to be turned over to the bearer.

All shook hands after the signin'. The vice-president signed, put his stamp on them, handed one to Hank, one to Slim.

The money was put into a carpet bag, the pair walked from the bank. Swan an' I sat on our horses across the street, an' would follow the men to the house. Chester was comin' too.

At the house we calmly had a drink. Swan passed out a cigar to each of us. When everyone was seated she poured all a drink, stood an' raised her glass, "To Will Chase, To the Sioux," we all toasted. As Swan poured the next round the room turned into an uproar of laughter.

After some sanity came back to the five of us, we started gettin' serious. At first all were talkin' at once.

It came around to my turn, to say what was to happen next.

"Here are your tickets to St. Louis." I said, countin' out five thousand to each man. They looked at me. "Your horses an' clothes are now at the station, the train leaves here at five o'clock. We'll make sure you're on it. You have about thirty days before all hell is goin' to break out here, maybe sayin' thirty days is too much, let's say twenty to be safe. In time they will know what has happened, you sure don't want to be here."

I counted out ten thousand for Chester, handin' it to him sayin', "Chester we need you out in Kansas City in about thirty days or less. Slim an' Hank are goin' to be there. They will rent a house in the country, like we have here. You keep a low profile, open a law firm, handle small cases until I get there. We need a Livestock Company there as well as a Tradin' post Company, buyin' supplies to ship West. You get that setup in the Turner an' Walker names.

"The Livestock Company, put your name in. You like to trade, you do good at it. We need also to rent pasture, quite a bit of land, say two hundred acres."

Chester was excited about it. "Loraine an' I have friends in Kansas City, I'm sure she will want to come with me, would that be alright?"

I thought about this a few minutes. Swan poured another drink. "Yes Chester, that would be fine, even better."

I counted out another twenty thousand, handed it to Hank, "Men this will get us a start in livestock. Bank with the same bank as I do business with. Buy some Hereford cows, a couple of good bulls, get the makin' of a good herd, to take west later on.

"Contact the man at the bank, tell him I'll be there shortly. Leave your address with him for me. Now you men drink up, get to the station and load up your horses."

All stood, shook hands. Hank an' Slim gave Swan a hug an' were gone.

Chester headed for home also, many things to do.

CHAPTER THREE

Kansas City

A week later I heard the first rumor about the gold. Fredrick Goodnight walked in, I motioned for him to join me. We had our drinks in our hand when he toasted me sayin', "To land, to gold, to greed."

We looked at each other, he started laughin'. He laughed so long an' loud everyone was lookin' at us. He finally got back to normal. We sat there smilin', had our drinks an' ordered another.

"That was the sweetest deal I've ever heard," Fred said.

I looked at him, calmly said, "I have no idea what you are talkin' about."

"Okay," he said, "Just wanted you to know, I admire anyone who could get to them four greedy bastards. Felter was a nice one, to take in. He's a real crook.

"He is also a killer of a woman in the west, Alice, she was very special to me."

"Fred, what will they do when they know for sure?"

"They will hunt you three down, try to get their money back. You have everything they own tied up. If they don't find gold, they're bankrupt!"

"Greed does that to a man," I said.

Swan had everything we needed ready to go, we were plannin' on leavin' at five the next day.

"Let's drive over and see the Browns this evenin', Swan. We can take our baggage to the station on the way." All our clothes were packed in five bags, these I loaded in the buggy. The money was all packed in the bottom, some in each bag. I kept five thousand. Swan had three. Mine was in a money belt, I had no idea where hers was.

We checked our bags in at the station an' drove to the Browns. They were all settin' on their porch havin' wine, we joined them.

We talked about the things that were happenin' around Washington. Veldon mentioned that four men who had put up money for the land rights in the Black Hills had came an' got their money back. Felter had been the first to get his back, three thousand. It looked like the Settlers Act was shot down, at least for two more years.

Chester an' Loraine were goin' on the same train.

As we started to the house, Swan took my arm, smiled at me, "We have succeeded for awhile Will Chase. It will be good to go home."

We put up the horses, walked to the house. It was dark, outside as well as inside. We opened the door, went in, I struck a match, as it flared I seen the house was a shambles. I droped the match an' shoved Swan behind the door.

I could hear movement from two different directions. I squeesed Swan's hand, moved over behind the couch.

Three shots came from the kitchen door, a single shot answered from behind the door where Swan was. There was a thud from the kitchen. I hadn't known Swan was packin' a gun but knowin' her she was always ready.

I heard footsteps retreatin' out the side door, later horses leavin'. I struck another match an' lit the lamp. The house was a mess, it had been searched thoroughly, every room. We picked up the clothes, then hung them up for tomarrow.

Swan looked at me an' smiled, that evil smile. In the kitchen lay a dead man. We took him outside. Later settin' in the front room with a small fire goin', havin' brandy, I put my arm around Swan, asked if she would miss this way of life. "No," she answered.

We seated ourselves, I settin' by the window. Just as the train was leavin' I saw two men I knew standin' on the platform. Moore an' Felter, they never returned my wave.

We had met the Browns at the station. Loraine had piles of luggage, had been worried about every piece. I had paid a man to take care of the horse an' buggy for a year. Said I'd "be back before then."

Loraine and Swan started talkin' of Kansas City, "Chester an' I were talkin' of the West, of the many opportunities that lay ahead."

We were about an hour on the rails when Chester suggested a drink in the smokin' car. We had to pass our sleepin' berth, I said I'd "get a cigar."

When I opened the door it bumped someone, I shoved it hard, he fell back on the bed. Before he could rise I had smashed his face three times, he went limp. I reached out an' pulled Chester into the tiny room.

"My God, you nearly killed him," Chester said. A knife was in his hand, I took it and tested the blade, it was sharp. I opened the window as wide as possible, then propped the man up. "What are you goin' to do Will?"

"Put him out the window," I said.

"Damn man, he may get hurt."

"He wasn't playin' when he came in here to rob me, nor when he pulled his knife. He was probably with the ones that tried to rob us last night. They shot at us. Swan killed his partner."

The man was comin' around, I hit him in the face again, cut off his right ear, shoved him out the window. He bounced an' flopped. The last I seen he was settin' up holdin' his head, the train turned, he was gone. I threw out his ear.

When I turned around Chester was settin' on the bed, he was very pale.

"My God! My God! You have marked him for life, you cut off his ear!"

"That way I'll always know him," I said, closin' the bag he had opened, then the window an' gettin' my cigars.

"Let's go get that drink," I said.

Chester went with me but he didn't have a drink, he was still sick.

We got into Kansas City four days later. Damn what a trip, it seemed like we'd been on the train forever.

As their bags were bein' unloaded Swan an' I got ours loaded into a carriage, then sat waitin' for them. When they finally got loaded we led the way to a good hotel. A man came an' helped carry our bags. We got rooms an' retired to change for lunch. I sent a message to the banker. I would like to have a meetin' with him at one o'clock if that would be okay.

We had an early lunch an' went to the bank. The ladies stayed at the hotel. I walked up to the guard an' asked to see Mr. Morecroft. We were shown into an office where a secretary said "Mr. Morecroft will see you shortly." She was lookin' at Chester, a smile on her face. They chatted while I waited. In a few minutes Mr. Morecroft came in.

We shook hands, I introduced him to Chester Brown. "He's my lawyer from Washington."

We went into his office, I sat the carpet bag on his desk. He looked at me with a question on his face.

"I had a very successful winter," I said, "Even got the Settlers Act blocked. Now I'd like to open some accounts with you, also have you hold some papers for me.

"I'd like fifty thousand in my account," I said as I emptied the carpet bag onto his desk.

"One moment," he said. "I'll get the secretary to come in to help count the money, also fill out the deposit slips."

She was impressed with the amount of money but very business-like about the countin'.

"Another fifty thousand in an account for Turner an' Walker Freightin' Company." We counted out that amount. "There will be three of us drawin' on this account. Slim Turner, Hank Walker an' myself. You have all our hand writin'.

"Forty thousand for Turner, Walker an' Brown Livestock Company. Mr Brown will give you his signature. Hank Walker has already left twenty thousand for this account.

"Fifty thousand to the Sioux Tribe. Henry Long, Swan or myself may sign for this account. I'll get their signatures for you. I can get Swan's here tomorrow. Henry Long's will take a while. I have his hand on an envelope if that will do, it is at the hotel. I'll bring it tomorrow also."

"That will do fine until he can give us a check or draft with his writin' on it," Mr. Morecroft said. "There is twelve thousand left, what account do you wish it in?"

"Put it in a company that we'll call Sioux Land Development. All of us can sign for it."

Chester filled out his card an' signed it. He opened an account for himself an' a thousand dollar one for his sister. He would bring her card back tomorrow. He then filed the papers, had it so any two of us could get them out.

Mr. Morecroft said, "Lets have a drink now gentlemen," as he brought out the whiskey an' glasses.

We all had our glass of whiskey, the secretary passed us the drinks but remained.

Mr. Morecroft looked at me an' smiled. "Veldon Brown wrote me, said you had gotten the bill turned down but never mentioned the fact that you had swung such a deal. You must tell me about it."

"Someday I will sir. Now the Indians have a chance for a couple more years of peace, I hope."

Morecroft said, "I have sent out some feelers about gettin' you off the wanted list. I'm gettin' a little hope from the army. You have a man out West that hates you badly. His name is Birtchfield."

"Will you dine with us tonight, Mr. Morecroft?

"I'd be delighted to," he said.

Chester asked the young lady to be his guest also.

He got her address, said he would send a carriage for her at seven o'clock. At the door he stopped, turned back, "Young lady, I'm sorry I never got your name."

"It's Dory Humphrey, I'll see you at seven."

When we returned to the hotel Hank an' Slim were settin' in the lobby. Both were in very good spirits, had some good news to tell.

Chester walked into the bar with us but refused a drink. Asked if he could be excused to go upstairs.

"Hell Yes man! Would you tell Swan we are entertainin' tonight at seven please."

He almost bounced with excitement, "Sure thing boss," an' rushed away.

Slim looked at me an' said, "What the hell got into him."

"Dory Humphery," I said.

They both laughted at this.

"Go West young man. Go West," Slim said.

We ordered a bottle and moved to a table. It seemed like a year since we had last seen each other. All three of us started talkin' at the same time. We turned it over to Hank. He told about the farm thay had located an' rented. The man wanted to sell, he was goin' west. They had also rented a large livery stable not too far from here.

It had always been the best in town. The man had died and his family wanted to sell. Hank an' Slim wanted to buy.

We were half way into the bottle when I remembered we had company for the evenin'. "Let's go up to my room," I said. "We better be straight for the banker is comin' to meet us for supper. So is Dory Humphery."

We went up stairs. Swan an' I had a bedroom an' settin' room with a bar. It was five o'clock so we sat an' talked, had more to drink an' smoked cigars.

There was a balcony, we went out an' stood, watchin' the carriages go past, people walkin', others ridin'.

Hank said, "This is where I want to stay. Look at all the horses out there we ain't never owned, look at all the people walkin' that should have a horse to ride."

I told them about the two times someone had tried to kill us. They had better be damn careful for them men were goin' to come lookin'.

Swan an' I were goin' to head home in a few days.

We had a fine dinner with the banker, he got a little drunk, started talkin' about the West an' wantin' to move out there.

After dinner we went upstairs, Loraine joined us for Chester an' Dory went for a drive.

Morecroft, Hank an' Slim got drunk as hell so I walked Loraine to her room. She opened the door as a bellboy came with a message. He handed it to her, I dropped a dime in his hand but he waited. He looked at me an' said, "I'm to take back a message."

Loraine gasped, handed me the note. Chester an' Dory had been taken, we could have them back for two hundred fifty thousand and the papers. She was to give the note to me, I'd send the boy back with a yes or no.

I gave him a dollar an' asked who had given him the note. "Another boy," he was to give my note to him. "Come with me young man." I took Loraine's arm, we went to my room.

Swan was gettin' ready for bed. "Swan get into your buckskins, lay mine out," quickly we changed. Loraine had Hank an' Slim up when I came out of the bedroom.

I told them what was goin' on. "Loraine stay here an' guard the banker, damn well don't let anyone but us in."

Swan was packin' two guns as I was. We each had a knife. I wrote a note for the boy, sayin' "When? Where?"

Swan was already gone. She would watch where they went. I went with the boy. He gave the paper to another boy outside, this boy got in a buggy an' it drove off into the night. I watched a horse ease away from the tie-rail in front of the bar an' follow the buggy.

I went into the bar an' had a drink. The men in there just stared at me. I guess they never seen a man wearin' two guns, a knife an' buckskins in this bar. The bartender recognised me, served me but there was doubt on his face.

I was almost finished with my third drink when Swan walked in. Wearin' her guns, knife an' buckskins, skin tight, an' a head band. She was one hell of a woman, these clothes proved it. The men stared at her as we went out the door.

"They are not far from here," she said. "We can walk." She took me down a side-street eight or ten blocks, then turned left, she hit a run. I had to hurry to keep up. The winter had made me soft. She finally stopped an' I was glad. She took one long breath while I was puffin'.

"They are in there," she said, pointing to a warehouse. "They are both tied in the pile of hides. Four men are still there with them. One took the note an' left with it."

We walked around to the back of the buildin', no way in. On the other side we found a door, it was unlocked. We slipped inside. It was darker in there than outside. A light was comin' from under a door. We moved to it. I could hear them talkin' on the other side.

One man said, "Hell lets have a little fun with her. W're goin' to be here all night, we just as well have a little fun." I heard cloth tearin', a strugglin' noise, more cloth tearin'.

I turned the nob, yanked open the door. Swan came through the door with me. Both her guns were shootin'. She had three down as I shot the fourth. Swan shot him twice more before he hit the floor.

I untied Dory, both her breasts stickin' out hard an' proud. She covered herself with her arms while I untied her feet. I untied the dirty rag that was her gag.

"Thanks Will. Thank you Swan."

When Chester could talk all he could do was cuss. He pulled off his coat, putin' it on Dory. She buttoned it.

CHAPTER FOUR

Guns Blazin'

We went to the hotel an' into our room. Hank, Slim an' Morecroft were up drinkin' coffee. Loraine was layin' down. Slim had let us in with a gun in his hand.

Swan took Dory into the bedroom to get her dressed.

We all turned to Chester for the story. Slim handed us each a large glass of whiskey. Chester killed his before he started.

"We were goin' to Dory's house when I seen a man layin' in the road. I stopped an' went to him. When I turned him over I was lookin' down the barrel of his gun. Another got Dory. We were helpless. They drove us to the warehouse, you know the rest.

"My God Will, I have never seen a man shoot like that much less a woman."

I walked to the door an' asked if all was decent, if you are, "Come out here."

Chester was tellin' Morecroft the story again. Of Swan an' I comin' through the door. Her with both guns blazin'.

Swan walked into the room then, all looked at her, her eyes had that flash of excitement, the smile I knew so well. I went to her, gave her a kiss an' a hug.

Morecroft came an' hugged her also, then he really hugged Dory. He was very thankful to have her back.

We decided everyone should spend the night so I walked down to the desk an' got three more rooms, I only needed two for Dory spent the night with Chester.

After everyone was gone to their rooms an' I returned to our room, Swan poured me a drink. She unbuckled her guns an' knife, made sure the door was locked. Walkin' toward me she slipped out of her shirt, ran her hands up her sides, under her breasts. The nipples were hard an' pointed. Her hands came up over the nipples, she slipped off the head band, droppin' it to the floor. She turned to the bedroom door, skinin' off the tight buskskins, turnin' her back to me she looked over her shoulder an' walked to the bed.

I sat down my drink, blew out the light an' followed her. I turned down the light in the bedroom, undressed an' crawled in with the wildest passionate woman I had ever known, the perfect lover.

In the mornin' Chester, Hank an' Slim escorted Dory home to change clothes an' were to bring her to the bank.

Swan an' I dressed in our city clothes, went with Morecroft.

We made two stops on the way. One at a gun-sales shop, the other a large supply house. Morecroft introduced us to both owners. Said, "I'd be shippin' to the West. I'd buy by the wagon loads." He guaranteed anything I signed.

We talked with Morecroft about thirty minutes. He told me of a place to buy wagons an' horses. I asked about Hatcher. He said he was retirin' this year but still stayed active on this end.

He said, Jordan was still in town. I'd probably find him at their warehouse this mornin'.

When the three men escorted Dory into the bank she was all smiles. She sure had things to tell of her dinner date.

Slim an' Hank went to the livery stable. Chester stayed an' talked with Morecroft about openin' an office here in Kansas City.

Swan an' I hired a buggy to take us to Shipp an' Hatchers. He stopped at the front door. I went in, the first person I seen was Hatcher. He was bent over a desk.

"Mr. Hatcher," I said.

He turned around, it took a second for him to recognize me in these city clothes. "Will Chase," he bellowed an' came to shake my hand warmly, "My God man, it's been awhile. Almost didn't know you in them store clothes. Come into my office."

"Just a moment, I have to get someone," I said, steppin' outside for Swan an' payin' the carriage man.

Swan an' I went into his office. It was more like a home. One the office, a small sleepin' room, the rest a front room with chairs, couch an' fireplace.

We had coffee poured when he asked, "What's been goin' on back East? I have heard you went to Washington to block the Settlers Act for the Black Hills."

"Yes, we spent the winter back there. Got it stopped, but only for a couple years at the most. Now tell me, what's the word in my country."

He started in, "It was a hard winter at Laramie an' up towards the Gap. It got cold early. They had lots of snow. Your people made it okay but word is a lot of the ones that stayed out in the plains late to hunt got caught out there. They had a tough winter, a lot of the old an' the young didn't make it."

"I have a contract for ten thousand buffalo robes so it's the beginnin' of the end for the buffalo."

We sipped our coffee awhile, my mind was seein' the snow an' cold on the plains. The hunger with my people.

"Do you have supplies out that way anyplace?"

"I have a post at Yankton. The army has a Fort there now an' I my post. What do you have in mind?"

"I want to buy supplies from you at your closest points. Have them shipped to the Indians."

Hatcher sat for awhile, then said. "Will, your lookin' at forty five days before delivery. By then your people won't need them. All that were to die already have. You must do that this Fall to see it don't happen again. It has been like this always for your people. About every ten years something happens to kill off the old an' weak. That's what has kept them strong."

We had more coffee. Swan said, "This is so Will, it has always been so.'

Hatcher turned to Swan sayin', "You have many songs you sang around the camp fires. Your people at the basin sing the loudest. It is said you are a great fighter, walk beside Will here, you make each other strong."

She dropped her head an' blushed. Hatcher smiled an' winked at me.

"What does Jordan say of me," I asked.

"He judged you hard at first over the generals you shot. Other than that he says nothin' bad. He don't even talk bad of the generals. He praises you for helpin' to clean up around Fort Laramie. You left the worst one free up there."

"Hatcher, what of Birtchfield?"

"He is out to see you under."

"Captain Bush?"

"He is still your friend but has his orders. In June there is to be a big push into your country."

"To survey?"

"Yes but they are takin' many soldiers."

We stayed with him until noon. Jordan never came in. Swan an' I hired a buggy to carry us back to the hotel.

Slim showed up so we, he an' I, sat an' talked. I was goin' back to the Gap I said. "Was goin' Monday." We worked out a deal for him to buy supplies an' things. I would make the gun an' shells deal. He would ship by train to the closest point to Scottsbluff. Then come by wagon. He'd send some word ahead an' we'd be ready.

I told him of the survey crews comin'. He said he could be there by mid July.

Swan an' Loraine came out an' said they were goin' to look around the town a bit, would be back by five.

Slim an' I went to the gun house. They had a large choice of weapons.

We ordered three hundred repeaters an' twenty thousand shells. Ten cases of dynamite, caps an' fuses.

We went into a saloon an' had us a drink. As I tipped mine up I was lookin' at a man I had seen on the train. Also I had seen him last night at supper. Casually I mentioned him to Slim. He never looked around but said he was across the street when we came out of the gun house.

We had another drink an' left for the supply house. We spent quite a bit of time there. We started orderin', I left most of it up to Slim. Coffee, sugar, tea, beans, peas, blankets, cloth, needles, thread, pots, pans, flour an' many more things. Beads, so many beads. I thought it far too many. "They don't spoil." Slim said.

When we left there we looked, the man was settin' on a bench out front of the supply house.

We headed back to the hotel an' stopped at the bar. Hank was settin' on a stool at the bar, had quite an audience around him. He was tellin' the story of how we three had taken the Moore gang.

Slim an' I orded a drink. The bartender hurriedly served us and rushed back to hear the end of the story.

They all oohed an aahed. Hank turned back to the bar. There sat three drinks in front of him. He seen us settin' there, said, "There is the other two men who was with me. Will Chase and Slim Turner." Some of them came over to shake our hands.

Fred Goodnight came in about then. He came right over to us. He shook hands an' we talked awhile. He was goin' west to meet his uncle in Kansas. He filled us in on the news from the East.

"Some mad people" was about all he said of the gold deal.

We had supper with Morecroft again that night at his house. We met plenty of important people. They talked about forcin' the army to drop the charges against me.

The police he had sent for had talked to Dory. They had been satisfied with her story. They had the bodies. They were known thugs from here.

Morecroft told the story of Swan stealin' a horse, followin' them. Then shootin' three men by herself, some of the city people looked at her settin' there all prim an' purty, shook their heads in disbelief.

They looked at me with questions in their eyes so I said, "Don't ever doubt her ability gentlemen. She's a fighter and damn tough."

Later at the hotel we sat talkin' of home. We went to bed, layin' in each others arms. Swan said, "Let's go home tomarrow."

I thought a minute and said, "Okay.

Ten days later we rode up to the edge of the basin. Swan led the way into the openin'. When we were half way to the bottom a shrill cry started. It was answered below.

As we rode into a big corral there were about twenty braves to greet us an' escort us to her teepee.

The great Buffalo Hump stood and waited for us to dismount. He shook my hand an' grunted to Swan before he hugged her.

We had a feast that night, much dancin' an' singin'. We stayed three days, then headed for the Gap.

Buffalo Hump had told of the hard winter. He had givin' cattle to the hungry, let many spend the winter in the basin. Some had died on the plains, the strong and wise had come through okay. To the north it had been worse.

We met some braves from the Gap the first evenin'. They camped with us. Chasin' Elk was the leader of this group.

They were out scoutin' for whites. It was the time of green grass, whites always came with the grass.

He told me of the Gap. Henry was okay but sad, Singin' Goose had died suddenly durin' the winter. Petey had a boy child. All had had a fair winter. Trappin' had been good.

They went southwest in the mornin', we straight west. A couple hours later we heard shootin' from the direction they had gone. We swung that way at a lope. Swan was smilin', that certain smile. We topped out on a ridge an' seen the battle below.

Chasin' Elk had baited a good trap. There was eleven cavalry men down, five that I could see still fightin'. All had lost their horses. They were in a shallow ditch, it was but a matter of time now.

We rode up to Chasin' Elk who sat back quite a ways out of range. "Ho brother, what is the story?"

"We set the trap like you showed us. Two came right in sight, the soldiers gave chase, shootin' at them, the braves led them into our guns."

"What are they up here for?" I asked. He looked at me, said, "They are soldiers, they shoot at us so we kill them."

Bein' that he was the leader I asked his permission to talk with them. He nodded his head an' waved his arm.

His braves pulled back an' came to him. There was only fourteen, this mornin' there had been sixteen. I asked of the others. He pointed south, said two died.

I tied a piece of cloth to my rifle barrel and rode forward. A soldier stood up an' came towards me. All others rose with their hands held up empty so I rode closer. It was a corporal I had seen before.

"Hello Will Chase, I was wishin' for you, but I heard you was in Washington."

"I was, corporal, now I'm back. What are you doin' up here?"

"We are a scoutin' party for a survey crew. They are south a few miles. Will Chase, this is the third time you have whipped a troop I was with. If you let me go this time I'll never be back, my times up today."

"This is not my fight it's Chasin' Elks', it's up to him."

"I thought you were the head chief?"

"No soldier, I'm just allowed to set at their council."

"What you say goes, I have seen it so. Speak for me this one time an' I'll never be back."

"Why did you shoot at his scouts?"

A private got excited, "They all fell to the chase, they didn't listen to orders."

I motioned Chasin' Elk to come join us. Swan also came.

"That is Swan ain't it," he said. "She is beautiful."

They stopped, I said to Chasin' Elk, "I have seen this one before, twice we have sent him back an' the army sends him again. He said today if we let him go he will quit the army an' never come back here again."

Chasin' Elk nodded his head. The corporal unbuckled his belt, walked to Chasin' Elk, handed up the belt an' said, "Thank you." Again Chasin' Elk nodded his head.

"How many men are in the survey party?"

"Fifteen surveyors, sixty cavalry. What of my men?" he asked.

"Will they leave their guns an' horses?"

"Yes."

"Then they can walk south," Chasin' Elk waved his arm, the braves rode forward. "Pick up all the guns." One brave said, "They have wounded," was he to leave a horse?

Chasin' Elk nodded an' sent a scout back to the Gap. The four to walk helped the wounded one on his horse. By the look of his wound he'd not see the sunset.

We headed south at a lope. Two scouts had already started a few minutes ahead of us an' were goin' at a faster pace.

Three hours later one scout returned. They had found the soldiers. They were about a mile ahead comin' up a draw. The other men were lookin' through something an' comin' behind.

"Are there no scouts?" Chasin' Elk asked.

"There is a spring at the head of the draw. They have a fire an' are goin' to eat there. The scouts are at the fire waitin' to eat."

We had been talkin' as we rode, now we whipped up to a long lope, eatin' up the distance in no time. We spread out an' slowed to a walk a quarter mile from the draw.

I went ahead an' looked into the shallow draw. Fifteen men were gathered around the fire gettin' served their food. The rest were still workin' their way up the draw. Two survey crews were workin' both sides, they were layin' out a road to come up the draw.

About ten soldiers were tryin' to get a wagon out of a washout, all others were behind the stuck wagon.

Quickly I waved five men to take the ones at the wagon an' the ones below. Nine other men an' I were goin' to hit the men at the fire. Get their horses that packed food an' supplies.

We charged the draw an' were all over the soldiers before any of them knew what was happenin'.

I'm not sure any soldiers fired a shot, we killed them all an' ran off all the horses. Five of the braves turned right an' poured more shots at the rest of the men behind the stuck wagon.

Soldiers were droppin' everywhere. The repeatin' rifles puttin' a deadly fire on them. Some ran back to their horses, they had been tryin' to get the wagon out of the ditch. The men holdin' horses were tryin' to return fire but had to turn the horses loose to do so. Horses were runnin' everywhere.

One sergeant charged the west ridge with ten men. Three were dropped from their saddles, another wounded on their way up. When they hit the top he dismounted his men. The Indians withdrew.

They dropped one brave an' wounded another. They then turned their fire on the east side. We were out on the flat, had to make a run for it. We lost two braves.

Swan had headed northwest with our pack horses. Now all the soldiers horses were behind her. All the saddles empty an' packs open. The first ways things had fallen out. I stopped an' picked up a side of bacon.

We had killed or wounded about forty men in the draw. Chasin' Elk had gotten ten earlier. The soldiers had also lost half their horses, all packs with supplies. I thought this would be a good time to regroup an' go back.

Swan stopped ahead of us at a small lakebed. There were several of these in the spring but they were dry in the summer.

We tied all the bridle reins around the horses necks an' closed up the packs that were open. Some of the men were carryin' three or four extra guns. We packed these on the horses as best as we could. All were to take more shells but the army's rifles shot a bigger shell so they were no good to our repeatin' rifles.

Swan an' three braves were to go on to the Gap with the horses an' supplies, that left nine of us to return.

Chasin' Elk was ridin' beside of me on the way back. He was sayin' how they would "never learn about fightin'."

"This was easy today Chasin' Elk because you sent out scouts, also their scouts were in to eat. They were havin' trouble with wagons. We came along at the perfect time, took them by surprise. It will not always be this easy. We must always keep out scouts, be ready." It hit him then what I was sayin'.

"Heya, Heya," he yelled an' two men took off at a lope.

He looked at me with a foolish face, "You scold well, Will Chase.

As we came up out of the draw the soldiers were all on the flat. They weren't goin' to be caught in the death trap again. They were a sorry outfit. A large grave had been dug. The bodies put in, they were fillin' it. They had a campfire goin' an a meal cookin'. When they seen us they lined up in battle formation. Four wagons were in a row an' they ran behind them, got in firin' position .

A brave behind me said "Hoo," I looked at him. He was pointin' to the north. Three men were walkin' an' one rode a horse.

Chasin' Elk an' I rode toward them. The one ridin' stepped down as we approached. We stopped in front of them. "Afternoon corporal," I said. "I want you to ride over an' have the officer come out an' talk with Chasin' Elk an' I. Who is he?"

"Goodwin sir. Captain Goodwin."

"Is he a wise man?"

The corporal, fidgety, said, "No Sir."

"Ride to him an' ask but you come with him. I think you know my word is good."

"Yes sir, Mr Chase, I know."

He rode away, I turned an' told the other soldiers to head over to our braves. "Just go there an' set down an' rest."

"What happened to the rest of our men," one asked.

I looked at him an' I guess he knew but couldn't accept that it could happen.

"We killed them," I said. The three men had never dreamed we, so few, could cut their strength in half. They had hoped for safty with the large group, now their hopes were shattered.

The corporal was talkin' an' wavin' with the captain who was sayin', "What the hell did you give up your guns for corporal! You should have fought! I'll have you court martialed for this!"

The corporal said, "The hell you will Captain, I'm not in your army anymore, I got out about four hours ago. You can stick your court martial up your ass, in fact Captain you can stick this whole army of yours up your ass."

The Captain got red in the face, who was this simple corporal to tell him how to command? "Captain if you go talk you have a chance, if you don't your dead as well as all your men."

"I'll go to hell first before I surrender my guns an' horses corporal."

The corporal said,"I'm goin' out there an' if you want to live you'll come with me." The Captain ranted an' raved but when the corporal started out he followed.

We rode forward, met them half way. The corporal looked me dead in the eye, "Mr Chase, I'm no longer in this army. If you let me live to get back to Scottsbluff I'll never ride with or for them again. I'll tell every man who will listen what a fair man you are an' have always been. This is Captain Goodwin, he's in charge."

"My names Will Chase, what are you doin' in Sioux country?"

"This country belongs to the U.S. Government," he answered.

"The hell it does. I just came from Washington, the Settlers Act has been killed. You have no business here with a survey crew. I sat in congress hall an' heard the bill put down. It can't be reopened for two years. The night before I left there I had supper with congressman Fairchild. He said I could come home an' know we'd not be bothered."

The Captain was caught flat footed, his mouth dropped open. He had expected to be talkin' to an outlaw, not a man that had traveled East an' had supper with congressmen an' senators.

"You are on our lists as an outlaw, what makes you think you can tell me what to do?"

I looked at him. "Captain Goodwin, how many men did you just bury?"

"Thirty one," he said.

"You have how many wounded?"

"Eighteen, but you caught us by surprise," he said.

"You damn fool, does that make any difference to them, the dead, their families. We took you with fifteen men. By mornin' I'll have one hundred fifty men here. Lay down your guns, turn over your horses an' supplies. I'll let you have a couple wagons for the wounded. If you don't I'll kill you an' your men."

He sat awhile, "What guaranty do I have you won't kill us anyway?" The corporal took over then, "Captain this man's word is good. These braves follow these two men an' are taught to do as they say." He stepped off the horse an' handed Chasin' Elk the reins an' started walkin' toward the rest of our band an' the other three men.

The Captain rode past us an' ordered him to stop, he walked on, the captain rode at him an' drew his gun. I yelled, the corporal ducked an' caught the reins, the horse reared, the captain fell to the ground losin" his gun. The corporal picked up the gun, gathered the reins an' walked to the first Indian, handin' him the gun an' reins.

He looked at the other three men an' said, "If you want to live you'll get up an' follow me," he turned an' walked south. They got up an' followed.

The Captain sat in the grass an' hollered at the men walkin' away. We turned an' joined the rest of the braves.

We sat our horses an' watched as two soldiers came an' led him back to the wagons. Him the leader cryin' all the way. A sergeant rode out to us an' said, "We will go if you let us."

"Go," Chasin' Elk said, "Tell the others this is Sioux Country."

We all watched as the soldiers drove two wagons loaded with wounded down the draw they had died in. At the bottom the sergeant looked back an' waved to us. We waved back an' they walked on.

CHAPTER FIVE

The Gap

When we got to the Gap it looked the same as the spring before, green an' good. Henry was glad to see me an' we had a good visit. He talked of the past a lot. I told him of the East an' suggested that Hank would be glad to have him come for a visit. "I don't think Hank will be back out this way again, he's awful happy there an' they do have a good setup there. I've been thinkin' of sendin' about a hundred head of horses back there this summer."

Henry said things had been the same at Scottsbluff. Beaver prices were good this year an' so were coyote an' wolf. He brought out a bottle an' we sat drinkin'. Swan came an' sat down on the other side of him, started tellin' him of all the wnderful things she had seen.

Henry said he'd sure wished Alice could have seen some of the good life as he called it. He then talked of her for awhile. I seen Standin' Elk an' Petey ride in, they had a deer on a pack horse. Henry was still talkin' of Alice when I walked away, he never noticed.

They were skinin' the deer when I got down to them. "Hey brother," I said. Standin' Elk just glanced over his shoulder an' went on skinin' the deer. He started sayin' to Petey, "You would think a man that was that great a warrior wouldn't need fifteen men to help him take on seventy or eighty soldiers. He should be able to do it alone. He only came back with sixty head of horses an' seventy or so guns."

Petey said, "Maybe they got too heavy an' he left them behind or lost them." Standin' Elk turned around then an' faked surprise. "Ho brother, when did you get back?"

We shook an' laughed. "Come Petey, we can skin the deer anytime." I shook Petey's hand an' said "I'm proud for you an' your boy child." He grinned from ear to ear.

We moved to the lodge an' a woman brought out the croc an' dipper. We sat by the fire an' had some. This was the strong stuff. I told how we had found Chasin' Elk with his trapped soldiers. How they had been turned loose to go south. How we had hit the others, after the tellin' of how the leader had acted an' his men had had to take care of him. We sat an' had the dipper.

Standin' Elk said, "It won't always be this easy. One day we will make a mistake, then our women will cry." I knew he was right.

I asked of the mother an' how she was doin'. She had moved up to Alice's room. "She takes care of Henry now. He needs somebody."

Swan walked up then an' sat with us. Standin' Elk passed her the dipper. Word had passed back here durin' the winter as to what a wild cat she was.

Sharps had heard an' told the story of the barroom fight as well as the one north of Scottsbluff. How she had fought off the soldiers an' taken me to Slim an' Hank.

We stayed until late evenin' before goin' to our room in the post. Both of us feelin' good, we sat an' talked awhile.

What do you really want of this life Swan?" She sat a bit an' said, "I have more right now than I ever dreamed of havin'. I have been places, seen two worlds but most of all I like makin' love with you an' fightin'. When there's danger it seems like something explodes inside of my body. Everything goes fast an' clear. I like to fight, I wish there were two of me so I could do two times as much." We then went to bed an' made love.

The next few days I spent talkin' to the people. They all seemed happy an' lookin' forward to another good year. Long Warrior was off with his family to the north. He had left two weeks ago. He had heard they were havin' trouble with whites. They were killin' buffalo as they were doin' to the south.

I sat around another ten days, then decided to send a herd of horses to Hank in St. Louis. Henry agreed to go an' Sharps was back an' would run the post for him.

We put together the best herd of horses I had ever seen. Half of them were sorrel with plenty of white. The rest were spotted horses. Even Henry got excited about them.

Swan made up two pack horses separate from the packs for the horse herd. We were goin' two days with them an' then swing west to see the Sheppards.

The horses moved out good an' we covered forty miles the first day, thirty miles the next. In the mornin' of the third day Swan an' I turned west. This was as close to Scottsbluff as I wanted to be

We spent a week with the Sheppards. Their cattle herd had made the winter okay but had gaunted a bit due to the big snows coverin' the grass. They had their three-room house an' a barn finished. I helped them work a bunch of cattle. They had a contract to sell the army fifty head of fat steers in September.

There had only been three white men through here since the last time I was here. The Indians had brought in a hundred head of cows the month before. Only eleven had brands so they butchered them. They made jerkey then branded the rest. Fifty-fifty, for them an' the Indians. Fred said the Indians were proud to have a cow herd.

We rode on up toward Fort Laramie just to look around. Swan looked at me an' grinned, "That's why you brought two suits an' had Henry cut your hair. You brought two dresses an' city shoes also."

We went past the Fort to Charlie Walker's place. We got there in the evenin'. We rode up an' started talkin' to him. It was two or three minutes before he recognized me. "Will Chase, in those clothes you sure look different."

"Charlie," I asked, "if I wore this suit an' the hair cut do you really think people wouldn't know or suspect who I was?"

"I'm sure they wouln't, what do you have in mind?"

"I'm not sure, most of all I want to know what's goin' on around this country. What Birthchfield is doin'. He's puttin' on a lot of heat from here to Washington. If he can make trouble for me he can keep it off himself."

Charlie started tellin' me how Howard was doin' at the post. He had built a hotel, "has the post office now, yes Laramie has a post office. He has a good cafe in the hotel. Jordan an' he have a partnership in a fur company. They are buyin' buffalo hides, haulin' them to Denver."

"Are there a lot of peddlers around now?" I asked.

"Laramie is a town now," he said. "There are three bars, a clothin' store, a saddle shop an' people everywhere."

After dark we changed clothes. Swan unbraided her hair, combed it out an' then we rode into town. It was amazin' how the post had become a town. There were houses every where, also tents.

We rode up to the hotel an' tied up our horses. Walkin' inside I felt a little nervous but as soon as I saw all the people I was okay. We got a room an' carried up our bags. I changed my guns an' went back down to find a place for the horses. A stranger told me where the livery stable was, it was half finished but open for business. I stepped upon my horse an' led the three others to where there was a big barn goin' up. A man came out into the corral an' said they had a place to put our saddles an' packs where they would stay dry but the horses would have to be put in the outside corral for the barn was already full.

I said that would be fine an' put up the gear where he showed me. I paid him the quarter a head an' went back towards the hotel. There were two shots, comin' from the saloon I had an interest in so I went to that side of the street.

One man came out holdin' his arm, another came behind him. Helpin' him on a horse they rode away towards the Fort. Huntin' the doctor I thought. I stood at the door an' looked in. I saw no one I knew or anyone who might know me so I went in. Standin' at the bar I ordered a drink, then stood there an enjoyed it.

There were miners, cowboys, peddlers, gamblers, Indian scouts, soldiers an' even ladies of the finer trade in here. This had all happened in less than a year. I had another drink an' looked the crowd over again. A man came up an' offered to sell me some land down by the creek. "Forty acres," he said "it sure would make a nice little farm. There were two houses on it an a nice barn." I bought him a drink an' kept him talkin'. There was lots for sale all around. A man named Jensen was sellin' out an' movin' East. He had gotten rich out here an' was leavin' in a few days.

I bought another drink an' he kept talkin'. I asked him, "Who had built the houses on the place." He pulled out some papers an' looked through them. "Man named Hunter," he said.

"Wonder why he sold it," I asked casually.

"Oh, he got himself killed for butcherin' a beef that belonged to a man named Blrtchfield. Anyway they hung him right beside the beef an' now they're huntin' his kid. The place was in the old mans name an' not paid for so this Jensen sold it to me."

"What do you want for the place?" I asked.

"Well now if your really interested in it I'll take twenty five hundred, that includes the three head of cattle, the hogs an' one horse."

The trader in me said to jew him a little so I said, "Two thousand." He said, "Two thousand, two-fifty." We called the bartender an' he signed as a witness. I paid the man an' he bought another drink.

I walked back to the hotel an' climbed the stairs to the room. Swan let me in an' asked where I had been. I told her about the deal an' we talked about Hunter. Swan had not known him but the man had worked for me for two years. I knew he was not a thief.

"I'm goin' down stairs an' get us a bottle. I'll be right back, wait up. We need to talk out a plan of some kind."

I went down an' the little bar was full. I had a drink an' ordered a bottle. Everyone was talkin' of different things. I asked a man how the gold was holdin' up around Denver. "Not only is the gold still good but the silver is really boomin' too," he said. "The cattle are comin' up there an' on this way. This is good cattle country. It will be all settled with ranches in another year or so."

I went back upstairs. Swan let me in again. I poured us a drink. There was only one tin cup. She was wrapped in a blanket. We sat lookin' at each other. "What are you goin' to do about Jensen sellin' all the land you an' he own," she asked.

The next mornin' I still had no sure idea or plan. We had breakfast an' sat watchin' the flow of people. I seen Howard Jensen walk past with some other men. He was gettin' fat. Over the third cup of coffee he went back towards the post. There was people comin' an' goin' in a steady flow.

Two wagons unloaded supplies into the post. I saw Captain Bush an' Sara ride past, stop at the post an' talk with a soldier. We went back upstairs an' I told Swan I need to go out awhile. I asked if she would like to walk with me. I worked on my hat a little an' was satisfied it was okay, we left the room.

We were walkin' along the path that led to the fort, as we passed the saloon Swan nudged me an' smiled. I knew she was rememberin' the night we had taken the barman out an' killed four of his men.

Three horsemen came down the street, Birtchfield, Buck James an' a man I had never seen. He wore his gun tied down an' looked young but very deadly. They stopped at the main saloon, sat their horses, talkin' to someone I couldn't see. He was standin' in the doorway. They turned an' rode on towards the post.

We crossed the street an' checked on our horses. They had hay an' water. We stood there awhile watchin' them. I turned to Swan, told her I wanted her to go to the post an' buy some clothes she could ride in. "Jeans or one of them split skirts, a couple of both. We may be around here awhile.

"Spend some time in there, learn what you can. I'll move around an' talk to some people. We are from Kansas City, our names Chasin'. We are lookin' for land to run cattle on." She nodded an' walked away.

I moved into the barn but all in there were too busy to talk, they were puttin' a roof on. I went on down the street, casually stoppin' an' talkin' here an' there. An old timer was tellin' me of beaver trappin' last winter when I saw Good Horse an one of his sons ride past. They stopped acrost the street from the post, stood by their horses talkin' an' lookin' at the post. They moved over to a bench under a cottonwood tree an' sat down. I crossed the street an' moved to them. Good Horse looked at me an' nodded. As I passed he said, "I know you, we must talk." I nodded an' walked on.

I went to the pens below the post, was lookin' at some cattle in one of them. Good Horse an' his son came, stood a ways off lookin at a scrubby colt, "We heard you had left us," he said.

"For awhile, now I'm back."

"Someone looks for you, he is waitin', but gets anxious."

"Who?"

"Young Hunter. He came to us when they hung his father. He has been with us ten days."

"I will come tonight," I said, "Where?"

"Big Teepee about two miles down the creek, south side. Jensen won't let us have our mares an' their colts. Now they are havin' colts again. He tells everyone you paid me for them."

"You were with me when we put it on the books," I said.

"That book is no longer in the store."

"How was your winter?" I asked.

"Very bad."

"Do you need supplies?"

"Yes," he said. I laid one hundred dollars on the ground an' picked up a rock an' pitched it at the cattle. They turned around an' I saw the brand on three of them. I walked away. The son took my place an' also throwed a rock at the cattle.

Walkin' back to the livery stable, goin' past the post I saw Audrey talkin' with Swan. I went on for Audrey would know me on sight. I stopped at the livery an' told the man to have our horses saddled before sundown. My wife an' I wanted to take an evenin' ride.

He looked at me an' nodded. I paid him for another day's board, asked if he had any corn. He said, "Yes it's a nickel more a horse."

I gave him another dollar an' said, "Feed them good."

Back in the hotel room I had a drink, was doin' something when I heard Swan at the door. I let her in an' helped her with the bundles. It looked like she had tried to buy out the post.

She had the rest of my drink an' smiled an' poured me another. She sat on the bed an' told me all she had heard. "Will Chase has moved to Washington, was in jail. The Sioux were lettin' settlers into the Black Hills. Great amounts of gold were found in the Black Hills. Captain Bush was bein' sent to Washington. Audreys husband had been killed six months ago. Howard Jensen was sellin' the post on Monday, they were leavin' for the East.

"I talked with Good Horse. He knows where Mark Hunter is. We will see him tonight. It's a good, thing we came here when we did." I told her of the Indian cattle in the pens. Had no answer to why they were there. We went to lunch then but heard no more talk or seen anyone we knew.

Swan went back to the room to try on clothes. I didn't want to be cooped up so I walked up to the saloon I owned part of. It was not busy so the bartender had time to talk. He seemed to know all that was goin' on in the country.

"Yes Will Chase was in jail back East." He had heard it a week or so ago. Ten head of cattle with brands like chicken tracks had been brought in by three braves. They were in the stockade at the Fort, had been for a week or so. Their women were camped east a ways. Some white men had went out there an' told them to leave but so far they hadn't left.

After three drinks I asked if there was "Any rumors of the Birtchfields?" The bartender said there were, "Always rumors about them." Wagons were still robbed along the trails but nothin' ever showed up here at the post. Word had it that they did a lot of business with the Mormons. He had a couple wagon trains go west last year an' word had it, one left already this year. A lot of cattle went with this train also. I bought another drink an' drifted over to watch a small poker game that had started a while ago. After I finished the drink I waved to the bartender an' went outside.

There was a bar west of the livery stable that I had not tried yet so I moved that way. I crossed the street an' looked at the roof of the livery. It was almost finished. As I walked into the bar I was surprised to find it had three walls of log. Only the front was sawed lumber. It was dug down a couple of feet into the ground.

A grizzly lookin' man stood behind the bar. He looked like my father an' Henry Long used to look. He wore buckskins as did ten of the fifteen men in there . Three Indians were settin' by the fire on the ground. There was no need for a fire, they had it by habit.

Old memories came rushin' back. I had spent many winters in houses like this. Our first post at the Gap had been like this. Everyone was lookin' at me with questions in their eyes.

I walked to the bar an' ordered a cup of whiskey. It was poured from a croc jug. The bear set it in front of me. I laid out a dollar, he kept it all. Everyone was watchin', waitin' for me to take a drink. I did, it was the strong brew that Standin' Elk made. Not as smooth but I had drank worse. I tipped it up, finished it, sat the cup down an' motioned it to be filled again.

The bear came back an' poured it full again. I never laid out any money this time an' he never said a thing. They all were baffled at a dude in here that didn't complain about the drink or the price.

The bear said, "You hungry youngin', there's a pot of tripe hangin'." Again he was testin' me. I walked over, got a plate, a piece of fried bread an' a spoon. A ladle was in the pot. I scooped out a good amount, picked up a knife, pulled up the tripe, held it with my fingers, cut off a good piece, dropped it onto my plate, cut it in three pieces, walked to the table an' ate, dobbin' up the last of the juices with my bread.

The bear came with my cup an' sat it down. He stood a minute, I pointed at the chair that was a log of good size. He sat, lookin' at me. I took a good drink an' belched as a trapper often does when he has finished eatin'.

He met my eyes when I looked up. "You're no green horn, you been over the mountain," he said. I nodded my head. "You look like a green horn but you ain't. What you want in this place?"

The other men had all went back to what they had been talkin' about or doin' before I came in. "I'm just tryin' to get the feel of what's goin' on around here. Heard Birtchfield's runnin' this country, the Captain's leavin' in the fall, Jensen's sellin' out, want to know what the locals think of this."

"Captain's okay but has to follow orders. Birtchfield's a crook. Jensens a chicken shit."

"In this order?"

"Captain just wants to retire, get out. Birtchfield keeps puttin' together outlaw whites an' Indians to do his dirty work. He makes the money, they get the blame.

"A bunch of his men got hung last year. Then a couple of Texans showed up with the bar man an' a herd of ragtags. After a trial they all were hung. It was said Will Chase had set up the deal to catch them. Chase shot hell out of the army east of here an' again, north of the Bluffs, hasn't been seen since.

"He was hard hit down at the Bluffs. For a long while everyone had thought him dead. Now Felter has come back an' said 'he's in jail back East.'"

"This Jensen was about starved out a couple years ago. Chase opened the post an' took Jensen in as a partner. Now he's sellin' off all he can an' runnin' out on this Chase.

"I knew Chase years ago when he was taggin' along behind his father. Saw him three or four times. His dad got killed when his horse fell on him.

"This Felter was in the army but got drummed out because of Chase. He's still mad about that. He's the one who complained to the Captain about the Indians tradin' cattle for supplies.

"How many of these men have bad feelin's about Chase helpin' the Indians?" I asked.

"Not a one in here now, cause when the Indians way of life is gone we go with them. These damn settlers raise hell with everything."

"I must go now, can we talk tomarrow?"

"Any time," he said, "I live in the back."

Back at the hotel I told Swan what I had learned so far. She was more interested in showin' me what all she had bought.

She looked damn good in one of the outfits. I had a drink an' we went to the livery. Got our horses, rode out goin' north. We went east after gettin' out of sight of the post an' Fort. We made a big swing an' came from the east into the Sioux camp. Three women an' two children were there.

Swan talked to them first. When she turned it over to me I told them to be ready to ride before mornin'. Two of them knew me so they believed what I said. Have your stuff packed within the hour, have your horses ready to ride. One woman said, "They have Plenty Arrows in the Fort."

"I know, I will get them out some how. I'm not sure what time yet, but be ready."

We took three horses an' rode on to Good Horse's camp. This time we dismounted an' tied our horses an' went in. Mark Hunter was settin' there waitin'. He smiled at me in my dude clothes, rose an' shook hands. "Damn glad to see you Will, you heard what happened?"

"Yes I have Mark. I don't go for it. I knew your father better than to believe it of him. I need some help Mark. We have to get some Indians out of the stockade first. Then we'll work on clearin' your name. I have the papers for your farm in my pocket so you don't have to worry about it."

I had Good Horse get Mark dressed in buckskins an' moccasins. One of the young boys had a horse saddled for him. "I'm not sure how we're goin' to get them out but they can't be too well guarded. I'll go to the Fort an' see what I can do."

"You'll have to leave here for all Indian camps will be searched for them."

"They will find you Mark. Where can I find you tomarrow about this time?" We agreed on a spring we both knew about, up a big draw. "Now Mark, I'll bring you some supplies as soon as I can but don't go away alone. If we work together we can make Birtchfield tell the truth about your father."

Swan an' I rode around the post to the stream. We tied the three horses we had brought for the braves. As we rode up the hill Swan turned, went onto the trail an' rode back to the hotel. I rode through the gates an' up to the dark side of the bar. There were eight head of horses tied at the rail, none I recognized.

Standin' next to my horse I slipped into an old coat. Dropped in two extra pistols, mussed my hair an' slipped on a head band. Walkin' toward the stockade door I pulled a bandana over my face. I just walked in. There were two privates settin', at the table. I pulled my gun an' pointed at the door to the cells in back. They raised their hands an' moved through the door. I grabbed the keys hangin' on a peg.

In the second cell all three braves were settin' on their bunks. I opened the door an' motioned the Indians out. As they passed me I shoved the privates into the cell, droppin' a smashin' blow to their heads, they never moved. Lockin' the cell I turned an' gave Plenty Arrows one of the spare pistols, the other to one of the others.

"Plenty Arrows, I'm Will Chase, don't you know me." He looked again. "Damn," he said, "no hair any more," he grinned.

"Go alone out the main gate, in a short time you other two follow. Walk slow an' natural, be calm, go straight. Your horses are down stream a short ways, your women are ready to ride with you. Go straight to the Gap. I will be along later this summer." We stepped out into the dark.

I left the coat, head band an' bandana on the bench in front of the stockade an' crossed to my horse. I put my fingers through my hair, put on my hat an' walked into the bar. Most of the men in there were watchin' the poker game.

I got a drink an' watched the games also. After two drinks I told the bartender, "Goodnight," an' went out the door. Nothin' had changed so I stepped on my horse an' rode out the gate, turned an' rode at a walk towards the settlement.

Half way there Swan joined me. We rode to the livery. The men came an' took our horses sayin', "You're out kinda late?"

"We got a little lost," I said. "Not used to the country yet." He was laughin' as we walked away to the hotel.

"Are you hungry Swan." She nodded so we went into the dinnin' room. She had a sandwich. I ordered whiskey an' a cup of coffee. As she was eatin', a soldier came in an' talked with the hotel desk man, who pointed at me, the soldier looked my way an' went out the door.

As I paid for the sandwich I asked what the soldier wanted. "They had a breakout at the post, the three Indians got away," he said.

While we were waitin' for the change a group of soldiers rode past in the street.

We went to our room an' had a drink. Swan sat smilin', waitin' for me to tell the story. When I told it she nodded her head, it had gone well. That night Swan was a wild woman in bed, later she snuggled an' clung to my body.

In the mornin' everything looked the same but the talk was excited an' strained. Twenty Indians had raided the fort last night, wounded two soldiers an' turned loose three killer Indians. The army was out chasin' them all night. It was all bullshit but the people were wild with speculation that we were about to be attacked by the whole Sioux Nation.

Swan an' I went to the livery, got our horses as well as the packs. The stable man warned us against the Indians. I said we had come to look at land an' would go look today. We rode to the hills an' wandered around as if we were lookin' over the country. By mid-afternoon we were at the spring makin' camp. Swan soon had coffee an' a meal goin'. Mark eased into camp about the time it was done.

He told me his father had found out something about Birtchfield. They had came to the house an' took him to the barn an' hung him. Mark had made a run for it before it was his turn. They must have brought the beef an' hide an' put it up beside his father after that.

"Mark I'm askin' you to go up into the hills an' learn all you can about the Birtchfield's movements. When an' where their cattle are, their horse herds, how their men come an' go.

"If anything goes wrong or you need supplies I'll leave them at Charlie Walker's place. Don't hang around there much cause Birtchfield may have someone keepin' an eye on his place. I'll leave another horse here if necessary but it will be a week or so. If you don't hear from me don't worry. Swan an' I will be back in seven days. I seen a young man with Birtchfield who looked fast, you know anything about him?"

"Billy Hagon, I seen him kill a man an' he's damn fast. He likes to kill. Him an' Rick grew up together. They are both bad, watch them close Will. They both have made the brag to get you."

We spent the night with him an' returned the next mornin'. I made a deal with the livery man for two more pack horses an' packs. He asked, "Where's ours?" I told him we had left them out where we were goin' to set up a ranch. I asked how I was to go about "buyin' the land."

"You have to file with the army an' put down money to buy it with. When it's surveyed you get your deed. This will take about two years."

I thanked him an' we went to the hotel for a late dinner. Slim was in there eatin' with a man in a suit. Seein' him on the way in I walked straight to his table. "Evenin' sir, my name's William Chasin' from back East." Slim rose an' took my hand. He knew when I started I was givin' him the layout of things. "My wife an' I are startin' a ranch north of here fifteen miles or so. We are stayin' here at the hotel but plan on movin' out an' building a house soon."

He had the drift an' introduced me to the man, Lee Henderson. He was goin' to buy out Jensen and take over Monday. "Pleased to meet you sir. That is sure moving fast."

Henderson said, "Well everything moves fast out here. I'd like to have it today but have to wait the extra four days for my cash to arive from Denver."

"Hate to run. I'll come out to the wagons after I take my wife to the room. We are goin' to eat a a bite first."

CHAPTER SIX

Sioux Lands

Swan was smilin' an' lookin' content as she ate. "How is Slim?" she asked. "We will see him shortly," I said. "As soon as you change I'm goin' next door to the bar an' see if there is any news on the Indians."

When she finished an' went up the stairs, I went to the door, headed for the saloon. The bartender I had talked with was there. He poured me a drink when he seen me come in the door. I was the only one in at the time. He told me all the Indian stories were just stories. The army had decided one of the squaws had gotten them out. They had gone back to the Black Hills. There was news of a raid on another wagon train south of here an' some miners had been robbed an' killed down that way.

I left an' went to the livery, picked up our horses an' Swan was waitin' on the porch for me. She was dressed in blouse an' blue jeans, with a hip-length jacket. The jacket was loose an' I'd bet there were two guns there somewhere.

We rode to the wagons to see Slim. Our Appy horses were tied to his wagon. Lookin' around I saw the grays in the rope corral. Slim came around a wagon an' he started tellin' of what was goin' on back East.

Swan asked questions of Chester an' Loraine. Chester an' Dory were talkin' marriage. Loraine was on her way out here to visit Swan. She had changed a lot since leavin' the East. She had learned to ride better an' shoot both pistol an' rifle.

Slim was proud of her. Hank was happy stayin' back in Kansas City. He liked the people an' the tradin' back there.

I said I wanted Slim to take my money to the fort an' file on this land. "Twenty thousand acres of it." We would ride out there this evening. I also told him everything to bring him up to date. Thanked him for bringin' our horses.

He had left the four wagon-loads of guns off down the trail a ways. They would be at the Pawnee draw by now. He had mostly old hands drivin' for him who liked the old days.

Slim said we could ride out now to the place where we were goin' to build but I asked him to look around here first. "Put the appys in the livery barn, tell him we bought them from you. Go an' see Howard an' have a talk with him. Learn all you can of his plans of goin' East or whatever.

"You haven't seen us since back East. Just go with the flow. I even heard a couple times I was dead. See what Captain Bush is doin'. We'll see you for supper in the hotel around eight if that's okay with you.

"I'm goin' to sell these loads of supplies to Henderson. I sent fifteen wagons with guns to the Pawnee draw." I said, We'd see him later an' went back, put up our horses an' walked to the west saloon. Heads turned when Swan walked in with me. The men watched her as a beautiful woman should be watched as she went to talk to the other women.

The bear of a man poured two cups an' came to a table where I stopped. He was smilin' as we sat down.

We had a drink before he spoke, "Heard the Indians got away the other night. Nobody knows who helped them though Bush ain't too worried they headed out of the country."

I nodded my head an' said "I'd heard the same." There was gigglin' over by the fire we both looked that way. Swan was talkin' in Sioux an' the other women were listenin' to every word she said. She was tellin' them of the huge buildin' back East. The women could not believe people lived on top of other people.

The bear looked back at me an' asked, "Is she as tough as I have heard?"

"She is tough," I said.

"What are your plans now that your back, oh," he said, "My names Albert Shaw," an' stuck out a hand big as a bear paw.

I shook it an' said "William Chasin'.

"I know, if you need help in any way let one of us know."

I looked at the other five men settin' around the next table an' said, "I'd like to know everything that Birtchfield is doin', everywhere he goes."

Albert said he'd put out the word to the others. They hunted meat in the summer for the people around here as well as the wagons goin' west. They could hunt up Birtchfields way tomarrow. He'd have some word in a couple of days.

I spoke to Swan an' she came to the door, lookin' over her shoulder, said something I didn't catch. She dropped her head an' all the women covered their mouths an' giggled.

Outside I asked, "What was all that about?" We had walked a ways before she said anything. Then she giggled an' asked me, "Do you know what the women call you up at the winter camp in the Big Horns?"

"No," I said, rememberin' some fine times.

"The Bull" she said an' giggled again.

At supper we talked of the East with Slim. I got a bottle an' we went upstairs to talk more in private. Slim had talked with Jensen, he had told him "I was dead or in jail." He was sellin' out an' movin' to Kansas City. Openin' a shippin' company. Beef goin' east and supplies goin' west. Audrey was all for it Slim said. She was goin' to do the bookkeepin' for him.

"What did he say about my half?"

"Not a word. The way he's talkin' an' actin' you don't have a half anymore. He figures you got it all when you robbed him last year."

"Robbed hell," I said. "That damn crook. I'll see him in hell before this is over."

Slim said he also heard that "there is fightin' goin' on over east of the Gap. A big bunch of soldiers are up there with some surveyors again. The Indians are givin' them hell but they are up against a smart man. He's a colonel from some officers school back East somewhere."

We had several drinks while I was thinkin' of what to do next. I wanted to work on Birtchfield an' Felter but felt I should go back an' help the Indians.

"What are your plans Slim?" I was goin' back after this deal was finished but "I can send the wagons loaded with furs an' hides to the new shippin' house we have in western Kansas an' stay if you want."

"Let's figure on you bein' around here for awhile. Hire some men an' get the land in your name. Let's start another ranch up north of here. I have about six thousand dollars left but will have more after Henderson buys the post. I'll get more by next spring. I can't write bank drafts out here because of my name.

"Don't worry about money. I brought a lot with me," Slim said. "Also I made a good deal on the supplies to Henderson."

I told him about Mark. "We could get in touch with him through Walker." He agreed to take care of him an' work with him. I had about made up my mind to head for the Gap. I looked at Swan, she had that damn smile again.

I told Swan to get into her buckskins an' be ready to go with me to visit Howard Jensen. Quickly I packed up, gave Slim my money, told him about Shaw at the west saloon. "Help me get saddled up an' take these bags to your outfit. Hell, I'm goin' home." I slowed down by the time we were saddled. The stable man had been mad for havin' to get up an' get my horses but five dollars made him happier to help.

"Whats all the rush young man, can't this wait till mornin'? Where are you goin'?"

We swung by Slim's wagon. He had our grays an' two pack horses ready. "Everything you need is there," he said. "Damn Will, some day your goin' to have to slow down."

"Take care of things while I'm gone Slim an' thanks." We rode off to the post.

"Swan," I said as we tied up our horses, "I'm not sure how this will go down but don't kill anybody. Promise me that. Don't shoot anyone in the house." She nodded her head.

As we went past the window I could see another man settin' at the table with Howard an' Audrey. She looked damn good. I rapped on the door. There was movement inside. Papers bein' moved. Howard asked, "Who's there?" I pointed to Swan. "Mrs. Chasin'," she said.

"One minute," he answered. Then the door opened an' Howard stood there. "What can I do?" he stopped when he saw me. "Hello Howard, looks like you gained a little weight since I seen you last." Swan an' I walked into the house. Howard was backin' up holdin' his hand out in front of him. Audrey rose to her feet sayin'. "Will how good to see you again," she held out her hand, I took it an' said, "I believe you know Swan.

"Mr Henderson my name's Will Chase, this is Swan. We didn't mean to interupt the business deal but were kinda in a hurry, our people need us."

Howard had found words again an' said. "Will, I heard you were dead."

Yes people have said that a time back but as you can see I'm not." Audrey came then with two glasses, one of wine for Swan, a large whiskey for me. I walked to the table an' sat down, I told Mr Henderson to continue. He was some confused but went right on with the conversation.

"Fifty thousand, that's for all the rest of the land an' livestock as well as the tradin' post. Half now an' the rest in one year."

"You're to hold a morgage on all of it for one year. That's what we agreed on wasn't it," he said to Howard.

Howard just nodded his head.

"I'll tell you Mr Henderson, Howard hasn't been all the way honest with you. Half this place is mine. Thirty head of the horses out there belong to an Indian named Good Horse. I know that for sure, the rest are mine.

"Now Howard how many dollars worth of land have you sold What is my share of the profits of the last year? Who owns the hotel an' bar? Also who owns the first saloon you set up? Tell you what I'll do Howard. You sign your half over to Mr Henderson. I'll take his twenty five thousand for your half an' let you keep what you have gathered in the last year. You do this an' leave in the mornin' an' I'll call everything even with you."

Howard just nodded his head. Audrey came loose then, anyway her mouth did, "How can you come in here tellin' us what to do? You're nothin' but an outlaw, you have no right to anything."

Swan said, "Shut up", pushed her down onto the couch, wine goin' everywhere. She was wise enough to shut up.

"What do you think Howard?" He nodded his head, "That would be fair Will, we can get the papers drawn up tomarrow. You got to believe I wasn't tryin' to cheat you out of your share."

"Damn right Howard, just like I believed you wouldn't cheat me last year. There was seventy five hundred in that sack."

Howard got red in the face an' he reached for the whiskey bottle an' poured again. Swan stepped back from Audrey so she stood an' came to the table. She looked at her father an' shook her head, then sat down.

"Mr Henderson, you understand that you have to run the post an' that they call me an outlaw. I'll leave everything up to you. All I ask is that you're fair with the Indians as well as all that trade with you. I ask you not to cheat me for I'll not cheat you. If something happens to me this is all yours. If this is okay with you write out two papers, one buyin' out Howard for him to sign an' one for our partnership. If not the post will be closed at this time."

Mr. Henderson started writin', I turned to Howard, "Now start gettin' out the papers on the land, you no longer have any of it." He went through his desk an' set out a pile of papers. I thanked him an' added, "You can start packin' now because in the mornin' you are to be gone. Do you understand that Howard?"

Audrey started to complain. I cut her off. "I remember a short time ago Audrey when I thought you were something special, but greed sure ruined you."

Lee Henderson said the papers were completed. Howard signed one. I witnessed it for them. I signed the partnership an' Howard witnessed it. Henderson counted out the twenty five thousand an' put it into the bag. I nodded my head, turned to Howard an' said. "It hasn't been as good as it could have been Howard. If you do anything foolish to break up this transaction it will be a mistake for you.

"Mr Henderson I'll have a man by the name of Slim come around an' talk with you in the mornin'. You bought his wagon loads of goods. I may have a war to fight for awhile. Would you like to join our company back to the hotel?" He said, Yes," picked up all the papers, his hat an' we walked out the door. Swan went for his horse an' Lee an' I went the back way to our horses. Swan walked up with his horse an' we all rode away.

At Slim's fire coffee was on. Slim was diggin' in the wagon, his head popped out, "Be right with you," he said; he went back from sight. We stood by the fire an' filled our cups. Slim came out holdin' three bottles of whiskey. Two he put on a pack horse, the other he opened. We all had a good drink. "Damn this is good whiskey Slim."

"I bought that for Sharps, he's always complainin' about that home-made stuff."

I filled Lee in on Good Horse. "Take care of him, go see him yourself, take him something, keep him happy. He'll be a big help to you."

We all shook, I handed Slim my sack of money. I nodded to Lee an' told Slim, "Take care of him."

We rode away headin' east. In four days of pushin' hard we were at the Pawnee draw. It looked like a real ranch with a lot of supplies waitin' to be unloaded.

I filled the Sheppards in on what all was goin' on at supper time. They took it all in an' smiled. Early the next mornin' I had the Sheppards get out the supplies they needed an' twenty rifles, five thousand rounds an' store them in the barn. I told the drivers which way to go an' we headed out. I'd need to tell the scouts this was our train so they'd let it through. Also a couple of braves could lead them into the Gap.

The next mornin' we hadn't gone five miles when we came upon Chasin' Elk. He was settin' there grinnin'. I looked around an' he had us flanked beautifully. We stopped an' got down, we sat an' talked. He filled me in on the fight with the soldiers. They had been hit hard once but now they couldn't be got at. Only now an' then one would be killed.

I told him of the train of supplies that were behind us an' asked if he could send back a couple men to guide them. He sent four men an' they left right then. "You must keep the soldiers off them also," I said. "They might try an' take the wagons to keep us from havin' our supplies." He said he would see that the wagons go there.

"Do you all have good rifles an' plenty of shells?" He said they did.

About noon we were at the post. Sharps was proud as ever of his two bottles of whiskey. "I knew Slim wouldn't let me down," he said. Sharps gave me all the news of the fort that was bein' built. The Indians had been snipin' at them all the time but these soldiers were good.

The next mornin' Standin' Elk an' I talked quite a while. They had set traps an' everything but the soldiers wouldn't chase them an' fall into an ambush. Now an' then they got a foolish one but not often. All the time the fort got stronger. I said I'd ride over an' have a look. I asked him to go with me. He said fine, he was tired of waitin'. All that night I thought about what might be done but had to look to see for myself.

Swan an' I were layin' in bed. "Will," she said, "I'm goin' with you."

"Okay," I said, "bring some of your city clothes an' the hat you bought in Kansas City."

"The big one with the ribbons," she asked.

I said, Yes." A plan was formin' in my mind. I'd need Petey if he'd go. I got up, it was all comin' together. If all was how Standin' Elk said maybe I had a plan. I'd need some bows an' arrows. I'd check it out in the mornin', see if it would work. Hell, I was gettin' all kinds of plans.

I was wonderin' about their horses, how could we get away with them, their food, supplies, could I starve them out? I didn't sleep much, was up early. Sharps had coffee ready. Evidently he hadn't slept either.

As we sat at the table drinkin' coffee Sharps started talkin' of some Romans he had read about. They built forts on wheels an' pushed them ahead of eight or ten bowmen. They had holes to shoot through. They had roofs on them so the enemy couldn't shoot down on them. They had built long ladders that they put up the walls an' got inside that way. Also they had fire pots, shot flamin' arrows into the stone forts, set buildin's on fire inside.

"Sharps you take some men with you but leave plenty here while you're up north. Don't go up there an' do something reckless. Play the waitin' game, don't waste men. When the wagons get here I'll send you up supplies. If you need to make you some forts on wheels make then backwards so you can steer them from the back. The men steerin' need protection also.

"Standin' Elk said the fort is out in the open as it should be but they have a little stream goin' right through it. Maybe you can change the stream. Most of their horses need to graze so they must come out with them each day."

We talked a long time, this Sharps was way ahead of me on ideas. He had done a lot of readin' evidently. He brought out a half a bottle of his good whiskey, took a long long pull an' handed it to me. I had as much as he. We walked outside.

Standin' Elk was there. We talked awhile an' I asked him for ten of the best men we had with a bow, also I asked where Petey was. When Petey got to me I walked away with him. "Petey if you don't want to do this you tell me an' I won't mind a bit. I have a plan that involves you. You'll be killin' white soldiers an' if this goes against your likin' just tell me an' stay here."

"Will, the Indians are my people, if that helps them I'm all for it."

"Okay, go up to the post an' get some new pants an' a shirt of bright color so you look like a white man. We may have a way of gettin' to them."

I walked to the cave an' came out with a box of dynamite. I took out ten sticks, goin' back down the hill to Standin' Elk who had ten bow men waitin'. I ask one for an arrow an' he handed it to me, lookin' at the dark red sticks of dynamite.

I got some leather strings an' tied the dynamite to the arrow. He was nervous when I handed it to him. "It's okay," I said. "Shoot it as far as you can, high an' far." He did an' I counted to eleven before it landed stickin' into the ground. I counted it off in steps, one hundred an' fifty, about one hundred thirty yards. As I walked back I was wonderin' what effect the noise would have on the braves. I decided the only way to know was to try it.

I walked back to the post an' called Swan. I went an' got a cap an' ten inches of fuse, capped it an' handed it to Swan. Goin' into the post I got a cigar, came out an' we walked back to the braves. On the way I asked if she could shoot a bow very well? She just nodded. She knew what dynamite could do. I borrowed the bow from the brave an' lit my cigar. Some of the braves backed up even though they had no idea what would happen.

Swan looked at the tree stump I picked out, lifted the bow an' as I touched the fuse she pulled back an' let it go. The arrow landed ten feet the other side of the stump an' for three heartbeats nothin' happened. When it exploded horses jerked free, Indians ran, some over each other, some fell down. All were yellin' in fear. One was thirty yards away still goin' an' not lookin' back. I just looked at the place where the stump had been.

This was a good idea but I could see it was goin' to be hard to get the Indians to try it. I tied another stick of dynamite to an arrow, capped an' fused it but no one would take it. Sharps said Petey would. He was good with a bow an' wanted to do anything that would help drive off the soldiers.

Petey came back carryin' the clothes. "What the hell was that noise?" he asked. "You got a cannon?" I explained the deal to him, "Sure," he said he'd give it a try. "Don't be nervous." I said, "Hell if you drop it, you have time to pick it up an' shoot it away.

He notched the arrow an' I showed him a rock. He nodded an' I put the cigar to the fuse. He calmly raised the bow an' pulled it back, raised it a little more an' fired. The arrow landed within inches of the rock an' exploded at once. Again the horses jumped, some ran but most didn't. The Indians stood their ground but none offered to shoot one.

I finally got two braves that would shoot an' that was a start. I packed the caps into three different packages an' loaded the dynamite on the same three horses, dividin' the fuses the same way. We made up four pack horses with shells an' supplies, an' by noon were ready to start.

We found the first Indian camp about four the next mornin'. We rode in on them an' they were all asleep. I raised so much hell they probably heard it back at the Gap. "What the hell kind of a party is this. You are all dead. Three whites could have come in here an' killed half of you. Who is leadin' this outfit anyway?"

A young man came forward, his head hangin'. Standin' Elk took over. "When the sun shines you go back to the Gap. You are no leader of the men. Go back to the Gap an' stay with the women. You are a danger to the men you lead.

"Where is the next camp?" Standin' Elk asked.

The young man told him they were "on the other side of the fort."

"Where is the large group?"

"About a mile up the creek," he answered.

It was gettin' light an' I asked Standin' Elk to show me the fort from a place I could see it good from. We mounted up an' rode to look. We rode out on a low ridge, a pencil of higher land with a few trees on it that reached out within a half mile of the fort.

The bugle was blowin' as we stopped our horses. The cavalry seemed to do everything by the bugle. The fort had three sides finished an' part of the fourth was up. Their gates were on the west side. It was a large fort as far as I could judge but I had only seen two others up this close. There were lots of buildin's inside. Men were goin' in an' out of one big buildin', this must be what they called the messhall, where they all ate.

The stream ran through the northeast corner of the fort. I had never seen this before but I knew it was a good idea. We sat on the ground an' watched for about an hour. Two men rode out an' made a big circle around the fort. Out a quarter mile or so they went in opposite directions. When they met, it was back at the gate an' they went back in.

Six wagons rolled out then with a driver an' five riflemen in each. They went to the north with ten mounted men bringin' the horse herd. The wagons were movin' along slow in a horse shoe. They went out about a mile an' stopped the wagons an' let the teams start grazin'. With the loose horses in the horse shoe the mounted men dismounted an' let their horses graze also. The men had their rifles ready at all times.

There were forty-six well armed men guardin' the herd with probably another two hundred close by. Three hours later they started movin' the horses slowly back towards the fort. All this time the men were puttin' up logs against the log buildin's. They had holes to shoot from the buildin's. They could also stand on the roofs an' shoot over the top of the upright logs.

All the buildin's had dirt roofs so fire arrows wouldn't start them burnin'. The stream offered little cover, it could be shot into from the towers at each corner.

The man buildin' this fort knew what he was doin'. After they had the horses back in, out came forty head with ten riders. These were grazed close to the fort.

Standin' Elk an' I rode to the big camp up the stream. As we rode in Many Arrows stepped forward an' motioned us to his fire. We were both ready for something to eat an' sleep. We both had to do some thinkin'.

We sat at Many Arrows fire an' filled our bellies. Our pack horse had been brought up here. Our packs were neatly piled under a leanto with room for us to sleep so we crawled in an' laid down.

It was awhile before I went to sleep. Many Arrows woke us about three hours later, askin' do you want to go down an' look at what happens at sundown? He had fresh horses for us, Swan an' I rode paints as did Many Arrows an' Standin' Elk.

About fifty braves rode with us. We rode out on to the flats toward the fort, goin' between the ridge an' the fort. We went to the east side an' crossed the stream, headed north, stayin' out of range. We turned west an' followed the stream. At one point I saw a place that looked like we could dam it up an' turn the stream away from the fort.

The grass was dry an' a breeze was blowin' from the northwest. I gathered a hand full of grass an' put a match to it. The fire started slowly an' others were makin' bundles of grass, makin' a long line of fire. It was workin' it's way toward the fort.

"If we burn all the way around tonight they will have to come out farther to graze their horses. Maybe we can get them that way." Many Arrows took one group an' Swan, Standin' Elk an' I went with the others. Soon we had fire all around the fort. We stayed awhile to make sure the fire didn't get into the hills. We could see soldiers workin' around the fort burnin' the short grass to keep our fire from gettin' to the logs of the fort.

We rode back to our camp. It would be a bother for them an' take more men to guard the horses but they could do it.

Early the next mornin' I was back on the ridge with Swan. I had told Standin' Elk and Many Arrows to start draggin' logs as close to the fort as possible, next to the stream an' push them in, a few at a time so they would float down against the fort.

It was afternoon, before they came out with the horses. This day they had ten wagons an' thirty riders. They crossed the stream an' went east with the horses. We could still see them from the ridge. The wind was from the west an' three braves came draggin' burnin' dead pine branches. Again the grass started to burn, this time towards the horses. About ten braves made a run at the herd but after three were shot from their horses they turned back. The soldiers hurried the horses around the fire an' back to the fort.

Swan said, "In about three days they will have to graze their horses again." The logs were pilin' up against the fort. Some soldiers came out an' started draggin' out what they could. The Indians took some long shots an' hit one.

That night we made plans to do the very same thing the next day. "Tonight some of us will go down an' beat drums an' dance at a fire up on the ridge. While they are watchin' some can go to the other side of the fort an' shoot at some of their loop holes. They may even have a hole open. Get right next to the wall an' shoot into the holes, if we're lucky we may hit a few of them. Most of all we can keep them awake all night. A few nights of this an' everyone in there will get on edge."

Thirty braves went to the point of the ridge an' built a fire, beat the drums an' danced. Standin' Elk took ten braves an' 'went to the east side. I took ten an' went to the south. We moved up to the walls with ease for after the burnin' the land was black with patches of color that had been missed.

Now an' then a shot or two would come from up on the ridge. My men spread out an' each found where a hole was. All waited for me to shoot first. I could see a head now an' then against the sky. I waited until I could see two men standin' together in the tower. I fired hittin' one in the head. The other screamed an' ducked. No shots answered mine. A full mintute went by, still all was quiet. I waited but seen no more heads look over the wall. All at once all hell broke loose along both walls. Some one had opened a hole to see what was goin' on. Two braves stuck their rifles in an' emptied them, sprayin' the sleepin' rooms. The rest of the braves on both sides shot into the firin' holes. Two had come open, guns had been emptied into each that was open. Others were shot to pieces, heads came over the top of the walls, here an' there an arm with a pistol would come over an' shots would be fired down at the braves. I hit two of the arms an' we melted away into the night.

The drums stopped as both our groups came up to the fire. I let out a scream an' wavin' my rifle started to dance. The drums started again an' all joined in the yellin' an' dancin'.

We had killed some soldiers an' had not lost a man. An hour later we quit an' returned to our camp an' fell asleep.

In the mornin' Swan an' fifteen braves were back at the ridge watchin' the fort. We sat around talkin' of the night before. Many had a story to tell, we listened an' laughed at each tale.

Today we would put more logs an' branches into the stream, like beavers buildin' a dam. The logs would pile up an' turn the water away from the fort. By that evenin' it was startin' to work, the water was backin' up from the logs.

I woke that night an' it was rainin' hard. I lay with Swan in my arms warm an' dry thinkin' of the soldiers in the fort, waitin' for something to happen.

The sun was bright an' warm in the mornin'. We took all the braves this mornin' to make a great show of strength. This was the third day the horses were without grass. It would happen today if they were goin' to try an' graze them. When we got to our places around the fort a brave came lopin' up to me, he was excited. "The logs have been pushed against the fort. We can crawl up them easily an' get into the fort," he said.

Swan an' I rode with him to that side, he was right, the logs had been piled high against the fort wall by the stream that had flooded out of the hills early this mornin'.

The soldiers were nearly shoulder to shoulder on this side guardin' against us rushin' an' tryin' this.

The stream had overflowed an' the fort must of been a mess inside, for water had ran all around it. Later that day the gates opened an' out came the armed wagons, then the horses rushin' out behind them. Hunger in their bellies they spread out, scattered huntin' something to eat. They took off in all directions, some runnin' straight towards Indians settin' back a long ways out of firin' range. The hungry horses could not be controlled. The wagons got spread out. The teams hungry also. The riders got scattered tryin' to get the horses back together. Indians charged from three directions, none fired until they had one wagon an' seven riders cut off. When they open fire it was a hot an' heavy battle. The wagon was tryin' to turn back. One of the horses went down, men spilled from the wagon an' were overrun before they could regain any form of order. All were killed. Five of the riders were killed, two got back to the gate.

The braves had a hundred horses, maybe a few more, killed eleven men. We had four wounded an' three killed. We picked up the dead an' wounded an' went back to the ridge.

The wounded an' dead were taken back to camp. The horses were grazin' away to the south.

It had been a great victory for us. We had hurt the soldiers badly this day. Again that night we danced on the ridge an' went to the fort. They were ready an' smarter this time. The holes never opened but we hit three where the logs were. This night we piled logs in a three-sided pile, waist high, walled it up good an' left five braves there to spend the day snipin' at the soldiers on that side.

CHAPTER SEVEN

No Demands

We left them plenty of water, jerkey an' bullets. More wanted to stay but I thought five was enough. They were told to not show themselves until after dinner when the guards changed. At the changin' there would be twice as many targets.

Swan an' I were settin' at the base of the ridge with Standin' Elk an' Plenty Arrows talkin' of what a good mornin' it had been the day before. We were ready for the horse grazin' again.

Swan said, "Look." We all looked toward the fort. Three men were walkin' our way. One was carrin' a white flag on a stick. They came at us in a slow walk. I started my horse forward. Swan at my side. The other men stayed behind. We stopped half way an' waited for them. One was Jack Henry, a captain, an' a sergeant. They stopped about ten yards from us .

"Howdy Will Chase."

I answered, "Howdy Jack, long time no see."

"Yea," he said, "I told them it was you back again two, three days ago.This is Captain Welter an' Sergeant Childer." I nodded to them. Jack Henry looked at Swan, tipped his hat an' said, "Mornin' Swan." She smiled an' nodded.

The Captain was eager, he took a couple steps forward an' started in. "We demand in the name of the..." I said, "Shut up." He quit talkin' an' went to sputterin'.

Jack Henry stepped up beside him an' said, "Sorry Will, he's excited about the army life," an' smiled.

The sergeant stepped up even with them. He was the same sergeant who had led the other leaders away last spring. He nodded.

"I'm glad you made it okay last time sergeant, you should have stayed away." He lifted his shoulders an' said, "Orders."

I directed my attention to the Captain. "Sir the first thing about this deal is, you don't demand anything. We can talk an' decide on things but you can't demand."

"We need to graze the horses," he said. His voice on the verge of breakin'.

"Give them to us, we will graze them. You have no need for them for you are walkin' out of here or dyin'."

The Captain said, "We have a fort you can't take in ten years."

"It's your prison Captain."

"We have food an' water for two months," he blustered, "An' reinforcements will be here long before that."

"No they won't. I know exactly where they are at this time."

"Where?" he asked. I never answered him. "We have two hundred men in that fort Will Chase."

"Jack Henry would you take a walk." He nodded. "Sergeant?"

He said, Gladly."

"Well Captain what did you have in mind?"

"We need to graze our horses or they will starve."

"I know that," I said. "Why should they have to starve, you can open the gate an' give them to us now an' walk away yourselves if you wish too."

"We have a right to be here, that is our fort."

"Take it with you then, we don't need it but you have no right here, this is Sioux land.

"What time is it Jack Henry?"

He looked at me with a questioned look but pulled his watch, "Three minutes to twelve. Why?"

I sat an' looked at the Captain. Countin' off the seconds, at sixty, shots were fired. Heavy at first then they stopped. All three men were lookin' back at the fort. The Captain whirled back to me, "What kind of trick is this? We have a white flag."

"That was no trick Captain, we just killed eight or ten men of yours when they were changin' guards. Jack, your watch is slow or theirs is fast." He smiled an' set his watch.

The Captain was furious now, "There is no sense in talkin' to a man who has turned on his own kind.

"I am Sioux, Captain. What is your deal sir? We will hear it if you wish."

"We want to graze our horses to keep them from starvin'."

"Okay, turn them out an' if all your men come out an' lay down their arms you can walk away. If you have wounded take one wagon for every fifteen wounded. If you put un-wounded in the wagons we will kill them. We will escort you as far as the Cheyenne River an' shoot your game for you."

"Go to hell," he said, turned his back on me an' marched away. I looked at the other two men. They shrugged an' the sergeant turned an' followed.

"Tell them Jack Henry. They can walk away." He nodded an' slowly walked toward the fort. Once he stopped an' looked back, then went on. I felt sorry for him. He wanted to walk away, to live but he had hired on for the job. Also I admired him for he knew it was goin' to get worse.

Later that evenin' out came the wagons. This time the horses passed at a dead run. A few of the horses were wobbly. One fell but got back up an' went on. The riders came an' made a try at herdin' the horses but when the Indians came out of two draws they all swung an' went back, wagons an' all, the horses were ours.

"I want twenty scouts to go east and south. They are ex-pectin' help an' we don't want it to get here. All we need is thirty men to finish this fight but all will stay tonight except the scouts. We need to know what's goin' on at the Gap.

"We may need more dynamite. Sharps was to send a wag-on. It should have been here today so we need to check on what's what."

The five men who had been in the pile pf logs came in all smiles. They had hit eleven men in the first shootin' an' three guards in the tower durin' the afternoon.

I finished makin' up the arrows with dynamite on them. I got out six cigars, two for each, Standin' Elk, Plenty Arrows an' a warrior named Shadow. We went over the way to light them, how to keep the cigar tip hidden from the soldiers I explained again, shoot an' move, shoot an' move. Each was to shoot five times an' then wait until I started again.

We slept for awhile an' then worked our way into position I an' Shadow took the main gate, Petey was to find a side door, they had one on each side. Shadow an' I waited to make sure all was in place. I notched the first arrow an' Shadow touched the cigar to it. I raised it high an' let it go.

The fuse sputterin', the arrow stuck into the log gate. I had an' arrow notched an' lit before the first one went off, let it fly an' it stuck into the other side of the gate. The third one stuck into the middle an' the gate came crashin' down.

We moved an' I put one into the southwest tower, another was on its way before the first went off. There was screamin' an' shouts from inside. The second one brought the tower crashin' down, a gapin' hole where it had been.

The rifle fire comin' from inside was hardly what you'd call steady. The explosions started on the east side then. There were two an' then one on the north.

I notched another arrow an' told Shadow to light it. I sent it into the middle of the fort. I was sure the men inside would be runnin' everywhere. I put the next four into the roof of a sleepin' buildin'. It caved in, fire was burnin' in four or five places now.

Shadow an' I took up our rifles now an' started pickin' off soldiers in the fire light. They were easy targets with the fire behind them. When we had emptied our rifles I let out a war whoop an' we loped away into the dark. There was no more shootin' anywhere. Some horses came rushin' out an' went to the south. We didn't know if they had riders or not, it didn't matter.

As we all grouped together an' stood watchin' the fort, Plenty Arrows came an' said a scout had come in. We walked to the top of the ridge where a fire had been started.

The drums were beatin', braves were dancin' an' yellin' war whoops. The scout stood with two cavalry flags in his hands. One was covered with blood, one said, Sixth Company A, the other Seventh Company A. Both shafts were broken.

"Ho," the scout said. He nodded at the fort an' laughed.

"Ho," I answered an' grinned.

"Chasin' Elk has a large party of cavalry cut off from their wagons but needs help or they will get back together. There are many cavalry an' many wagons. Two wagons have guns that shoot plenty fast."

I didn't understand but that was all he could tell me. He circled his arms an' said many times, "Plenty fast."

We had a quick council an' decided thirty men would stay with Swan an' I. All the rest would go help Chasin' Elk. Petey said he knew how to fix the dynamite arrows an' could handle that end.

I called Standin' Elk, Plenty Arrows an' Long Warrior aside an' said, "Remember now be patient, do not be foolish, watch an' wait. Petey will make some mighty arrows for you but use them wisely."

There was much excitement an' all wanted to go help Chasin' Elk. Shadow called out for some to stay an' thirty stepped forward. The rest went south, the scout in the lead.

I took up the two flags an' rode with Swan to within three hundred yards of the fort. They were gettin' the fire under control. I planted the flags twenty yards apart, deep in the ground. Then we returned to the ridgetop an' slept.

When mornin' came the fort was a total disaster. The roofs had fallen in on many buildin's. Two corners with their towers were down, the gates lay on the ground.

Swan an' I rode to the flags an' stopped between them. Soldiers were lookin at us from holes all along the fort walls. Jack Henry came through the gate an' walked to us. He had a bandage around his head an' was limpin' badly.

"Mornin' Will," he said.

"Mornin' Jack Henry."

He turned an' looked at the fort, then at the flags on each side. "Guess you did it again Will, wonder when they're goin' to leave you alone."

"I don't know Jack, seems they don't learn too good. I'll talk with the General this time Jack, I didn't like the Captain much."

"Just as well, he's dead. General's hurt a little but we can get him out here. Sergeant wants to talk also if that's alright. He'll come with the General."

"That's okay, he's got some brains."

Jack turned an' then turned back. "Will, I tried to tell them four days ago. They wouldn't or couldn't believe you could do this. They'll be back again you know."

"I know. I'll be ready."

He limped back to the fort or what was left of it. He went out of sight an' we waited. I looked at Swan, she was beautiful settin' on her horse, wind blowin' her hair a little. She had that damn smile again, she enjoyed this.

They came out then. There was five of them. Two I did not know. As they got up close I could see the General was beaten. He looked old an' very tired.

Jack said. "Will Chase, Swan, this is General Shellman. The other two gentlemen are surveyors. If you an' the General can't make a deal they want to speak for themselves."

I nodded, the General was very formal. "We have many dead an' wounded. We'd like time to bury the dead before we move out. Our horses will have to be returned before you can expect us to go."

"General you have no horses."

"But yesterday..." he started in.

I cut him off. "That was yesterday today is today."

"Mr Chase, what do you propose then?"

"Leave everything, go south an' never come back."

"But we can't go without the wagons."

I looked at Swan, then Jack, he shrugged.

"Swan tell Shadow to gather up ten pullin' horses an' bring them here." She turned an' rode away. I knew that she was thinkin' me a fool. She wanted to kill them all.

"Mr Chase where did you study?" the General asked.

I was confused for a second then replied, "Right here, you're only allowed one mistake."

He then looked at the flags, "You have beaten the two best outfits the U.S. Army have, they even had gattlin' guns."

I was feelin' sorry for this old man so I said, "The braves call them guns 'shoot plenty fast.'"

"Who has trained this army you have? Did you?"

I guess I had done it, so I said, "Yes."

"You did a good job."

Swan returned then, she spoke in Sioux. "Shadow wants to kill them all."

"No! Bring the horses." She waved her arm an' the horses started our way. "Water them first General, then go easy with them for a couple of days."

"Now let's start bringin' out the arms an' the wounded an' General, don't let any of your men think they're safe for if anyone so much as tries to hide a knife all will be killed. The braves want to kill you all anyway."

"Jack Henry can keep his guns for I trust him. I'm not worried about gettin' shot for I'm all that's keepin' you alive. Jack can tell you that."

They brought out the wounded an' each man laid down his guns, rifle an' pistol, shells for both. The dead were brought out an' stripped of their guns. When they were finished there was two hundred fifty rifles an' that many pistols. A large pile of shells for each.

I let them take some of their medicine, some supplies, the rest was left. By mid-afternoon they were loaded an' on their way.

Each brave could take a pistol an' shells for it. Some took rifles an' shells but most were already usin' repeaters.

Ten of the braves an' I headed south. Swan stayed behind to see to the movin' of the supplies. They were moved to a cave up the canyon along with other supplies. Everything of value was taken an' the fort burned to the ground.

Noon the next day we joined Chasin' Elk. They still had the two groups split. We laid a trap in a valley that the cavalry would have to come through if they were to help the wagons. A hundred braves, half on each side, were waitin' for them. The braves on the eastside were up in the rocks to shoot down, the others were hid in the brush an' trees.

Petey opened up on the wagons with the dynamite arrows, A few of them were destroyed an' the horses ran off. The wagons were on a rise in the open an' it was imposible to get closer without facin' heavy fire. We lost fifteen braves, that many more were wounded.

About sundown the cavalry had sent out a scout twice. Both times he had been allowed to come an' go through the trap. He was sure it was there but couldn't see it. When the cavalry came we open fired. I never seen so many saddles emptied. The braves were gettin' better an' better with their rifles .

Of the two hundred maybe forty got through. They never stopped at the wagons but went right on past as fast as their horses could go. Officers were whippin' their horses along side the privates. All were only concerned with livin'. About twenty braves fell in behind them at a more casual pace. They would keep them goin' all night.

I rode back to the wagons an' called for the man in charge. A Captain showed himself from behind a wagon. "What do you want Will Chase?"

"Do you want to walk?" I asked.

"Hell no," he said.

We talked at the council that night. I asked, "Are there any scouts out?" Chasin' Elk said, "There were about thirty of them all the way south an' east. Nothin' was comin' from anywhere."

That night we crawled close with the dynamite arrows. We were down to twenty sticks so Petey an' I went in alone.

He dropped ten into the circle raisin' hell. We had a few rocks to get behind an' needed them for everytime they seen a fuse in the air they laid down a heavy fire at where it came from.

I had a bad cut on my cheek either from a bullet that had hit a rock or from a piece of rock. It was bleedin' badly. We laid where we were for about an hour. Me with some cloth pressed against my face. Finally the bleedin' stopped but I felt weak as hell.

"Let's give them another one Petey." He notched an arrow an' I touched it off. He let it fly. I took a bullet through the right shoulder. It went all the way through an' knocked me flat.

The dynamite went off an' so did their camp. He put one right into a box of their dynamite. There was such an explosion we were lifted off the ground by the force of it. Then the fast shootin' gattlin' guns were goin' off, hitin' in the rocks. Their men were on the run now, were runnin' straight into the Indians layin' out there. The light of the fire behind them, bullets explodin', most of them never knew they were bein' killed from in front.

I must have passed out about then for it was gettin' light enough to see by when I opened my eyes. My face was wraped up as well as my arm. Nothin' hurt much so I sat up an' reached for the coffee pot settin' by the fire.

Petey said, "Hold on," an' poured me a cup. He started to fill me in on what happened.

The soldiers had been wiped out. The braves had stayed away from the wagons cause there had been some fire up there an' nobody wanted to go close. There might be another explosion. After it got a little lighter I'd go up an' look around.

We finished our coffee an' waited a little longer. Braves were sleepin' all over around us. Petey helped me up an' we walked up the hill. There were eighteen wagons still in good shape but you couldn't tell how many had blown up. It looked like four or five had gone. There were pieces of soldiers flung all over.

I asked Petey where the horses were. He had some braves watchin' them a mile or so away. "You know what to do from here on Petey. I'm goin' to the Gap. I have some rest comin' an' you can take care here.

"I'll take Plenty Arrows with me if it's okay with you. I may need his help."

"That's fine, I'll get all the guns an' stuff an' bring in the wagons. See you there." he said.

I walked to where Plenty Arrows was settin' by the fire an' joined him. He said he'd go home with me an' started gettin' things ready. An hour later we were goin' through the pass. There was one hundred twenty one bodies I counted as we rode along. Seventeen more at the place they had been held up in. This was the biggest loss the cavalry had ever suffered to the Indians.

Later that afternoon we met Jack Henry. He was ridin' an Indian horse bareback. We stopped an' asked him what was he doin' off here by himself.

"General sent me down to get help from the Seventh Cavalry," he said.

"Jack there ain't no Seventh Cavalry. We counted one hundred thirty-eight bodies in two spots, about thirty-five or forty went runnin' south as fast as they could go. They never stopped to help at the wagons.

"Jack we got all their supplies an' amunition. Their gattlin' guns an' all. You best ride back an' stay with your soldiers. If the other Indians see you out here alone you're a dead man.

With them you can make it. I like you Jack Henry but I'm tel-lin' you , don't come back up here."

"Thanks Will, I'll go back an' tell the General, hope you get well soon."

"Thanks," I said an' we rode on.

That night we rode into the Gap an' again I was very glad to be there. I got down an' made it up the steps an' to the ta-ble in the post. Half a quart later Sharps an' Swan got me into bed. The last I remember was Swans warm body wrapped around me.

Ten days later Swan, Sharps an' I were settin' on the porch when five braves came with a white man. They brought him to the porch step. It was the old trapper. He looked like a bear. I thanked the braves an' told them to give back his guns. They did an' he thanked them in Sioux.

"Hi Albert, get down an' have a seat." As he walked up the steps Sharps got up an' shook his hand, gave him his seat an' moved another stump over, then went into the post an' came back with four cups an' a gallon jug. He poured all around. When Albert finished his in one drinkin', Sharps was still there to fill it again.

"That's the first time I ever been took, ever, these Indians of yours are sharp as hell. All the time I was tryin' to sneak in to see you they were herdin' me. They had me anytime they wanted," he said.

He an' Sharps talked awhile as mountain men do. They were goin' over old times. Swan went into the post to help someone, came out an' filled our cups again.

Albert finally looked at me an' said, "Boy you sure have raised hell with the army. You can walk up behind a soldier an' say, 'Will Chase,' they all jump. Half the young ones want out of the army so they can come join you. There have been more court martials this summer than in the last ten years.

"Captain Bush sent word that there aren't anymore cam-pains comin' your way until next spring. I'd say that's straight. Also he said there are some men to come in here an' take you out alive. You have some papers they want. He said you'd know what it was.

"Lee Henderson said to tell you everything is fine. He has Good Horse an' one of his sons workin' for him.

"The bad news is that Felter an' thirty men are somewhere here in the hills, over north of here. Word came to Good Horse. He's the one had me come out here to tell you."

We had more of the jug. I got up an' put Albert's horse up. Swan was fixin' supper. I left Albert an' Sharps alone for awhile an' walked to the creek. It felt good to be movin' again. At the creek I worked on my draw. It was gettin' better. Another week an' I'd be faster than before.

I knew exactly where Felter would be an' he knew I'd know. He'd have something up his sleeve. He'd not kill me until he had them papers back. The other three men wouldn't be happy until they had those papers. Gold he could get from that stream but the papers were in the bank in Kansas City. It took two of us to get them out.

I'd work out something or some way to get rid of Felter. Let him get out the gold. I'd take it later.

Back at the porch Albert told me Slim had said he had "a good line on Birtchfield." Said, "That kid Mark had them stirred up like a hornets nest. He'd killed three of them an' wounded three of four more. Run off a big bunch of their cattle he needs for evidence. Birtchfield is down in Texas again. Lester an' Mary don't have anything to do with the outlaws' end of the ranch. It's the kid Rick an' the old man.

"Lester an' Mary started their own outfit south of the fort. Slim has you a house, barn, bunkhouse an' corrals done. He bought some Hereford cattle, they are doin' good. Also he has bought about five hundred head of long horn Heifers."

We went in for supper of elk steaks an' squash. Then returned to the porch. Swan an' I walked on to the creek.

We sat on a log awhile. I stood up an' undressed an' waded into the creek. I heard Swan laugh, then she was beside me. We swam, later after we were dressed walkin' back we stopped at Standin' Elks lodge.

"Ho," I said.

"Enter my brother," he answered. He was settin' by the fire.

His woman brought the croc an' dipper. She was swollen with child. I laughed an' shook Standin' Elks hand. He was proud an' slapped her on the rear with pride,"Damn fine woman."

We talked of the fights we had had this summer. Then our talk turned to the hunt comin' this fall. I told him about Felter bein' up north. He nodded an' said, "This we can take care of."

"Not now," I told him, "Let them dig the gold for us. We will need it to help the people again in two years back East."

Swan an' I went to our room in the post. "What is botherin' 'you Will?"

"There are three places I should be an' this is where I want to be."

In the mornin' I had decided to go to the fort but out the west way. I could look at the horses we had put there. We left about noon an' Albert went with us. He was in bad shape but had brought along a gallon to get well on. We camped early on a nice stream up in the hills. Next mornin' we started early an' ran into a band of Sioux an' Shoshone. They were huntin' buffalo an' havin' bad luck.

The buffalo had not come back, not as many as had went south last fall. I told them of the whites killin' them for their hides. "That's all they take. Whenever you see them becareful, their guns shoot far. The Indians in the south skin for them an' get the meat after shooters are gone.

"We must keep them from our lands or we will have no buffalo in a couple of years.

One of the Shoshone laughed an' said,"There will always be buffalo."

"In three years when your children cry from hunger then remember what I have said."

Another Shoshone was ridin' an outstandin' Appy stud. I asked him if he would trade?

"For five good horses an' a fast shootin' rifle, three hand fulls of bullets." I agreed, told them to follow along an' I would trade by evenin'. I had a spare rifle an' hundreds of bullets, plenty of horses.

We rode over a ridge an' there were horses everywhere below us. There was three hundred or more in a big lush valley that you could see for miles. It was blocked on this end by this high wall an' ran wider the further it went. Water was runnin' right down the middle of it. Buffalo were grazin' far below on the valley floor. "I give you ten geldin's an' this rifle, five hand full of bullets but don't kill the buffalo in this valley." I got out the rifle from our pack horse an' the shells. He was lookin' at the rifle with pride.

"Now make a trap on this end of the valley. Go easy, move the horses slow, they are all broke to ride I'm sure. Don't take any mares an' don't take any with brands. Look good to make sure they have no brands for if they do, the Army will say you stole them.

"When you have your horses then turn the stud loose with the rest of the herd here in the valley. Do not run them an' chase them out of here, do you understand."

All said, "Yes."

Swan an' I rode on an' Albert rode up by Swan. "He sure trusts them don't he, how do you know they won't take the whole herd?"

"They won't" I said an' rode on.

We came into the place we had chosen for our ranch, sat lookin' at a ranch. There was hay cut an' stacked. Three big stacks here an' I could see three more down the valley. The big log house was beautiful as was the rest of the ranch.

A man came out of the house an' said. "Howdy." I asked for Slim. He said he was Slim's forman an' asked who I was.

"Will Chase," I said.

He came to full attention. "Mr Chase, I should have known you by the description I had. Do come in. Have something to eat won't you."

We went into the nicest little kitchen I had ever been in. We sat at the table an' had coffee. Swan was tickled with the house an' asked to see the front room. The young man was proud an' glad to show the rest of the house. The front room had a nice fireplace, it was damn nice.

We went back to the kitchen an' had more coffee. "Are you expectin' Slim tonight or soon?"

"Oh Yes, he should be here anytime. He's been around all day. I'll go put your horses up for you if you like," he said.

"I'll help you," I said an' got up. Albert said he'd be ridin' on into his saloon an' came outside with us. He rode off down the valley. He still looked like a bear to me but I'd bet he'd be one tough man.

At the barn the young man said his name was Chester Marrow. It was a big barn, room for ten horses. It had a saddle room an' a crib for corn.

We put up the horse an' he brought in some hay from outside. "I'll fill the mangers, there are three more horses to come in yet.

"Have Swan make herself at home for it is her home," he said as I started for the house. On the porch Albert had left the gallon jug. I picked it up as I went into the house. Swan was busy at the stove. She had a pile of steaks cut layin' on the table. Potatoes were on the stove an' some carrots of all things.

She had to show me the house again. One bedroom was ours for our stuff. It was hangin' there in a homemade closet. There was sheets on the bed. Slim had done a remarkable job.

The other two men had come in with Chester, eaten an' gone to the bunk house. Slim got home before dark. After puttin' his horse up he came to the house. Swan hugged his neck an' told him how she loved the house. He blushed but was proud.

We sat an' worked on the jug. He told me all that had happened while I was gone. Bush was waitin' for Birtchfield to come home so he could arrest him. Mark had brought in three hundred head of cattle with reworked brands an' left them at the fort. He brought us up-to-date on all that was goin' on.

"Be damn careful when you go in because Hinkel, Lestergood an' Morre are there. There is a big reward for you alive. Also Swan. They know they must have two of us at the bank to get back the papers. Hank is right there so they really need just one of us an' him.

"There is some ruff men in town. Bush has orders for your arrest also.

"In fact I don't know what the hell you're doin' down here anyway." We were gettin' a little drunk by now. Swan was drinkin' also. Slim got up, went to the cupboard an' came back with some labled whiskey. We continued it on into the night. We ended up goin' to bed without supper.

CHAPTER EIGHT

The Riders

In the mornin' I was up an' had the fire goin' an' coffee on before anybody else had stirred. I didn't know where Slim got the glass but it was nice to be able to look out without openin' the door. I looked out the east window as I was waitin' for the coffee to come to a boil, something had moved behind the haystack. I moved the coffee to the back of the stove an' stood there lookin' around the ranch yard. There was a pile of poles layin' down by the corral. A good spot for someone to cover the front door of the house. North was a pair of large rocks, another good place.

I seen him then, he darted from the haystack to the barn. I had a good look at him. A western dressed man carryin' a rifle an' wearin' a pistol. He couldn't be friendly or he'd not be sneakin' around the place instead of comin' to the door.

A magpie flew up an' started to land on the rocks, then darted away. Something was there. Slim came into the kitchen then an' seen me lookin' out the window.

"What's up?" he asked.

"We got company out there an' I don't think they are here for breakfast. One's in the barn an' I'm sure there's one behind them rocks just north of the haystack A magpie started to land then changed his mind.

"You watch. I'll tell Swan," I said. She was up an' I laid it out to her. She smiled an' nodded, reached for her pistol, belt an' buckled it on. I went back to Slim. "When do the men come from the bunkhouse?" I asked.

"They will be stirrin' around about now. They have coffee down there an' feed before they have breakfast. One cooks an' the other two do chores. They take turns. Reckon I should holler at them?" he asked.

"Let's wait a minute. I think there is someone behind the pile of poles down there." We both had our rifles in hand an' were standin' on each side of the window. "Where did you get the glass Slim?"

"Man up from Denver, had a lot of it."

"Let's slide open these two windows, I hate to see it shot up." I slid the glass open, it was safe from bullets. Slim waited ten seconds an' done the same, like one man opened both windows.

"There's a door in the front room goin' south an' one in your room goin' north," he told me. "Put in three for just this kind of a deal. There's two in the bunk house also," he said.

Swan was lookin' out the west window when I looked in the front room. "There's two in the rocks back here," she said. I slid the window open an' looked, I could see an arm behind a log an' a knee an' part of a leg behind a rock.

"Swan we have to warn the men in the bunkhouse. You take the arm an' I'll get the leg." We fired together. She shattered the arm, I nailed the leg. The arm staggered out an' she killed him. The leg was gone but I knew it was hit. There was three shots from the front an' I heard bullets slap into wood.

The leg's shoulder came out a little an' I shot it. A man rolled out from behind the rock, I shot him again.

Two bullets came through the window. Swan gave them an answer, cussed, she must have missed.

There were three shots from the bunkhouse. A man came staggerin' down the hill. He took one in the chest an' was flung to the ground.

I heard Slim cuss from the kitchen. I went to see how he was doin'. He'd been creased on the left arm. It was bleedin' some. I tied a dish towel around it. "One behind the rocks, one in the barn an' one behind the poles," he said.

"We still have one on the hill out back also," I told him, "Maybe more."

Two rifles opened up on the pole pile. They were shootin' hell out of it. A man came runnin' an' almost got to the barn corner. He was hit hard, done a flip an' never moved. It got awful quiet then for quite awhile. Then we heard a horse runnin'. A man popped up an' was over some rocks so fast no one shot. Shortly another horse could be heard.

I hollered at the bunkhouse an' got an answer.

"Anybody hit?" I asked.

"Wayne got killed," Chester said. "Bill got his ear nicked."

Swan called from the other room, "This other one got away also." I looked around outside. It looked like it was over.

I had a long drink an' passed it to Slim. He had some an' I took off his shirt. The bullet had cut deep along the arm, takin' a chunk of meat with it. I took the bottle an' washed it out good, then wrapped it again with the dish towel.

We each hit the bottle purty good. I then poured some more on the towel an' let it soak in. Chester came in with Bill. His right side was bloody. Swan went to work on him.

I went to the barn an' saddled my horse. I had filled my pockets with shells. At the house everything looked under control. I had another drink, told Swan to wait here. I'd be back later. She nodded an' kissed my cheek. I had another drink an' took the bottle with me. Stickin' it into the saddle bag I mounted an' rode south.

Half a mile I found where the riders had come together on the little road. They were goin' south. Five miles later they turned up a side draw. A stream came down the draw. There were cattle in it, the bunch had been split by the riders an' hadn't gotten together again. I swung to the tree covered ridge on the right an' went on.

The draw narrowed an' got rough with big rocks on both sided. Another half mile on I could smell smoke so I left my horse an' went on foot. Damn these men, if they'd leave me an' the Indians alone I'd not be out here huntin' them.

I could be gettin' ready for the fall hunt. It was time lookin' at the color of the trees.

I came upon their camp shortly. They had been here a while, half an elk hung in a tree. A leanto was put up. Five men sat at the fire, they were deep in talk. I crawled with in twenty five yards of them. They never had a clue I was there. Lester Morre was talkin'.

"God Dammit, I told you to get them all. I want Will Chase dead, either or both the squaw an' Slim alive. We can get Hank anytime. Our man in Kansas City said it took two for them to get the papers. We have one man workin' for Hank, another watchin' him at night. That old basterd chases more women an' parties almost every night. Where are they now?"

I was proud of Hank. The man I had seen go to the barn spoke up. "There probably buryin' their dead about now, along with ours."

"That's wrong," Morre said. "That Will Chase can't dig a hole big enough to bury his dead, don't give a damn, he just leaves them lay."

"We killed one an' wounded two of them for sure, maybe more. We'll go back tonight an' get the ones you want Mister Morre."

I thought, the hell you will mister. I shot him between the eyes as he took a drink of coffee. I got another one on the rise, missed twice, the three were pinned between two big rocks. A brave one made a long dive for a log layin' ten yards away. I got him in mid-dive. He was floppin' a little so I put another one into him.

I sat there an' fed my rifle full again. "Morre I'll let you two walk if you throw out your guns an' come out."

The other hired hand yelled, "Go to Hell Chase," an' came out shootin'. He thought he knew where I was from my voice, wrong again. He shot a tree three times. I killed him. I shifted an' fired into the bigger rock behind Morre. Chips of the rock an' lead was spittin' on him. He yelped at each shot.

"Enough," he yelled an' stuck his hands above the rock. I shot through his right hand. The hands disappeared. There was some whimperin' an' cussin'.

"What's the matter Morre. Ain't this like Washington?"

"You said I could come out."

"Hell man, you forgot to throw out your guns." A pistol flopped out into the grass.

"That's better, now is that all you have, cause Morre if it isn't an' you have another one I'm goin' to kill you when I find it." After a pause he threw out a derringer. "Is that all?"

"Yes," he answered.

"Now walk out so I can see what a skunk looks like." He came out slowly, expectin' to be shot again. I walked down to him an' pushed him to the fire. I then picked up the guns layin' around. "Set down Morre." He did, holdin' his hand. His left shoulder was bleedin' also.

I drug away the dead man, pulled his pistol an' put it with the rifles. "I wish my cousins were alive," he said. "They would take care of you".

"Mr Morre they tried don't you remember." It seemed to hit him then. They had tried an' died.

"Got any whiskey?" I asked.

"Over by the leanto," he said. I got it an' tore a piece off a shirt there. Walkin' back to him I said, "Stick out your hand." I poured it full of whiskey. It ran on through so I poured more. I took a drink, handed him the bottle, he had one, then another. I took the bottle from him an' poured some more on his hand.

"Mr Morre I'm goin' to let you live on one condition. I'll let you walk but if I ever see you in this country again I'll kill you on sight. Do you understand?" He nodded.

"Empty your pockets," he did, pocket knife, wallet, money an' six extra shells for the little gun. "Now start walkin'," I told him. He looked at me, started to say something then walked off down the valley. He never looked back.

I gathered all the guns, gun belts, rifles, shells, a new coffee pot an' the money the men had. It looked like Morre had paid up front. I took a horse that wasn't branded puttin' everything on him. There was bacon in the pan so I ate it. Looked through the food pack in the leanto. I took the coffee an' sugar. I passed Morre on the way down the valley. He was stridin' right along.

Neither one of us said a word. I thought he might turn back after I was gone but decided he wouldn't take the chance.

Chester had Wayne in the ground when I got back. They were all settin' at the table . When I rode up they came out an' helped unpack. Slim walked to the barn with me an' I put my horse up. His arm was wrapped better than I had done.

"Hurt much," I said.

"No it will be good as new in a couple days. Quite a pile of guns you brought in," he said.

"I let Morre go back, walkin'. He had a hole through his right hand an' was actin' mad. I told him 'I'd kill him on sight.' He may leave."

I told everyone what I heard about them havin' Hank staked out. He was safe as long as they didn't have one of us.

That bunch is out to get them papers back an' they don't care who goes under."

We ate a bite an' I said I was goin' down to Charlie Walker's place an' see what Mark had goin' or where I could find him.

"I'll not be back tonight so don't get nervous if I don't show up." Swan said she was goin'. After a year of bein' with her I knew not to say no an' was glad she wanted to come along.

Charlie was at the barn so we rode in, tyin' the horses up. He was glad to see us an' said he knew where Mark was goin' to spend the night. "Do you remember where you found Jim Knight?" I nodded. "Up another three miles theres a little spring. He's camped there. It's in the left hand canyon." I thanked him an' we went on.

We were havin' coffee when Mark eased into camp. We shook hands an' Swan poured him some coffee. He started in tellin' me all the news he had from Charlie.

"We got most of that Mark, also heard about the cattle deal at the fort. That was a good trick. How did you get all them cattle there alone an' with no one knowin'?"

He was proud of that deal. Good Horse had lent him some of his braves. They are good cowboys when they want to be. "Also heard you been slingin' some lead around." He told of that; he had some run-ins with the Birtchfields hands that brought cattle up from the south. Had a battle with them up here once an' run in with them once south of the fort.

"Lester don't have anything to do with this deal. He an' Mary live on a small place south of the fort. They run a couple hundred cows an' only three hands. Old man Birtchfields is the kingpin. He has a one-eyed man works for or with him.

"They bring cattle up here, put Tto brands on them an' push them on west. They go with two herds a year. Also they take a wagon train of stolen supplies with each herd. The Captain has a warrant on them both right now, but they ain't been here so he's been unable to do anything until now, they are back.

"I have a place located to build a ranch on when I get my named cleared. Have been puttin' some cattle up there all summer. I cut out unbranded cows from their stolen herds an' go on northwest with them. There are a couple Indian families that have been helpin' me. Just like your Indians work with you."

We had more coffee an' he told me the Birtchfields were at the house right now.

"Where is Buck James?"

"He's with Lester an' Mary. He's a good enough fellow but he's awful tough an' fast. Did you know his sister is their mother? She was killed many years back. He has worked for the old man an' watched after them. Guess he lived with Birtchfield from the time his sister married him."

He saddled a different horse an' we rode on out. "The moon will be up early tonight. I know the way back here by heart anyway," he said.

As we rode along I asked him if "he always came the same way."

"Most of the time," he said.

"Why?"

"Cause they probably have someone tailin' you by now."

"Let's go another way," I said an' turned up into the trees. "Another thing, were not goin' back to sleep there tonight either," I told him.

We came to their ranch from the south, leavin' our horses half-a-mile back in some cherry brush. It was quite dark so we just walked up close with no worry. There was lights in the house as well as the bunkhouse.

We laid awhile an' listened. Then eased on to the house. We could look into the front room. Floyd an' Rick were both in sight. Three women were settin' with their backs to us. The Birtchfields were talkin' to them. Rick walked over an' slapped one of them. Her head rocked back an' he slapped her again.

I couldn't figure out why a woman would just set there an' put up with it. Rick pulled his hand back again but Floyd said some thing to him. Rick dropped his hand, swung around an' faced him. They had some words. Rick lowered his head an' went out of sight. Another man came into view, had the women get up an' led them into another room. All of them had their hands tied behind them.

The man came back an' got a lamp. He went back into the room where we had seen them go. Rick came out onto the porch. We all laid flat an' still. He was within twenty five feet of us smokin' a cigarette. His dad came out. They talked. "Son I don't like this at all, but you know what them other women brought out there. A girl is worth a lot more than cattle an' horses. He gives a thousand apiece but he don't want them all beat up. It's also hard to explain if you should meet anybody on the trail.

"We'll leave them here for the night. Jack can go with them early in the mornin'. I don't want them around here. This could sure get us hung."

He went in an' Rick walked off to the bunkhouse. The other man hadn't come back. Floyd sat down in a chair with his back to the window.

"Stay here," I said an' moved away, goin' around to the other side of the house. I stayed out of the light from the window an' moved so I could look in. First I saw the man. He was settin' by the door readin' a book. The girls were settin' on the bed, all had their backs to me. They just sat there.

I went back around, moved up on Swan an' Mark. I touched Mark's foot, scared the hell out of him. "I'm goin' in an' try for the girls," an' moved away.

I walked up the three steps an' through the door, closin' it behind me. Floyd never looked up. I just walked up behind him an' stamped my gun down on his white head. He slumped in his chair with blood comin' from his skull. I reached down an' got his gun. I moved to the door where I was sure the girls were, opened that door, tried to break the man's head open that was settin' there readin'. He ducked but I got him with the second swing. He went down to stay.

I got his gun an' looked up at the girls. They had surprise on their faces but were quiet. "Stay quiet," I said, "We're goin' to walk out of here." I talked as I was cuttin' them loose. Their first reaction was to rub their wrists.

I cut the last one loose, "I'm takin' a man with us. You stay behind us an' don't ask questions. There are two people out there to help, come on," I said. They followed as I walked out into the front room

Together we got Floyd on his feet an' over my shoulder. I had my gun in my hand. Just as we got to the door it opened.

There stood Rick an' another man. I shot both of them in the chest. We walked on out. Men came scramblin' out of the bunkhouse. I open fired on them. Swan an' Mark were firin' also. I saw two men go down an' the rest were divin' back for the bunkhouse. "Keep them there a few minutes," I said.

"Come on girls." We went through the meadow at a trot. "Untie one of them horse." The black-haired girl did. "Now you other two get on the other side an' help me load him." He was tall but thin an' we never had much trouble. "One of you get up behind him," the black-haired one did.

I grabed my rope an' put the loop on his feet an' then threw it under the horse, went to the other side an' finished with his arms an' tied it to the saddle horn. "Don't let him slip girl, I want him alive."

We rode back toward the ranch. The firin' had slacked off to spaced shots. The lights had been put out in the bunkhouse. Now an' then a gun flash would show. We stopped out a ways. I had the girls wait here handin' one my reins.

I ran toward the corrals an' barn, grabbed a rope an' two bridles off the fence where saddles were hangin'. Someone fired from the barn. I pulled out the gun from the "reader of books," shot five times, a man staggered out of the barn door an' fell.

I caught one horse easy but had trouble with another I was gettin' scared now. Finally a horse stopped in the corner.

He let me catch him. Back at the gate I opened it wide an' jumped on one horse, leadin' the other I pulled Floyd's gun an' drove the other horses out the gate.

The damn horse I was leadin' didn't lead worth a damn. He drug it seemed. I felt like a settin' duck goin' along at a walk. Mark came along an' chased him for me. We got some distance out when Swan came ridin' up on my horse. We stopped an' Mark jumped on the horse I was leadin'.

The moon was peakin' up a little over the ridge. We needed to be gone. When Mark asked the horse to go he just swallowed his head an' bucked. Mark was jerkin' his head an' cussin'. He finally got his head up an' we got under way.

Men were comin' out of the bunkhouse shootin' at us even though we were out of range. We headed south at a lope. Mark's horse would lope a ways an' then buck a ways.

Swan turned up the hill an' went over the ridge headin' due north. We came down to the stream an' sat waitin' for Mark. When he caught up I asked him the best way back to the fort. "Down stream," he said, "The road's just on the other side of them bushes.

"The next time you steal a horse Will, check an' make sure he's broke to ride." About then I hoped never to steal another one.

Just as we started we heard horses comin'. Three riders loped past on the road. The moon was up full now. It was nearly as bright as day but they never seen us. Guess they figured we were ahead of them yet. Mark said, "We're cut off from the fort now, let's cross an' head up to our camp. We can get me a better horse there."

"Okay," I said, "But go in another way than usual. Some one may be waitin' for us there." We hadn't gone far when the black-haired girl said, "This man's startin' to kick a little." We stopped an' I had the girl get down an' help me get him loose. Floyd sat on the ground with his head in his hands.

"You all may as well get down an' have a rest. Looks like it's goin' to be a bit before Mr. Birtchfield is goin' to feel like ridin'.

He looked up at me then said, "You're Will Chase."

"You're right Floyd," I said.

"You'll be sorry when we turn you over to Bush also," I said. "They might hang you as fast as you did Ed Hunter."

He talked without thinkin', "Had to do that, he seen the women," then he stopped an' looked at the three women standin' there.

"You girls heard that, remember to tell Captain Bush when you see him." They all said they would. We talked then of how we was goin' to get these women an' Floyd to Captain Bush.

"You all head for the ranch instead of the camp up the draw. It's about twelve of fourteen miles but you can be there by mornin'. I'll head for the fort an' get Albert Shaw to bring the Captain out there."

Swan said, "I'm goin' with you."

I never said no. "Put Birtchfield on his own horse, he won't, get away ridin' that plug. You four can double up on the oth- ers." We all got mounted up an' headed in our directions. By one o'clock Swan an' I were at the little log cabin behind the saloon.

There were three horses in the corral an' a light in the window.

I rapped on the door an' Albert said, "Who's there."

"Will Chase" an' the door swung open. His women was in the bed. Swan an' I stepped in an' he pulled the door closed behind us.

"Sorry to bother you Albert but we need to see Captain Bush." He never said a word, just pulled his mocccasins on an' started out the door, "Wait Albert, maybe you beter know the story." He said, "No, I'll let you in the saloon an' bring him there alone."

"Okay if you can get him to come alone. One more thing, I want you to lead a horse away from here."

We went out together an' he caught his horse an' saddled up. I handed him the reins when he had mounted up. "Can we borrow these other two horses?" I asked.

"Help yourself, there's another saddle an' bridle in the saloon. What about this bridle?" he asked, holdin' up the reins. "Throw it away when you turn the horse loose." He rode away toward the fort.

I called Swan after I had changed her saddle to another horse an' turned hers loose in the small pasture. We went into the saloon an' I put a couple of sticks on the fire, she lit a lamp. I found the saddle, bridle an' blanket an' went out an' saddled the other horse.

Swan had coffee an' meat on the table when I came back. She brought a cup of coffee for herself an' another cup which she poured half full of whiskey. We sat down an' waited, nether of us havin' anything to say. It wasn't long until we heard horses comin'. Only two of them.

Albert came in first, then the Captain. Albert went for a cup an' Bush walked up to the table.

I stood an' stuck out my hand. He never hesitated, took mine in both of his warmly. He sat down an' took off his hat, said, "Evenin' Miss Swan." She nodded her head an' smiled. "What's the rush to get us all up at this hour of the night Will? You could have come an' seen me anytime, that fancy suit might have fooled some people but not me. Swan you look awful good in dresses, like the lady you are." We all four laughed.

"What kind of a mess you in now Will?" I took a good drink an' started in with this mornin', cuttin' out all the little stuff."This mornin' we were attacked by Morres men. Four didn't make it. Three got away, they joined Morre an' another man. I caught up with them, killed four an' sent Morre in walkin'. He's to go back East an' leave me alone." This never got much reaction from the Captain.

"Heard this from Morre this mornin', said 'you robbed him an' killed his men.'"

"We then went to Birtchfield to snoop around. Mark Hunter met us an' went along. Rick was slappin' hell out of a girl. He died an' so did one of their men. Couple of others got hit. I don't know if they lived or died.

"We got the three girls an' the old man Birtchfield on the way to Slim's ranch. They will be there when we get there.

"Birtchfield fessed up to hangin' Ed Hunter cause he had seen Floyd with some women. He sells them to a man out West for a thousand each."

Captian Bush asked, "You didn't happen to kill a man with a patch over one eye did you?"

"Not that I know of," I said.

Bush said, "Too bad, he's the one that's been swipin' the gals."

"We'll ride out an' talk to the girls whenever your ready," I said.

The sun was up an' breakfast was ready when we got there. The girls said they had been kidnapped from Denver, they had all been taken the same night an' brought right here. "Now tell the Captain what Birtchfield said about Ed Hunter." They told what he had said. Bush looked at Mark an' asked, "Why didn't you tell me about this?'

"Dad never had time to tell me so I had no idea why Birtchfield came an' hung him, there was no beef hangin' there when they hung him. I had to run or I'd have been hung also."

Captain Bush then looked at me an' asked if I knew "about Morre's partners."

I said, "Yes," but didn't know where Hinkel or Lestergood were. I then told him about Felter killin' Alice up in the hills. "You know I trade for gold like my father used to. I went back to Washington to help keep the Black Hills for the Indians an' ran into them. If it hadn't been for Felter's greed as well as theirs they wouldn't have bought the land an' lost their asses so bad.

"Now their tryin' for the hills again even though the Congress turned down the Settlers Act bill an' it can't come up for another year an' more. Felter is up here now diggin' in them hills. When I get this settled down here I'm goin' up an' run him out again."

"What are you goin' to do next spring Will when the army comes in to survey?"

"They can't next spring an' if the bill gets passed the next an' they keep the army out the survey crews can come an' do what they must."

"It's comin' Will, you put it off one more winter but not forever."

"I know," I said, "But the Indians are learnin' to farm an' 'they already have cattle an' ranches.

He looked at me an' said, "I have heard this but didn't believe it."

"We have set them up so they have the good land an' water. It won't happen to Sioux like it has with the rest of the Indians."

"Are they as well trained an' armed as everyone says?"

"Better now. We have three gattlin' guns to help us. Every brave has a repeatin' rifle an' is a good shot.

We decided to sleep for awhile before startin' back. Captain Bush took Slim's room an' we went to ours.

CHAPTER NINE

Legend of the West

We left for the fort an' post early in the afternoon with Mark, Captain Bush, the three girls an' Birtchfield. Mark rode in the rear with the black-haired girl. It looked like they were gettin' along fine. Mark was busy tellin' about the ranch he was buildin'.

Before we got to the fort Swan an' I told the Captain good-by an' turned off into the trees an' let the rest go past. Birtchfield said "I'll see you in hell Will Chase, in Hell, I say."

I just waved at him.

Swan was wearin' a ridin' skirt an' blouse under her hip-length jacket. I knew she had her pistol on also. I was wearin' my suit with my pistol on the left side.

We rode to the post, tied up in front an' went in. The place was as it had been a year ago. Lee Henderson came from behind the counter an' shook my hand. "Good seein' you again Mr. an' Mrs. Chasin' come an' have some coffee. We can talk awhile." He was rather insistent so we went. He poured us coffee an' added whiskey to mine. He sat my cup at the end of the table. Swan's to my right with her back to the door. He than sat on my left.

"Sorry about bein' so formal," he said, "But there are men in town huntin' you. Mr Morre left town but you have others that wish you trouble." He said he was doin' real well with the post. He would show me the books at dinner if we would come or right now if I wished.

"Lee I know nothin' of books an' I trust you. Have all the way or I'd not be your partner."

"I can get your share right now," he said.

I don't want it either. Can't I just come an' see how your doin'?"

He looked embarased. "Oh," he said, "I'm sorry Will, guess I'm just nervous."

We talked of the post an' how it was doin'. I asked him if he had "gone through the papers I'd left him?" He had an' gave me a run down.

We owned the sawmill, it was doin' good. The hotel, half the one bar, the blacksmith shop, he had a man break up more land an' farm the field on shares. We had a good corn crop again. The hogs were ready to butcher an' he had a man doin' it, curin' the ham an' bacon. Once he got started he got carried away. When he slowed down he filled my cup with whiskey an' poured Swan more coffee. We talked more. I asked if he knew "any of the gun hands that were huntin' me."

He described one as a man dressed in black clothes, a white hat. Another was part Indian wearin' a buckskin shirt. He suspected two more were short men that looked like brothers. They both wore their guns tied down low, one was left handed.

"Say Lee for an Easterner your awful keen on the lookin'."

"Thanks," he said, "But they are after my partners."

"Let's go over to the hotel Swan an' get a room, everybody knows were in town anyway."

We mounted an' rode up the street. Albert Shaw an' a couple other men were standin' outside the west saloon up the street. The sun had gone down but it was still full light. We rode on up to them an' said everything looked okay as far as we could see. Shaw said, "Keep an eye peeled."

At the hotel Lester an' Mary were havin' supper. I tipped my hat an' they both nodded. Mary's eyes turned on Swan, studyin' her every move. I got a room an' we went back out an' started back to the livery barn to put our horses up.

Billy Hagon was standin' in the street when we came out. He waited until we were halfway across the street an' then called to me. "Will Chase, you killed a friend of mine, never gave him a chance." He had himself primed for this.

Several people were on the street. The ones behind us moved as the ones behind him did. Horses bein' ridden stopped, their riders sat motionless.

"I killed seven men yesterday Billy, none I'd be proud to call a friend. They were all back-shootin' slime." He was gettin' mad. "Why don't you get on your horse an' ride back to Texas little man, ain't no place up here for your kind."

Swan an' I kept walkin', straight at him. "Ain't no one to pay you now, you're dyin' for free." He licked his lips. We were on top of him, less than three steps. We never stopped, we split an' there he was. Swan on one side me on the other. I reached down an' pulled his pistol from the holster an' stuck it into my belt. He was red faced an' sputterin'.

Someone on the street laughed then another, eight or ten men were now laughin', it sounded loud in the still street. He broke an' ran, then he ran between us an' went across the street to his horse. Swan an' I stepped up on the porch, a shot rang out. We both dived for the ground. Swan an' I both comin' up with guns in our hands. Billy Hagon was layin' in the street, his rifle on the ground where he had flung it.

I looked around but no one had a gun out, many had their hands up. I looked up the street an' Shaw waved, his big rifle in his hand. I waved back. Swan an' I straightend up an' went into the hotel. Many people were in the street now. Lee Henderson was in front of the post, a rifle in his hands.

We sat down an' ordered two coffees an' two shots of whiskey. Mark came hurryin' through the door, seein' us settin' there sippin' our coffee, he came over grinnin' an' joined us. The waiter brought him a cup of coffee, a glass an' the bottle.

"Damn Will I never figured Shaw would take a hand in this."

"Mark that's probably the toughest man in this country. He takes no chances an' bothers no one."

Lester an' Mary came to our table an' stopped. Lester said, "Mr Chase, we have no stake in this that's goin' on between you and father. We, Mary an' I split with them almost a year ago when they first started with the women. Buck had nothin' to do with it either or the stolen cattle."

I rose an' asked them to join us an' they accepted. Lester pulled out a chair for Mary an' they sat down. Again the waiter came with glasses. Swan asked if the hotel had wine. The waiter rushed away an' came back with a bottle of labeled wine. He poured for Swan, she tasted an' nodded, then he poured for Mary. He smiled an' sat the bottle down an' left.

Lester started askin' questions about the heavy bodied Herferd cattle. He wanted to know if there was a way he could bring eight or ten of his best longhorn cows up an' have them bred.

Better yet would we sell him one of our bulls. Swan an' Mary were talkin' of the East, both were smilin' an' sippin' their wine.

"Lester why don't you an' Mary ride up next week an' have supper with us, spend the night. We have thirty or forty head of full Hereford calves about ready to wean. Maybe you an' Slim can work out a deal on a couple bull calves. He is buildin' a fine ranch up there."

Swan an' Mary were laughin' now an' it sounded good, honest laughter.

The three girls came down the stairs then an' we lost Mark. The black-haired girl flashed him a smile as he met them at the foot of the stairs.

The Birtchfields excused themselves. They were stayin' the night at the hotel. "Maybe we can have a drink later," Lester said.

We had a nice supper with Lee. He apologized several times about the cookin'. He said he'd never been married but did like the idea of havin' the comfort of home an' all that went with it.

Swan in her open way said she'd "bring over some ladies tomarrow for him to talk to. You need a woman or two workin' in the store anyway. I think the dark-haired one is goin' to stay up here. If the others had a job they would stay also. I think they have to be here for the trial of Floyd Birtchfield. That won't be for a week or so."

Lee was embarrassed but pleased with the idea.

We talked of the post awhile an' he said, "Good Horse an' his family had gone on a hunt," but would be back in awhile.

Swan an' I walked to the door, then she decided she needed a change of clothes. Asked Lee if she might get into the store. He gladly opened the store for her. Lee an' I waited on the porch. She came out with quite an arm full of clothes. "I wrote everything down an' left the paper on the counter," she said.

As we walked back to the hotel she said, "Most of these are for the girls," I chuckled, "A woman out to trap a man," I said. A few steps on she said, "Self protection."

"What," I asked.

"If they're all married off then you can't have them, Bull."

At the hotel door I stopped an' turned her to me. "You need not worry," I said.

Lester an' Mary were settin' in the lobby when we came in. Mary joined Swan an' they took the clothes up to the girls. Lester an' I went to the small bar an' ordered a drink. We talked of many things. Land, cattle, horses, gold an' many other things.

A man came to our table an' asked if he could join us. Lester an' I both rose an' he introduced himself as Whitehead from Washington. "I'd like to ask you some questions about the gold, the gold deal in Washington, the fights with the army this past summer an' many more things. Some people in Washington think you are a hero, others think you're an outlaw fightin' your own kind."

"The Sioux are my people."

"Tell me of Swan, is she always by your side in battle? Is she a born killer?"

"I'll let you talk to her in the mornin'. You can be your own judge." He bought us a drink an' turned his attention to Lester. This man brought your father in on very serious charges. How do you feel about this? Lester just raised his glass an' said, "I'm drinkin' with him ain't I."

We went up stairs an' knocked on the door. Swan let us in. The girls had all changed an' looked good. They were happy an' laughin'. They had been drinkin' wine. Mary was watchin' me closly an' it made me nervous as hell.

Finally everyone was gone. I picked Swan up an' swung her around an' kissed her. She tipped her head back an' looked me in the eyes. She was very serious. Then she smiled an' kissed me again. We sat an' talked of the newspaper man. She said she would talk with him in the mornin' an' not tell him of the gold.

In the mornin' at breakfast Mark said the girls were goin' to stay at his dad's old house if that was "okay with me."

"Hell yes," I said, "It's your house anyway."

Swan said she wanted "the girls to meet Lee Henderson." He needed to hire some help, one maybe two people. Maybe the girls could help him out. Sherry was twenty-one, Kathy was twenty-two. Both had taught school a little.

As they left the hotel I noticed quite a few men hangin' around outside an' smiled. Word was out about three good-lookin' women bein' in town.

Lester excused himself an' said he needed to put an order in at the post also, an' went along behind. He was taken with Sherry.

Mary an' I sat an' had more coffee. We talked of small things. Finally she asked me if I had ever "thought of settlin' down."

"I think I'm purty well settled now," I said. "I have an interest in three ranches, this hotel, two posts an' a horse outfit."

Mary looked at me an' said, "An' always on the go. Don't you ever want to just stay in one place?"

"No," I said, then, "Yes, at the Gap." Then I told her of the Gap. The "beautiful hills, trees that sing even when you can't feel the wind. How the stream started from under a rock an' came tumblin' down through the valley. How the snow never gets deep an' when the wind was howlin' everywhere else the high hills keep it from pilin' the snow deep in the valleys.

The stream never froze in some places. There were all kinds of wild berries in the summer, game everywhere. I told of how happy the people were, of children laughin' an' playin', of the dances an' singin'. Now the white people wanted to take all this away.

I stopped, embarrassed that I had gotten carried away talkin' of the Gap. Mary sat lookin' at me for awhile. Then she asked, "Is Swan from there also?"

"No she is from the basin, east three days easy ridin' from the Gap. I have cattle an' horses there. Buffalo Hump is the chief. He trades an' things for me."

Swan came back then. She was smilin' that happy smile. She sat down an' said, "Lee hired both of them an' they are already workin'."

The newspaper man came in an' joined us. I introduced Mary an' Swan. Mary excused herself an' went to the post. Whitehead looked at Swan an' said, "No one will ever believe that you are a killer."

Swan looked him up an' down. When he dropped his eyes she calmly said, "Mr Whitehead I'm not a killer. Everyone who has fought me or Will has shot first or were tryin' to take what is ours. If they want to live they shoud not bother us or our people."

Whitehead said, "No offense Swan, I'm here to get an honest story to send back East. If I offend you it is only by my stupididty. May we continue?" She nodded an' they started. He went from where she was born up until today. When he finished he sat writin' for awhile.

I had ordered a bottle an' glasses an' had four drinks before he had his first. I had learned things of Swan I had not ever thought about.

"Could we quit until after lunch?" he asked. "I have so much to write now it will take all night." We agreed to talk with him at four up in our room. Swan went upstairs an' I went to the saloon down the street. The newsman was still writin' when we left him.

At the saloon I ordered a drink an' stood talkin' to the bartender of the frost we'd had last night. We then talked about Birtchfield, the girls an' all the wagons goin' west that were tryin' it late.

We had three more drinks an' the people were driftin' in after dinner. A couple card games at the tables started.

Suddenly the bartender froze, lookin' over my shoulder, he stepped away, I unbuttoned my coat an' turned around. There was Lestergood an' the pair of brothers. They came a couple steps closer. "We don't need you anymore now Chase. We have Swan an' with you dead the papers will be ours."

I guess they thought I would plead for her to be turned loose or for my life, I'm not sure what they were thinkin', maybe they weren't thinkin' at all.

As the word, "ours," came out of Lestergoods mouth I drew an' shot the left handed one, then the right handed one. Him I shot twice, his gun went off into the floor. Left hand was raisin' his gun, I put a bullet into his chest. It slammed him into the floor. His gun went off an' hit his own foot.

Lestergood was fumblin', tryin' to get out his gun. It came out of his pocket. I had walked up on him an' as he looked up with his gun in his hand I slapped it away, puttin' mine between his eyes.

"Get down on your knees you cheap snake," he did, whimperin' an' sobbin'. The newsman came through the door. He stopped dead in his tracks.

"Tell me where you have Swan." He gasped for air an' started beggin' for his life. The newsman said, "Don't Will, don't kill him."

"Shut up," I said. "Where's she at Lestergood?" I pressed the barrel against his forehead, he leaned over backwards.

"Where? or I'll kill you." He gasped for air. "Tell me or I'll kill you." I pressed harder, he choked an' sobbed. "Two miles south in a cabin up a draw, turn at a big rock on the right, turn right."

"How many?"

"Three, Hinkle an' two others."

I stepped back an' started reloadin' my gun. Lestergood colapsed on the floor. I kicked all the guns away from him an' walked to the bar an' downed my drink. The bartender hurried to refill it.

The newsman came up an' said "I'm sorry Will. Would you have killed him?"

"Yes," I said an' walked back to him. He was shakin' an' looked up at me. "When I get back you be gone." He nodded.

My horse was in the stable an' I hollered across the street at the livery man who was out front, pitchfork in his hand, "Get my horse ready." He turned an' went back in.

I went for my rifle at the hotel. My horse was at the door when I came down. I thanked the livery man an' went south at a lope. When I could see the big rock ahead I swung up the hill. Fifteen minutes later I was crawlin' over the ridge. The cabin was below me an' up a bit. There were four horses saddled an' two pack horse all ready to go. They must have been goin' to kill me an' head right out.

I laid in the shade an' had rocks on both sides of me. A man in a huntin' shirt came out an' stood awhile then went back in. Thirty minutes after, the one in black came out. He went to a horse an' pulled a bottle from the saddle bag. He had a drink an' looked down the road. Then went back in. They were gettin' nervous now. The sun was behind the hill an' it was gettin' late.

They built a fire an' the smoke was raisin' straight up. By now they were talkin'. They still had Swan an' needed to get her to Kansas City. Hank was already there.

Both hired guns came out then an' looked down the road. They made a discussion an' went back in. If they didn't leave purty soon my shootin' light would be gettin' bad. They had Swan an' needed her alive, to kill her was to lose.

I knew I could get two of them before they knew what was happenin'. Also I knew when the first one was hit Swan would be off an' gone if her feet weren't tied. I knew what two I'd shoot first.

Just before dark they came out an' put Swan on her horse not tyin' her feet but tied her hands in front an' then tied them to the saddle horn. All three men mounted an' the man in black took her reins, started off leadin' her horse. Hinkel an' buckskin were behind.

Just as they started, I seen how it was I shot the man in black dead-center. Swan kicked her horse an' I killed the other man in the huntin' shirt. Swan was off an' runnin'. I shot Hinkel's horse from under him. It was a hell of a wreck. Horse's legs, man's arms, legs, when it came to a stop Hinkle was on his hands an' knees, his head hangin' down. I ran up behind him an' smashed him in the head with my rifle butt. He went down onto the ground.

I ran down the road an' caught a horse, went on down the road at a dead run. I came around a bend an' met Swan. She was comin' back at a walk. She had caught a bridle rein as it flew back. The other one was broken off short.

I slid to a stop an' cut her hands loose, leaned over an' kissed her. She smiled, "I knew you would come," she said an' we rode back up the trail.

Hinkle was still on the ground. We gathered up the bodies as well as the live one, puttin' their guns all on the pack horses. We got out the bottle an' had a few snorts on the way into town. When we got to the stream I stopped. Swan looked back at me.

"Swan I'm goin' up to the west saloon, you ride into town an' ask at the hotel for Captain Bush. Don't answer any questions, there will be plenty asked, just ask for Captain Bush.

That newsman will have something to write about by mornin'. I'll see you at the fort."

I went around the post area an' came to Shaw's corral, tied up my horse, walked into the saloon. Albert looked up at me an' reached for a cup an' poured it full of whiskey.

As I sat the cup down I laughed. He gave me a funny look but said nothin' until he had a drink from his cup. I laughed again.

"Well shithead, let me in on it or get the hell out of here," he told me.

There were four other mountain men in the saloon so I motioned them up an' bought a round. I told the story of the newspaper man, an' then told how I'd sent Swan in with Hinkle an' the two bodies.

Albert said. "Damn man she will end up bein' a legend of the West." We all had a good laugh an' finished our drinks. We went out the door an' looked toward the other saloon. Swan was comin' up the road toward us. A large crowd followin' her. She rode on past. "I'll wait here." She looked back an' nodded. I could see that smile of hers.

About half the crowd followed us into the saloon. Albert was busy as hell. Everyone was askin' questions of anybody that wasn't talkin' at the time. I never said anything until Swan came through the door. The newspaper man rushed to her an' begged her to tell the story.

She came to me. smilin' an' took my arm. "Captain Bush said 'Thanks.'" People were crowdin' around so tight we were nearly crushed. I picked Swan up an' put her on the bar. Everyone got quiet an' she told how they had taken her out the back door, on to the cabin, started to Kansas City, how I held a mortgage on all they owned an' they couldn't pay so they had taken her because she could sign to get the papers out of the bank.

She told how I had waited outside. When they came out they had pulled their guns an' the fight was on. They were dead an' we were here. She held out her hands an' ten hands came up to help her down. There was applause for her.

We finished our drinks an' eased out the door. I went to get my horse and Swan had all the horse, saddles, as well as the pack horses. She patted her pocket, the Captain gave me a piece of paper sayin' they are ours. He said them men wouldn't need them. We put all the horses in the livery an' went to eat.

The newspaper man came an' asked if he could join us.

I looked at Swan, she nodded an' he sat down. "Now Mr Whitehead do you see how things work out here? There ain't any law so a man kinda has to take care of himself or he won't make it. You throw the army an' Sioux into this an' tell me there ain't a lot of killin'. Look at the men today who came to kill me. "

"Can we talk again tomorrow?" he asked.

"I don't know," I said. "We'll see what tomorrow brings, now were goin' to our room."

CHAPTER TEN

Hell if I Know

The next mornin' we had people waitin' for us at breakfast. Lee an' the two girls. Sherry an' Kathy were havin' coffee. Swan was all smiles an' asked where Linda was. "They hired some men, bought supplies an' left early this mornin' for the country where Mark is buildin' his ranch. They are goin' to get married when the house is done."

"Well good." Swan said. I asked if they wanted breakfast. They did so we all ordered. The women talked all through breakfast, Lee an' I talked very little. He sat watchin' Kathy most of the time. She kept glancin' at him. The redhead cast a couple looks at me also. Swan never missed them, kept layin' her hand on mine in a way that said mine. Lee an' I excused ourselves an' walked to the post. Outside he started talkin' of many things. He was a happy man.

I asked him if he could sell some saddles. He said. "I can sell anything." Them girls had people comin' an' buyin' he had never seen before. We laughed at this an' he opened the post. I said I was "goin' up an' see the livery man, have him send down the three saddles."

At the livery the man said he could sell one of them today. He had a man who was after a saddle just like one we had. I said, "Okay," an' told him to "send the other two down to the post."

As I came out of the livery I heard someone choppin' wood behind the west saloon so I walked over an' watched Albert gather an arm load. I did the same an' we went into the saloon. He already had a fire goin'. We put the wood in the corner.

Albert poured coffee an' we talked awhile of old times. He told me stories of my father, they had been good friends. "Aw hell," he said an' went an' got a jug. We sat an' remembered the past.

"What are you goin' to do now Will, you got a long winter ahead of you?"

"I still have Felter to deal with," I said, "An' he's got thirty men with him." We sat an refilled our cups an' never talked for a long time, just sat sippin' our drinks.

Albert asked, "You need any help?"

I finished my drink an' said how much I appreciated the offer but "I better go with the Indians so if anybody got away, made it out, all they could blame was us that was already in trouble."

As he was fillin' the cups again Swan came in an' joined us. Albert handed her a full cup. I got up an' threw more wood on the fire. Three customers came in an' Albert waited on them. The woman came in with a pot of soup an' hung it on the fire. Albert aways kept a free stew for his customers.

Swan reached over an' touched my shoulder an' asked, "What is wrong?"

"Nothin' Swan, maybe I'm just tired. We have been settin' here talkin' of the old times before the whites came.

"He knew my father an' we talked of him."

"I knew him," she said. I just looked at her for a long time, we said nothin'. Then she started in. Jacob had been her step father. Her real father had been good friends with him an' after he died Jacob had stayed with her mother. They had been very happy together.

I asked, "When?"

"About fifteen years ago," she said.

"That was about the time he had quit takin' me with him to the basin." I finished my cup an' she poured it full again.

"He talked of you all the time," she said. "He was very proud of you. Is he the one who taught you to read an' write?"

"Yes he brought me books every year. We spent a lot of time together the last three or four years. He told me of how it was at the Gap."

"I knew you even though we had never met. What are we goin' to do now Will?"

"Guess we'll go up to the ranch with Slim for a few days. I told Lester to come up an' look at the bull calves. What time is it now, do we have time for dinner?" I asked.

"Well it's nearly four o'clock, have you been here all this time? Guess we talked longer than I thought."

We walked back towards the hotel. I had wasted a day. What the hell was I doin' mopin' around. There was a hell of a lot I had to do yet before winter got here.

I stopped at the saloon an' told Swan to go on to the hotel. She stood lookin' at me for a while an' said, "I should not of told you," an' walked away.

I had several drinks an' was gettin' purty drunk an' feelin' full of hell. There was a poker game goin' an' I stood watchin' it. There was an argument started over a pot an' it looked like there was goin' to be a fight so I walked up to the bar an' talked to the bartender. He asked me, "What was the problem over there?"

"Hell if I know, I don't know how to play cards. Thats one thing my father never taught me. Let me have another drink." I killed it, paid him an' started out the door.

When I got outside I made my way to the hotel. Damn I was the drunkest I'd ever been. I made it up the stairs to the room. Swan wasn't there. Now where the hell was she anyway? I had another drink from the bottle but it didn't taste good. I sat down on the bed, what about that woman? My dad had raised her … we were almost brother an' sister.

I got the bottle, hell tomarrow I was goin' back to the Gap. Maybe I'd go see the Sheppards. Maybe the Birtchfields. Damn that Mary might give a man a run in the bed. Maybe I'd give it a try tomarrow. Sleep got me before I had made up my mind about tomarrow.

When I awoke there was no one in bed with me. Damn this bed was big an' empty. I got up an' found the bottle, had another drink. Man my head hurt. I had another one. Diggin' around in my bag I found some cigars. I lit one over the chimney an' sat thinkin'. Wonder where the hell Swan was. It wasn't like her to not be here with me.

There wasn't much taste to this cigar. I had another drink an' more of the cigar. I heard foot steps in the hallway, they sounded like Swan. The door opened an' she came in. She had a bottle of wine in her hand an' had Lester an' Mary with her.

Lester had a bottle of whiskey an' a silly look on his face. He looked around for a cup or glass. There was none so he drank from the bottle an' handed it to me. I drank. "Well old man how do you feel?"

I drank again an' said "Gettin' better. Where the hell you all been?"

"Last two hours we been huntin' you. Swan said 'you were upset an' gettin' drunk,' so we thought we'd join you an' could not find you. Never looked up here though."

Lester reached for the bottle an' had a drink an' handed it back. Swan found a cup an' poured Mary a big drink of wine. She killed it. Swan filled it again an' she killed it. The bottle was empty. Swan got the whiskey bottle an' had a drink an' handed it back to me. I handed it to Mary, she had a drink an' said, "A toast to Will Chase an' Swan, may they always be happy."

It was one hell of a night. The last I remember Swan was tellin' the story of the great gold swindle in Washington. As I dressed the next mornin' the night was comin' back in pieces, never had I been that drunk.

I remembered Lester singin' an' later cryin', wantin' to go get Sherry. Hell he'd only seen her twice but had been sure he was in love. Swan was sleepin' soundly. I'd go get some coffee an' bring some back for her. The last I could remember of her she had been cryin' about something. I looked into the mirror, decided that I looked as good as could be expected.

As I came into the dinin' room Captain Bush an' Martha were settin' there. Bush rose an' shook my hand, "Good mornin' Will." I smiled an' said I wasn't "too sure," I tipped my hat to Martha. Captain Bush an' I sat down. The waiter brought coffe for me an' asked if I would "wait for Miss Swan to order." I said, "Yes," but could he get me a cup of whiskey. He nodded an' left.

Martha asked where Swan was. I told her she'd be down in a bit. When the waiter came with the whiskey I asked him to "take up a pot of coffee an' wake her."

I was wearin' my buckskins an' was thinkin' of the hills when the Captain asked, "What my plans are?"

I drank half the cup of whiskey an' chased it with coffee, sat lookin' at him. "Hell if I know Captain. About the only thing I know that needs doin' is Felter but I'll bet the scouts know right where he's at."

Bush said, "We're movin' to Washington in two weeks. Next week my replacement will be here an' he has made the brag that he would take you in Will."

"He won't hear of me until next spring I'm sure. I'm goin' up into the hills, today I think, been around here too long."

"You know the army is goin' to make a big push up your way next spring. They are sendin' some top generals an' plenty of men an' supplies."

"Why do they keep this up?" I asked.

"The people in the East want more land," he said, "An' there is the gold. You missed three men who got out with quite a bit a few months ago. They are in Denver gettin' together a large minin' party to come up here shortly."

I had the coffee cups refilled an' I asked Captain Bush if he'd "take three letters to Washington an' one to Kansas City for me."

He said, "Yes."

"I'll get them written up today. There not real important but I want my side told to these people.

"One is to my lawyer in Kansas City, also I'd like Slim to come in an' put money down on another piece of land. I have quite a bunch of horses up there an' some buffalo."

"Don't the Indians steal from you Will?" Sara Martha asked.

"No Ma'am for what I have is theirs also. If we need horses they just go an' get them but they always leave some. I traded for a great Appy stud an' put him up there on my way down."

Bush asked, "How's the mare an' colt?" I had gotten from him.

"Some time next spring I'm taken her over an' put her with this stud. If she has a good one I'll give it to you Captain."

Sara had came in an' joined us, she was friendly. I asked how she liked the East? "Great, there are some wonderful people there, Will. How did you like it?"

"It's better out here," I said.

"I heard some wild stories about you back there. Seems you stirred the hearts of quite a few ladies. You better be careful if you ever go there without Swan."

Lester an' Mary came down with Swan then. We all had a big breakfast an' more coffee. We decided to ride to the ranch an' look at the Herferds. As we all got ready to go our ways I shook hands with the Captain an' told him I'd probably see him in Washington later in the year.

We spent three days at the ranch. Lester an' Mary were excited with the cattle an' our location. The last night we were to be there we had a big supper of turkey an' dressin', wine an' squash. Lester asked if Slim an' I'd mind if he "scouted this country for a ranch." It was far better land than his.

"Why don't you move back to your old place?"

"Do you think that possible?" he asked. "After all dad has done."

"Just go an' see the Captain tomarrow before he leaves, talk with him, I'm sure it would be okay. I'll write them letters an' you can give them to him for me if you don't mind."

He said, "Fine," an' we went into the front room.

We about talked out everything there was to talk about. The men went to the bunkhouse an' the women went to bed. I got out pen an' paper an' wrote the letters encouragin' all three men in Washington to again get the Settlers Act stopped an' told them of the past summer, how the Indians were fightin' for survival, if they thought resevations were the answer take a look at every one they had set up so far.

The Indian people were starvin' due to crooked Indian agents. Only about ten percent of the money alloted ever got to the Indians. The rest went to crooked agents an' politicians along the way. Our Sioux nation would never quit fightin', I'd never quit fightin' for them. I put a ten thousand dollar check in each letter, the money to be spent to fight the bill in a way each man saw fit. I signed them "Sioux Nation, Will Chase."

The letter to Chester Brown contained his next year's wages an' money to go to Washington to fight the bill. It gave him the power to act in the Indian's behalf.

Just as I finished these letters an' my cup of whiskey Mary came into the kitchen. She had slipped into her jeans an' blouse.

She poured herself a cup of coffee an' poured me more whiskey an' sat down at the table with me. I sat lookin' at her. Her hair was loose an' hung around her face. She was beautiful. Her blouse was open quite low an' I could see her large breasts. The nipples were makin' points in the material.

"Will Chase, what are your plans for the rest of the night?" I took half my cup in one drink an' coughed.

"Mary, I know what I'd like to do."

"Then do it," she said. I rose an' came around the table, she stood an' met my arms, kissed with a fire I had never dreamed was there. Our mouths clung together, she pressed her breasts to my chest. We came apart, walked to the door an' went out to the haystack.

As we later lay in each others arms she snuggled her face into my throat an' nibbled my neck. "When are you goin' to Kansas City?" she asked.

"I'm not sure how long it's goin' to take with Felter. I'm not sure I'd be able to make Kansas City until January late."

"What hotel do you stay at there?"

"Hatchshire."

"I'll be there," she said an' we made love again. It was toward two o'clock when we got up an' started for the house. I seen a shadow go around the north wall.

When I got into bed Swans body was cold as she snuggled into my arms. She had been the shadow I'd seen. She held me tighly to her. It was an hour before I went to sleep.

At breakfast the next mornin' everything seemed the same. When we said goodby to the Birtchfields Swan gave Mary a hug. Chester an' the other two hands went with them to sort out the bulls an' their mothers they were takin' home. We'd get the cows back another time.

CHAPTER ELEVEN

The Colt

By noon Swan an' I were packed an' on the trail to the Gap. We were goin' back the way we had come. Evenin' found us camped in the valley where the horses were. We had found where the Indians had made the trap an' they had built a good one. Our horse were in for the night.

After eatin' an' before dark the Appy stud came to check out the new horses. He stopped at our fire first. I walked out to meet him, he liked to be talked to an' petted, he was some horse.

That night when we crawled into our blankets Swan was a volcano of passion.

Three days later we rode into the Gap. Every teepee had much meat hangin' on their dryin' racks. All the people were happy, talkin' of another great hunt. The leaves were fallin', the trees were gettin' rather bare. There had been hard ice the last three mornin's.

Sharps an' Plenty Arrows were in the post when we put our horses up an' went in. They were waitin' for us. Plenty Arrows said the guards had told them yesterday we were comin'. Standin Elk an' Long Warrior were usin' boys as young as ten as guards an' scouts. The boys were proud they had a job to do an' it was good trainin' for them.

Everything was quiet around here. There had been no whites since the soldiers last summer. Henry was two days south comin' in. He had two whites with him, a man an' woman. The Sheppards had a little trouble with some Pawnee an' a couple white men. One white man an' the three Pawnee had been killed.

The other white man had a patch over one eye. He an' two Pawnee had been chased back south. They had been tryin' to steal cattle.

Later that afternoon Petey came ridin' up leadin' the Appy colt or what had been a colt. He stood sixteen hands and weighed about eleven hundred fifty pounds. He handed me the reins an' asked how I liked him. "Sure has grown, I got him purty well started," he grinned, "Thought you might like to ride out the Gap with me an' look around a little."

I saddled him up an' mounted him. Lookin' down on his neck an' withers I was surprised at the width of his neck. When I turned him he did a perfect pivot half way around. As we rode off at a walk he dropped his head straight out an' walked with power in every step. We kicked up to a lope an' his head stayed at the same level. He moved out with ease an' sureness.

Petey was watchin' the colt with pride. I told him what a "hell of a job" he had done on him. "Wait until you hunt, he loves to run to buffalo. He will cut one out an' almost lay into him. There's no way they can get away from this colt. He'll also stay at it all day if you ask him. Hope you don't mind I used him."

"Petey you have made a good one out of him. I traded for a stud the same color as this one. When that mare has her colt we'll go catch him an' bring him down here. I got him runnin' with a bunch of horse I got over near the new ranch. You can have her first colt".

"Thanks Will, damn that would be fine."

"You ain't goin' to cut this one are you? I bred him to some of my mares this year, hope you don't mind."

"I don't Petey." We stopped an' the colt sat down on his tail an' slid to a stop. Petey smiled again.

"Where are the gattlin' guns Petey?" He showed me a big dead tree in a tumble of boulders. I sat an' looked a long time before I could see it, then not it but a slit where it could cover a large area, over a hundred yards or more either way from where we sat. Turnin' around I finally saw it, after still lookin' a long time. It was under an' overhangin' rock, with rocks piled waist high all around. The gun wasn't there now Petey said. It sat back under the overhang. One man could set it up in less than a minute. Sharps had taught twenty men how to operate the guns. Five of them stayed at the Gap at all times.

The other gun was in the cave by the post, a place had been built for it next to the rocks that made up the east side of the corral.

"Did you notice how the new pole corral ran all the way across the floor of the valley?" I nodded. "When the poles are put up for the gate it's too high to jump an' too strong to ride through. It puts the cavalry at the mercy of the gattlin' gun. It can control the whole valley floor whether they come from east or west."

We rode on out an' made a swing around the country. The colt rode beautifully. As we passed back into the Gap I looked again at the guns, they were reassurin'.

When we had unsaddled I spent a long time brushin' the colt. His hair was long. He was ready for the winter. I left him outside of the corral an' he went down an' got a drink, then went to stand with Petey's horse.

I turned an' Swan was settin' on the porch watchin' me. As I got to her I bent an' kissed her cheek.

"Your War Horse?" she said.

"Yes, now I have two appys an' you one to ride into battle next spring. We'll have to get you a couple Appy geldin's to ride later this winter for I'd like a colt out of your Appy mare by this colt."

"So would I," Swan answered.

I told her of given Petey the next colored colt out of the big mare, how he had hunted on him this fall. "That is good, for the horse of my father's needs to be let run the easy life. I know a young boy who would be good to him."

The next day late in the afternoon Henry, Chester an' Loraine rode into the post. Swan an' Loraine laughed an' hugged. Loraine said, "Hi Will," an' they went into the post. Chester an' I unpacked, I noticed there weren't all the bags an' junk Loraine had hauled to Kansas City. Chester was happy to be here. He said the reason they came was because we needed to be in Washington in February or they might get the bill through. His father had sent word that there was many hard feelin's toward the Indians after the past summer. A man had taken rock samples laced with gold back to show the Senate an' Congress that this was a rich country.

We turned all the horses loose an' went into the post. There was laughter, Henry was tellin' a horse-tradin' story on Hank.

"That man has them people filled with so much bullshit about comin' out here an' capturin' them horses from the Indians, they are fightin' each to buy them. He had a big ad in the paper." Henry brought the ad out. I took it an' read it out loud.

Notice people of Kansas City, we have for sale one hundred fifty head of horses straight from the Black Hills. These horses were captured from a War Party of the Great Chiefs, Long Warrior and Chasing Elk. This may be the only time you will have the opportunity to buy these magnificent animals for the risk is almost too great to ask even the bravest man to go again. There maybe one small bunch later on for we.had to leave three brave men behind bringing another herd but two of the men were wounded and have not been heard of.

Turner, Walker and Brown Livestock Co.
1902 State Street, Kansas City, Mo.

We all laughed again. Wait until the great chiefs hear this – their liable to go an' steal them back. We had a good supper an' then walked down to Standin' Elk's teepee. Petey an' Plenty Arrows were there an' I read the news ad to them. They nearly rolled on the ground laughin'. They wanted to go tell the rest of the people this great joke. We talked them into waitin' until mornin'.

Standin' Elk's woman had gone back to her mother's to have the child so Swan got his dipper an' croc for the group. Petey's woman also brough a croc an' dipper. We put more wood on the fire, passed the dipper an' all listened while Henry told his story of Kansas City, the dipper kept passin'. We had to help Henry along goin' to the post later on. He was singin' a song about New Orleans an' a cajun woman.

A couple days later I asked for a council to be called for the next day. It was gettin' colder every day an' we needed to go after Felter before the snow got deep. There had been no word from the scouts that they were comin' out so I figured they planned on spendin' the winter. If it took us a month I'd be pushin' goin' East an' I sure wanted to spend some time in Kansas City, in fact I was plannin' on it.

Loraine an' I were standin' on the porch that night after supper. The night birds were singin' now an' then. It was beautiful but cold. Loraine shivered a bit an' I offered to get her a heavier coat. "No," she said an' moved closer, got against me. Someone was comin' so I stepped aside an' called out. A young boy rode his horse up to the porch. He was leadin' another horse. "I have come for Swan, Standin' Elk's woman has trouble."

I went in an' told Swan. She quickly gathered some stuff, slipped into her coat, kissed my cheek an' was gone. When I got back outside she was ridin' hard, the boy whippin' to keep up.

I had brought out a blanket an' now I put it around Loraine. As my arms went forward with the blanket she stepped back against me. My arms went around her, she turned an' kissed me. I just started kissin' back. We walked to the creek an' enjoyed what seemed like hours of lovin'.

Later settin' on the log we talked. Wrapped in the blanket Loraine told me how she had changed since comin' West. What seemed important back East didn't mean anything out here. We sat a while longer an' listened to the coyotes howlin'. Loraine said, "Now I know why you are fightin' so hard for this land."

We walked back to the post. She went to the teepee an' I into my room in the post. Swan came in later an' woke me, "Will, Standin' Elk has a boy child." She lay in my arms, later sayin', "I wonder what it's like to watch them grow up." I drifted off to sleep, that's one thing I had never wondered about.

Much meat was in the camp again this year so we didn't worry about the women an' children that we would leave behind. All the men wanted to go but I only asked for thirty. Petey, Chasin' Elk, Plenty Arrows all asked to go. Long Warrior an' Standin' Elk were to stay home. Shadow stepped forward an' asked to go. I nodded my head, he let out a yell an' jumped into the air.

Chasin' Elk, Plenty Arrows an' Shadow were each to pick nine men. They must be trained an' follow orders to perfection. The man we had made walk back stepped forward an' asked to go. "Have you learned?" Chasin' Elk asked.

"Yes, learned well, Chasin' Elk."

He was accepted.

"I will leave the rest to you Chasin' Elk. They must not fear the dynamite for we are takin' it. That is one of the reasons Petey is goin'. He knows how to handle it if something happens to me. Take good horses an' plenty of shells. Each man is to know we will be gone thirty days.

"Pack for that long. We will hunt our meat so only take meat for a week. Plenty Arrows, each man must be good with a bow. Take a few young braves who will be controlled. If we are to be strong the young must learn now an' teach others."

Petey an' I walked to the post an' sat at the table with the others. We talked of what we must take. After all else were asleep I sat at the table smokin' a cigar an' sippin' on the whiskey. There were four men up there who had been watchin' for a month or so. Maybe they had it all figured out. We must know where the gold was. We would need it to buy lobbyist in Wasington.

Swan eased from the bed an' came to join me with a blanket wrapped around her. She rubbed my shoulder a bit then poured us both whiskey. "Don't worry Will, it will work out good, it always has."

We were up early an' busy. Petey went to the big cave an' got a whole case of dynamite, caps an' fuses. I checked him when he got back to make sure it all was there. I had plenty of good strong string this time, as well as plenty of thongs. Swan an' Sharps had the supplies of beans, flour, coffee, salt an' tobacco.

In our packs she had matches, cigars, our jerky, some things of hers, plenty of shells, both pistol an' rifle, hatchets, our bed rolls, coffee pot, fryin' pan an' a stew pot, some sugar, salt, coffee, an' extra knives. I put in ten sticks of dynamite, caps an' fuses, five bottles. We put a folded tarp over our pack horse as well as the one with the dynamite.

CHAPTER TWELVE

Death Hole

When we headed out there was plenty of yellin' an' whoopin'. The ones left behind were singin' the song of war. Swan an' I rode appys, her the mare an' I the War Horse.

Three days later we turned up the big canyon Swan an' I had come down what seemed like so long ago. The first two camps had been dry but this one was in the snow. There was already snow on the ground an' it was snowin' harder all the time. We pushed until almost dark huntin' a good camp site.

Just before dark we came to a stand of cedar, made camp, we had coffee an' roast meat of a deer. We all slept under the cedars that night.

It was clear an' the sun was shinin' when we started the next mornin'. We came to a big meadow that evenin' an' made camp early. We would leave everything here. The grass was good an' the extra horses would do good here. We set up camp, some went huntin'. They came in at dark with two deer an' a big cow elk. We all ate good this night. The big stream we knew the men to be at was over the ridge an' up stream five or six miles.

A scout came into camp that night. The men were broken up into three groups. Each had nine men an' two had been killed in a rock slide. Felter had also killed two of them. They all had built cabins an' piled rocks around them. They were set up for the winter an' prepared to fight. Two camps kept two guards all the time. The other had three guards.

Each kept their gold in the cabin somewhere. They all worked together at each camp. The horse herds were in three different bunches.

The scout sat an' thought awhile then said, "There is anger at the middle camp. They do not trust each other."

"Where is Felter?" I asked.

"He's at the middle camp. Sometimes when he's on guard at night he meets a man from the upper camp.

"We will go an' watch in the mornin'. Shadow, Chasin' Elk, Plenty Arrows, Petey, Swan an' I will go with the scout. He knows the way that is best. All scouts have done good. Now let, us rest."

Swan an' I had our own fire away from camp, a leanto made of a tarp. We sat an' talked, sippin' the bottle. Could they have fought over the gold or could they be gettin' more gold workin' this way. I sat an' thought about it a long time sippin', finally I went to bed, decided to wait until I seen what was goin' on.

In the mornin' we seven headed out to the camps of the whites. We watched six men workin' a sluice box. Three were spread out guardin', one up stream, one down an' one across the stream. We watched an' hour before they stopped an' emptied the box. It must have been a good mornin' because thay took out quite a lot of gold. It all went into a sack, two men took it to the cabin. They all came up to the fire except the guards. They had coffee an' warmed their feet. The water must have been cold enough to nearly freeze their feet an' legs. They stomped them an' moved around to get the circulation goin' again.

We watched until they went back to work. To shoot from here was too far. We'd have to wait until night an' watch where the guards spent the night. We moved on to the second camp.

This one we could get closer to but we never tried. We went to the upper camp. It would be harder than the first for the stream went slower here an' split a wide valley. This also would be too far for good shootin'.

Back at camp we talked it over an' came up with no sure way to take all three at once. We could get their horses an' not lose any men I was sure. They may send out some men to get them back, we could kill these an' cut the number down some. We would try an' get the lower camp's horses first but keep the other two covered at the same time.

Swan an' I went to our leanto an' talked again. This would be the best way I thought. We never left until after dinner the next day. The five men left to guard our horses were un-happy but never said anything. We split into three groups, the upper ones were to try for the horses at that camp but take no chances, kill as many as they could.

Petey was to start it all by shootin a couple of the dyna-mite arrows into the roof of the middle cabin. The men could be picked off for they were in range.

We bedded down an' waited at the first camp. As I watched Swan nudged me an' said, we could get closer from the other side. I looked where she was pointin' to a bunch of cedar trees next to the canyon wall. The trees started out of sight of the lower guard an' ran almost even with the sluice box. About a hundred yards out the horses were grazin' along the stream. One was in a corral near the cabin. He was their wrangle horse. I had two men move into a place they could shoot the horse from.

"Do not leave him alive," I said. Both looked at me not likin' it. Swan got out four arrows an' we headed back down stream to cross an' get behind the trees. We made it within one hundred fifty yards of the sluice box. I had a cigar goin', we waited for Petey to start the show. We waited, it was thir-ty minutes before it came. I was on my second cigar.

Swan had an arrow notched an' waited patiently for the boom. When it came she pulled back an' I put the cigar to the fuse. The men at the box looked in the direction of the next camp. The arrow Swan shot stuck into the sluice box. She had already fired the next one. The first one exploded while the men were lookin' at it.

The explosion destroyed the box an' knocked men down, killin' some an' woundin' the rest. The lower guard ran out to see what was happenin'. I dropped him where he stopped. The braves had opened up on the horse an' the guard on that side of the stream. They killed both. One man crawled up out of the water an' I shot him.

The upper guard opened up on Swan an' I. We ducked back into the cedars an' moved to the next tree but goin' towards him. The horses had scattered everywhere. The guard was shootin' into the trees all around us. Swan notched an arrow an' moved back from the tree so she could shoot over it at the corral again. I touched the fuse an' she let it go. When it went off I took a run at the place I had last seen him. The dust my cover, I ran through the dust, when I located him he was runnin' up stream. I stopped an' shot him in the back of the head. He turned a flip an' never, moved.

There was a shot from behind me, I whirled around an' dropped. Swan had shot another man who had come out of the stream. Braves were comin' down the cliff. We gathereds up the guns an' crossed the stream.

The braves were startin' to gather up the horses. They were confused an' easy to handle. The braves had them all in the corral in no time. Swan an' I went into the cabin. It wasn't hard to find the gold. It was piled in bags. Five an' a half of them among the supplies. I just searched a pack an' carried it out side. Then searched the next one, carried it out. In the third one was the gold.

The braves started saddlin' an' loadin' the supplies. These men were runnin' out of supplies for there was little coffee or tea, no sugar. We rolled the bedrolls an' took everything that could be used by the Indians. We had poor families an' old that could use it all. They had a large supply of rifles, pistols an' plenty of amunition. We took it all.

We could still hear shots from the middle camp. As these men took the horse an' supplies up the mountain trail Swan an' I started up stream on two of the horses we had just taken. Shadow would see that our horses got back to camp with the taken ones.

At the second camp the cabin was half down. I could see two dead men by the sluice box an' we had seen the lower guard dead. This cabin was backed against the cliff face. Now an' then shots were fired from it an' shots would answer from the rocks around

I seen Petey up the cliff, he was ready to shoot another arrow. We watched as it arched out an' landed on the cabin roof. When it exploded there was dust but the cabin still stood. A brave made a run to get closer, he was cut down by three bullets.

The sun was gettin' low and in a bit would be settin'. It was already gone from this deep canyon. Petey seen us an' worked his way down an' came to where Swan an' I were. "We got both guards an' one explosion hit the cabin good, killed two men by the box. The others dived into the cabin. We can't get them out. I put five arrows in it but it still stands. Nearly two sides are solid rock. They built it right against the cliff face. The upper side is a big boulder. You can see the big one by the door. Five men made it into the cabin. We have lost three men so far."

We sat an' looked at the cabin. "Let's get closer," I said an' ran in a crouch from rock to rock. A couple shots came my way but I never seen where they hit. I had gotten fifty yards closer an' was in a better shootin' position. Swan was as close as I for she had ran at the same time. Now she was behind a rock big enough for her to stand behind.

I put some shots into the window, got some in return. Stuffin' shells into my gun I looked around for some better place but this looked like about the best place to shoot arrows from. Petey an' Swan could both hear me. "Petey you shoot first, don't put it on the roof but as close to the door as you can. Swan you shoot after he does an' put it as near the window as you can. When the first one goes off I'll rush the cabin, get as close as possible."

When Petey's went off I was runnin' toward the door in the dirt an' snow thrown up by the dynamite. I never seen the arrow Swan had fired. It had went through the window as I got to the door, there was a loud boom from within. Screams, shouts an' cries of pain. I went right on through the door. There was so much dust I could not see. A man jammed into me, I turned an' shot him, another went for the door an' I shot him. He went down but crawled on out the door, an' was shot from outside.

I heard moans but the dust was so thick I still could not see. Someone in the corner started shootin' at the door. The shots were spaced evenly. At the third shot I had the gun flashes located, on the fourth I shot three times, one centered on the flash and higher, then quickly put one to the left, one to the right. All sounded like hits. I waited

Petey called my name from outside. I never answered for if anyone was alive they would fire at my voice. It seemed like forever before I could see. It was nearly pitch black in there an' was gettin quite dark outside. I couldn't hear any breathin' inside so I took a chance an' called Petey He answered immediately. "Ho, we thought you had taken one," he said.

"Light a branch an' throw it in here."

A couple minutes later a pine bundle came through the door. It landed in about the middle of the room an' flared up good. I could see fairly good in the room. There were three bodies. I picked up the fire bundle an' put it in the fire place. This wasn't right, there should be one more.

I added wood to the fire an' waited for it to get to blazin'. Petey an' Swan came in an' drug the bodies outside. The braves had gathered wood for a fire outside. They had collected the guns, shells an' knives as well as anything else that was worth takin'. I looked around the room an' found a cave with an openin' just big enough for a man to go through. It had been caused by runnin' water for it was smooth. How far back it went I didn't know an' I wasn't crawlin' into it to find out, not right away anyhow.

We searched the cabin an' found the gold. There was two small bags of it. A rock had been fitted into the fireplace that could be pulled out an' had a large storin' area in there. Petey an' I sat while Swan was makin' coffee. There had to be more gold than this if this place was as good as the other. There should have been four times this much. Felter should have been here.

"Petey are you sure five came in here."

"Yes I'm sure."

"Felter ain't here, he's the main one I wanted. He's the bastard that has caused all the trouble."

We searched the room again. All we came up with was the same thing. I checked the rocks in the fireplace, nothin'. I sat lookin' at the cave, was he in there or did it come out some where an' he had escaped?

The braves refused to move inside even though it looked like snow would be fallin' by mornin'. A young brave came in an' looked around, "death hole," he said an' went out. It was snowin' in the mornin', the trees were heavy with it. The smoke went straight up slowly.

After we had eaten we had a meetin' outside. The braves agreed to take the horses down the stream an' come out on top, double back an' watch for smoke, I'd build a fire in the cave an' we'd see where it came out on top. I found a log that had been lightnin' struck an' cut some pitch out of it. I had three as long as my arm an' big as my wrist.

I lit one an' crawled into the cave. Five feet in it got bigger, big enough that I could stand up an' walk. The floor was covered with sand. I squatted down an' studied the floor, there were footprints goin' both ways. Someone had been in here many times. I picked up a hand full of sand an' it sparkled in my hand. It was laced with gold. Hell there was no tellin' how much gold was in this cave.

I hollered back at Petey to start shovin' in branches so we could build a fire. He came in draggin' a rope. He then pulled it in with a log an' some branches. "Damn," he said, "This is a big cave." I showed him the gold in the sand. His eyes sparkled when he looked at me, I have heard of places like this but never believed they existed, always thought they were just stories. "There are tracks," he said, "Have you been back there?"

"No but lets follow them." The cave forked in another hundred feet, the tracks went to the right an' we followed them. The floor had no more sand an' was gettin' steep. Then it got narrow an' steeper but we climbed on. It leveled off for a ways then split again. My branch was burnin' low so we lit another one. There were pine needles an' leaves on the floor here so we must be gettin' closer to the openin'.

Another turn an' we could see light ahead. We came out in a deep ravine about half way up its side. "Petey you go up on top an' tell the rest. Swan an' I are goin' to the upper camp. You put the best trackers up there on this trail. We don't want Felter to get away. He will just cause us more trouble. He's carryin' a bunch of gold you know. He can't get out with it again."

"What should we do if we catch him?"

"Kill him an' make damn sure he's dead." Petey went on up the hill an' I turned back down the cave.

When I got back to the sandy bottom I looked at it again. It was full of gold. Maybe this was close to where Swan an' I had camped last year. Maybe this mountain was full of gold all over. I came out an' Swan was settin' there waitin', a silly smile on her face. "What's so funny woman?" She showed me another bag of gold. "Where did you find that?"

She went around the fireplace an' moved a big rock that had been rolled against the back wall of the fireplace.

There was a hole in the wall, she reached in an' pulled out three bottles an' said the gold had been there also. She handed me a bottle. I tasted it first an' then had three big swallows. It burned all the way down an' exploded when it hit my stomach, spreadin' through my body an' limbs. I drank again an' handed it back to her. She had a drink an' sat it on the table we had propped back up.

"We are goin' to walk up the draw an' see what's goin' on at the next camp," I said. "Swan said she had heard shots from up there."

"At one time there had been many of them. Maybe it's over," she said, "There ain't been any lately."

A half hour later we could see the Indians around the cabin out in the open. They were loadin' packs on the horses. Petey was among them.

As we walked up they were all excited about the fight. All tried to tell the story at once. They had lost four men but it had been a hard place to attack. There were windows on all sides. The whites had fought well.

Petey told me they had followed the trail of the man easily in the snow. He had come to this camp, scouted around, stole two horses an' rode south. He had left durin' the night an' had a big head start.

We all rode back to our camp. Some were sad their friends had died but all were happy we had killed so many whites. We spent the night there an' had a good feed when we got in. The horse guards had meat an' beans ready for us.

Swan an' I were settin' in our leanto havin' some bottle later that evenin'. She reached out an' touched my arm, "You are troubled Will, what is it?"

"We let the one man that can hurt us the most get away. He will go to the East. He has much gold to show, a story of how we killed his men. We can't go there as we did last year. We have angered the whites back there when we killed their soldiers."

"But many will go back an' tell of the ones you let live. They will tell how you gave them a chance everytime."

"The big soldiers are angry about their fort. They will come an' build another an' this time maybe we will not win."

"Then the Sioux are done for the whites will come by the thousands."

"We cannot stop them. The free life will be over."

We sat awhile an' then crawled into our blanket. We both lay awake a long time.

CHAPTER THIRTEEN

My Side of the Story

Four days later we were at the Gap. There was much dancin' an' singin' that night. Swan an' I went an' watched for awhile. I told the story of the warriors great fightin' ability, bragged on each warrior. I divided the horse an' guns equal among the dead braves' wives.

I thanked everyone for followin' me again. Wished them a good winter, told them I would go East, try to get help from the good men back there. I'd be back in the spring.

"Keep out the scouts always, stay ready. The whites will come in the spring, you must be ready. If I'm not back before the fightin' follow the leaders, do as they say."

Swan an' I walked back to the post, she was holdin' my hand tightly. "You are sad an' angry Will Chase, would you talk with me?"

"Yes." We went to our room an' closed the door. She sat out a jug an' cups, we talked of the good times we had had, our life together.

"I don't know if we can go to Washington," I said. "Chester is there, also Captain Bush. Maybe they can do what I cannot – If I'm seen back there the soldiers might put me in jail. All I have been fightin' for is goin' to be lost anyway. Maybe I even made it worse for our people.

"There is no way to win now. Felter has gotten away. This I'm sure or the other braves would be back by now with word." I was drinkin' again, anger was in my heart. Most of it at myself for havin' failed in the fight. I had won all the battles, made fools out of the whites but they kept comin', more an' more. Maybe bigger battles were what was needed.

Maybe I should of killed instead of lettin' some go. We went to bed then. We made love an' Swan was the perfect lover as she always was. Later layin' in my arms she said, "Will I'm not goin' with you."

"What!" I lay a long time then asked, "Why?"

"I would slow you down in a fight or if we had to run."

"Swan, you have been with me goin' on two years, you out-fight any man I have ever known. You're always ready, you read my mind. You know my next move sometimes before I do. How could you slow me down?"

A while later she answered, "I am with child."

I didn't know whether to be happy or sad. A child would be wonderful but what of this world now. Would he ever see the good days we had, the happy times. I held her tight in my arms, "We'll talk of this in the mornin' Swan."

"No, we won't in the mornin', I'm goin' to the basin. There is still happiness there. The whites are not there yet. You can fight from there an' when we win we will come back here."

After she went to sleep I got up an' put wood into the fire, lit a cigar an' drank a long time. Nothin' could be worked out in my mind so I crawled back into bed an' slept.

In the mornin' I got my packs made up, saddled the gray Swan liked an' my War Horse. For her I caught the Appy mare an' her gray, loaded them an' was ready to ride. I went into the post, Henry an' Sharps were settin' at the table havin' coffee. Neither said a thing.

Petey came in an' poured himself some coffee, stood by the fire watchin' me. I walked into our room.

Swan was there in her winter Indian clothes, her hair braided. She was beautiful. I walked to her an' held her in my arms a long time. We walked out the door an' all three men came an' hugged her, shook my hand. Henry said, "Ride slow son."

We walked out an' mounted up, ridin' from the Gap. I looked back at the openin' an' it hadn't ever changed since I could remember. I stopped where the trails split. Swan's horse was headed east. I turned the War Colt an' leaned an' kissed her. "I'll be back in the spring."

She looked at me a long time, then said "I'll be at the basin if you want us. I hope you do for I love you very much." I kissed her again an' rode south. I never looked back for if I had I'd probably have gone with her.

I spent two days with the Sheppards, enjoyed myself a lot for they were good men to be around. They had sold cattle to the fort in Scottsbluff an' were full of news. We talked of cattle an' I told them next spring I'd bring them a couple Hereford bulls or have them sent down.

I rode on toward the new ranch. It took me four days to get there. I spent three days with Slim. We done much talkin', got drunk as hell the first night. By mornin' he was ready to go to Kansas City with me. Marrow the foreman said he an' the other two men could handle things until he got back. I told them if they needed anything to see Henderson.

The afternoon of the third day Slim an' I headed for the post. We got there at full dark, put our horses in the leanto, went around an' knocked on the door.

Kathy answered the door an' let us in. Lee wasn't home at the time but he'd be right back. Sherry came out of the bedroom. She was smilin' an' glad to see us. We talked for awhile. Kathy poured us drinks, was refillin' them when Lee came in. He shook our hands, he was glad to see us also.

"How do you like my bride?" he said.

"Why hell man, she didn't tell us." We slapped him on the back. He poured us another drink, we congratulated Kathy with a toast, "To happiness."

There was a knock on the door an' we all looked at it. "It's Lester," Lee said an' opened the door. Lester came in an' Sherry went to stand by him. She stood on her toes an' kissed his cheek. She turned an' told us they were gettin' married on Sunday. We gave him a ribbin' an' then wished them luck. We had a few drinks before Slim an' I turned in.

We left the next mornin' an' headed for Denver. The tracks were all the way to there now, we could get a ride to Kansas City from there.

Lester told me with a smile that Mary was at the Hatshire Hotel. "She's waitin' to hear from you," he said with a grin.

In Denver we sold the gold for thirty-one dollars an ounce. It came to twenty-one thousand, five hundred, seventy-six dollars. We bought train tickets, a boxcar for the horses, plenty of feed an' headed east.

In Kansas City we got unloaded. Slim took the horses an' headed for Hank's place. I took the bags an' went to the hotel.

Hank an' Slim were to meet me there for supper. The Appy horse had gotten some admirin' looks when he came off the train.

At the hotel I got a room an' ordered three complete suits from my tailor from last year. The desk man remembered me from last spring. He was glad I was back, anyway he said he was an' seemed so. My bags were taken to the room. I asked about Miss Birtchfield bein' in. He said she was out at present should he tell her I was in town? I said, "Yes, I'll be in the bar for awhile."

The bar had two couples an' five other men besides the bartender. He also remembered me from the last spring. He started tellin' me of the write-ups in the paper of the fights with the army. "You're either a great general or a damn out-law," he said with a smile.

Another young lady came an' joined the two couples. They must have been talkin' about me for she turned an' looked my way. Our eyes met an' she smiled. I turned away first an' said to the bartender, "Probably half that was in the paper was bullshit."

He said,"Probably but it sold papers."

We talked about my lettin' people go but makin' them walk. I got carried away an' started tellin' how it realy was. "Wait," he said, "Let me get drinks for these people first."

When he got back he asked, "Mr Chase would you mind a reporter from our biggest paper listenin' to what you were tellin' me."

"Not at all," I said "but I have never talked with a reporter before."

"You won't mind this one," he said an' went to the table again. The brown-eyed woman came to me an' introduced herself. "Mr Chase, I'm Lucy Morgan an' very pleased to meet you." She held out her hand. I took her hand in mine, my hat in the other an' bowed at the waist, "The pleasure is all mine," I told her. She was very attractive.

"What do you want me to say?" I asked, "An' is this goin' in the paper?"

"Yes," she said, "No one has ever heard your story, just the army's side, now I'd like to tell yours. Where are you goin' now, Mr Chase?"

"I'm on my way back to Washington to try an' get the Settlers Act put down again. Last year it was voted down. It was not supposed to come up again for two years. Now the lawyer who speaks for the Sioux Nation came an' told me it was comin' up in February. His name is Chester Brown. He's from back East an' his father is a statesman back there. He's a fine man.

"Would you like a drink?" I asked.

She said, "Yes," an' told the bartender what she wanted. I'd never heard of it before. I ordered another also. "Tell me the story of the first fight last spring, the one with the surveyors. They all spoke good of you."

"Swan an' I had camped with some of our people from the Gap. The next mornin' we went west an' they started southwest. A couple hours after we heard shots an' went to see what was goin' on. A cavalry patrol had taken after two Indian scouts an' ran into the rest of the Indians.

"All the soldiers were killed except five, I'm not sure but four or five. I talked with Chasin' Elk, he said 'The soldiers had opened up on two of his scouts.' I asked him if the ones livin' could walk out. Chasin' Elk said, 'Yes.'

"One of the soldiers knew me so we talked. He said 'They would walk.' They had one man wounded so we gave them a horse, an' we let them go. Swan an' I joined Chasin' Elk then for there was 'more soldiers south of us' a scout said. They were crossin' the Cheyenne river. We kinda used it as a boundaßry. Fifteen of us went with our scouts out an' found them again. They were in a draw gettin' ready to eat. Anyway part of them were. Some others were still surveyin' an' some had a wagon stuck. We got their food an' horses from the ones at the fire. All the men were killed. Swan headed toward the Gap an' their horses were followin' her. We split up, five in each bunch, one bunch chasin' their horses, five on each side of the draw. We fought them for awhile killin' thirty or forty gettin' more horses. We took them towards the Gap. Swan waited for us, we had a talk, a few of the braves had been killed."

Lucy stopped me, "How many?"

"Four I think an' a couple wounded."

"An' how many soldiers were killed?"

"Thirty or forty, I'm not sure. Why?"

Lucy said "I'm not real sure but the officer said 'There were one hundred fifty Indians an' his men had killed half of them.'"

"No, I know we never lost more then four an' a couple wounded."

"Can you prove this?"

"Not unless we can find one of the soldiers or surveyors who walked.

"What about the Captain who told his story to the paper?"

"I don't know what he might say, his men had to help him away, he was beggin' an cryin'.

"He what!"

"After we had talked he tried to kill a man who was with the first ones. He had walked the year before an' knew I'd let him go. Anyway his time was up that day, he didn't have to take orders anymore. The Captain tried to ride over him. They fought, the first one threw me the Captain's gun an' walked away, takin' the other three men with him. They had waited with the braves.

"I told the sergeant an' the men who came to help their Captain back to their wagons. They could walk if they left their guns an' horses. He talked with the other soldiers an' said 'Okay.' We gave them wagons for the wounded an' men to shoot their meat an' they went south."

"How many Indians were with you at the time?"

"I'm not sure, maybe sixteen to eighteen."

"And they surrendered an' you let them walk away?"

"Yes."

Mary came in then, I swung her around an' kissed her.

She hugged me tight. I remembered my manners then an' introduced them. The three of us went to a table an' sat down. The bartender came an' brought drinks for Lucy an' I an' asked what Mary would like. She said, "Wine," an' he went to get it.

Lucy asked, "Will are you sure of this battle or fight as you call it?"

"Sure of what?"

"How many men you had?"

"I know ther were fifteen an' Swan to start with."

"Where is Swan now?" Lucy asked.

Mary was lookin' at me with the same question on her face. "She is not here," I said.

Lucy asked, "Why, has she been killed?"

"No we only lost four men in the last two days fight," I said.

"How many men did you fight?"

"Thirty," I said, "but one got away. He was the man. Captain Felter who caused the Indians all this trouble."

"How many men were fightin' with you?"

"Thirty an' Swan," I said.

"Will, can I print all this tomarrow an' will you tell me more of what has really happened out there?"

"Will it help the Indians?" I asked, "An' keep the soldiers away?"

"It sure can't hurt them any," Lucy said.

"Okay then I'll talk with you more. I have to go now so I can get this set up for tomorrow."

A man at the bar called out. "Hey Lucy did you find the great Indian lover?" She looked back at the man an' motioned him to be quiet. "What's the matter ain't my hair long enough or ain't I killed enough soldiers?"

She said, "Please excuse me." She went back to the man, I unbuttoned and loosened my pistol. Checked my knife at my back, both we ready.

"Well Mary have you been havin' a nice time here in the city?"

"Yes but I missed seein' you. Tell me all that has happened while I was gone."

"Biggest news I know is Kathy an' Lee are married."

Mary squealed with excitement, "When? Where? Are they happy?"

"Yes to all of them," I said, "Now get ready for this, Lester an' Sherry are goin' to get married next. Hell, they are married now."

Mary bounced with glee, "Good for them," she said. "That will be great for Lester."

Miss Morgan came back an' apologized for the man. I just shrugged my shoulders.

"Many men talk of things they know nothin' about," I said.

Here he came, he shoved Lucy aside. "Who knows nothin'?" he demanded. I said nothin'. "If you had any guts Indian lover you'd git up an' fight." He reached for me. I kicked his knee cap off with the toe of my boot, grabbed his coat front an' jerked him down on the table, flat on his back with my left hand. My knife point was up his nose hole. Mary said low, "No Will, these fools back here fight with their mouth, not like men do in our country."

The man was whimperin' but was afraid to move. "Let him live Will, he's just a town fool anyway." I shoved him off the table an' put my knife away. No one had seen it. We rose an' I walked to the bar an' asked for a bottle of wine an' one of whiskey. The man was layin' on the floor. Mary an' Lucy were at the door. The first shot hit my left arm at the shoulder. The next shot hit where I had been an' broke a bottle of whiskey behind the bar. I was facin' him, my gun in hand. His gun had fallen to the floor. It was a double barrel derringer an' now was empty. I put my gun away, pulled my knife, walked to the man an' cut off his ear, dropped it on the floor in front of him, put the knife away an' walked back to the bar, paid my bill. I picked up the two bottles an' walked to the ladies. A bottle in each hand I offered an' arm to each lady an' walked up stairs. My arm hurt like hell but I never said a word about it.

Lucy had been in a hurry to go, now she was in a hurry to open the door to my room after I handed her the key.

Inside I sat the bottles on a table an' pulled off my coat, vest an' shirt. The hole was bleedin' so I pressed the shirt to it. Both women stood lookin' at my naked body. It was tanned an' rippled with muscle. There were scars everywhere. Both looked at each other an' then back at me.

"Open the whiskey Mary, there are glasses on the dresser for your wine." She jumped to open the bottle. She handed it to me, I had three big swallows then two more. Lucy had opened the wine an' drank from the bottle.

"Mary get a towel," I started sayin' when there was a rap on the door. I drew my gun, as I turned I had the gun coverin the door. "Come in, it's open." Slim, Hank an' two ladies stood

135

there. Puttin' the gun away I said, "I'm sorry, please excuse my appearance ladies."

Hank walked up to me an' looked at the hole. He handed me the bottle, I drank an' heard his pocket knife come open. I handed him the bottle he poured whiskey onto the shirt an' the knife. I felt the pain as he probed for the bullet. He was good, this wasn't the first for him. It popped out, he wiped the blood an' poured whiskey in the hole. He got a washcloth, soaked it in whiskey an' pressed it to my shoulder. Slim had torn a towel in strips an' they wrapped up my shoulder.

Both women were still standin' there when I turned around. "Get your glasses an' have your wine," I said as I looked for a shirt. I pulled out a shirt an' slipped it on.

Lucy asked, "What are all the scars?"

"Most are from gettin' bullets out," I said.

Mary said, "Some are from knives."

Hank started in then, "Damn Will why don't you get shot up out West, this is tame country back here."

Mary laughed at this. Lucy still hadn't spoken but she had been drinkin' the wine. Everyone was introduced an' the women sounded like a herd of magpies.

I told them what happened. Slim said, "Will your goin' to have to quit cuttin' off the ears. These gentle people don't understand about that."

We laughed an' turned to the women, they had settled down an' were havin' a glass of wine. Lucy asked me, "Will, do you always cut off the ear?"

"No Lucy, just the cowards that I let live. That way I can always tell who I can't trust. Who was he anyway, one of your boyfriends?"

"No, he is just a dandy as they call them here. His daddy has money an' son don't have to work so he spends his time gamblin', drinkin' an' goin' to parties, chasin' girls. This one's name happens to be Archie Tompson. His father owns several saloons here in town an' a couple houses of ill repute, or so it's rumored. You'll have to watch him, he won't try again but he will hire it done."

Lucy took my arm, "Will, does it hurt bad? I have to go get this story in, is it okay if I came back later?"

"It sure is if you don't mind seein' three old friends drunk an' talkin' about old times when the country was wild. What is Archie's dad's name?"

"He's called C. J. his name's Charles James Tompson."

After she left we sat around hearin' what Hank had been doin' all summer.

He told of horse trades, horse-prices an' all the fun he was havin' in the city.

"What did you think of my Appy colt, Hank?"

"Biggest damn colt I ever seen an' the best. I'll bet he'd be bringin' a hell of a price here if you want to sell him, can he run?"

"Like the wind," I said, "Ain't nothin' on the plains can beat him." There was a knock on the door. We looked at one another. I got up an' asked, "Who's there?"

"Police, open up."

I turned the knob an' opened the door. Two men dressed in blue were there. They each had a long black stick in their hand. "What can I do for you gentlemen?"

"Get your coat, we're takin' you downtown."

"What for?"

"Attempted murder, give me that gun."

"Come in," I said, "There must be some mistake."

"We were told to come an' get you, now give me that gun."

Hank got up an' walked up to the two policemen. "There must be some mistake officers. This man never tried to kill anyone."

"The report says he tried to rob a man an' cut off his ear with a knife."

Mary said, "Let's go downstairs everyone." We all followed her. The officers bringin' up the rear. At the bar she called the bartender. "Sir would you tell these officers what happened in here today?"

The bartender told the story as he had ten times before to customers. The broken bottle was still settin' on the back bar. "Archie Tompson was on the floor right there where the blood is.

"He shot Mr Chase in the back an' Mr Chase drew, ducked as he turned," the bartender was now actin' out what happened was in a crouch his finger pointed like a gun. "Mr Chase seen the man's gun was empty. The coward then dropped it. Mr Chase put his gun up, pulled his knife an' cut off the ear. Comes back smiled at me, paid his bill, picked up his whiskey in one hand the wine in the other, stopped at the door gets this lady on one arm the other lady on the other arm an' walks up the stairs. Thats exactly how it happened."

"What doctor came an' fixed your back?" one policeman asked.

Hank stepped forward an' said he had. All the people were crowded around now. The police man said, "Show me Mr Chase."

I unbuttoned my shirt an' pulled it an' the coat down over my shoulders. The bandage was soaked with blood. I flipped them up an' buttoned my shirt. "Are you satisfied?"

They both nodded their heads, the bartender produced the derringer but would't give it to the policeman…

"You can read this in the mornin' paper," I said. "The lady was Lucy Morgan, she was doin' an article about the West when this started." The policemen shuffled their feet an' then said for me to "stop down in the mornin' at my convenience." I said I would.

We then went to the dinin' room an' had some dinner. We were havin' wine when Lucy came in. She had two men with her an' they had some stuff in there arms.

She came to our table an' asked if she could take my picture for the paper? I said, "Okay," an' got up.

They set up their equipment an' I stood where they told me, there was a bright flash an' I jumped, everyone laughed.

She thanked them an' they left. She took my arm on the way back to the table, gave it a squeeze an' thanked me.

Back at the table Mary wasn't too happy with all the company but smiled an' sipped her wine. The bartender came out an' asked if we'd join him in the bar for a drink. I nodded an' said we'd be over shortly. I signed for the meal an' we left for the bar. Mary took my good arm an' said, "This ain't exactly what I had in mind for our first night together Will."

"This won't last long an' we'll be alone Mary."

She squeezed my arm an' smiled up at me.

We had a couple of drinks an' I said I'd better go change the dressin' on my shoulder. Lucy offered to but Mary said with a smile, "I'm sure I can handle this alone," an' we left.

She helped me take off my coat an' shirt an' unwrapped my shoulder. It had bled but was not now. She folded another wash cloth an' put it on the hole an' wrapped it again.

I stood an' pulled her into my arms. We kissed long an' hungrily. When we parted I walked to the door an' slid the night bolt, blew out the light an' we walked into the bedroom, she bent to blow out the lamp.

"Just turn it down Mary," she did an' came an' pulled off my boots. As I stood to remove my pants she started kissin' my chest. I reached around an' started on the buttons on the back of her dress. We helped each other out of our clothes an' crawled into bed. The soft light was golden on her naked body.

Her nipples were hard an' looked like dark berries waitin' to be eaten. I ran my mouth gentle around her swellin' breasts an' touched her nipple with my tongue. Mary moaned an' pulled my head to her breast. We made love for what seemed like hours, until we were both satisfied beyond our wildest dreams. Mary lay in my arms an' we rested.

"Would you like a cigar?" she asked. I lay there for a while an' then got up. She followed me out of bed, slipped into my shirt an' handed me my pants. I pulled them on an' went into the other room an' relit the lamp. I poured me some whiskey an' her some wine. I lit my cigar an' she came out.

Damn she looked good in one of my shirts. We sat on the couch an' drank our drinks. "May I taste your cigar?" she asked. I handed it to her an' she had a puff, held it in her mouth, then blew it out. I showed her how to inhale it. She tried it, then blew the smoke out slowly. "I like it, they make some little one's for ladies, would you mind if I bought some tomarrow."

"Not at all," I said.

We went back to bed an' snuggled together an' drifted off to sleep.

We made love in the mornin' an' got out of bed smilin'. Goin' down to breakfst we were arm an' arm. I had her on the left so my right had was free.

Hank an' Slim an' their ladies were at a large table so we joined them. The ladies were all smilin'.

After breakfast we were waitin' for a carriage when one stopped at the hotel door. In it was Lucy an' an older man. Lucy introduced him as Silas, the owner of the newspaper.

He wanted to do an interview with me. I said, "Okay," if he would ride to the police station with us. We got another carriage for Slim, Hank an' their ladies. We all rode there at the same time.

I told Mr. Humes about the deal in Scottsbluff an' how it had went. "I'm not takin' any chances, that's one reason Hank an' Slim are along. Havin' Mary an' Lucy as witnesses is more insurance an' to have you along is an extra ace in the hole."

When we arrived I was nervous as hell. Mr Humes took charge as we walked in. He introduced himself to the desk sergeant an' ended up in the police chief's office right away. The chief shook his hand an' said he was glad to see him. Silas told him why we were here. He said it had been "cleared up an' not to worry about it."

He shook my hand an' said he had read about me many times. "Hoped to get the true story." As we started to leave he asked if "Swan was in town."

"Not this time," I said.

He looked at Mary an' said, "I see."

We climbed back into the carriage. I asked Mr. Humes if he minded "a ride to Hank's livery stable?"

"Not at all Mr Chase, I have until two this afternoon."

Our horses were in a lot when we got there. We all stepped out of the carriage. I asked the carriage man to wait. Both drivers were glad to, it was seldom if ever they got to see a horse like this.

I whistled an' the colt bucked an' played across the lot to me, the gray followed.

I petted them an' rubbed their ears. Hank said, "One minute," an' went into his office to check on things. When he came out he was smilin'. "I have the day off, them horses I been expectin' won't be here until tomorrow," he said. They had to take the ladies home but would see us at the hotel later in the day.

We four went to the hotel an' stopped in the dinin' room. Lucy an' Mr. Humes asked questions an' I gave answers to the best of my knowledge. When we got to the battle for the fort I told how it was the best fort I'd ever seen. Told how they could have left but due to pride an' stupidity they had chose to stay an' fight.

I told of the water an' rain comin' an' helpin' us. Then how six of us had wiped out three sides of the fort. I told about Jack Henry, how he was a brave an' fair man. That he had been a scout for Felter when he was in our country the year before. Told how the cavalry had ran an' left wagons in that battle.

How we were armed to hold out for years. The gattlin' guns that we had improved an' how they now could turn an' shoot all the way around.

Lucy an' Mr. Humes asked questions for a long time. Finally Mr. Humes asked why Swan wasn't with me?

I said, "She's on a mission to improve the world of ours," an' would say no more.

Finally they all left so Mr. Humes could make his meetin'. He asked Mary an' I to have dinner with them the next evenin'. I looked at Mary, she nodded an' I agreed.

He asked if it would be okay to have some of his friend an' a couple Generals join us. I said, "Yes."

Mary an' I went to the bank to visit Mr. Morecroft. He was very happy to see me an' to meet Mary. Dory was goin' to marry Chester Brown. We agreed to have dinner at his house the day after tomarrow. We again returned to the hotel.

We stopped at the bar, a note was there for me from C. J. Tompson. It asked if I'd see him at my convenience at his bar on Twenty-Second street.

As Mary an' I sat havin' a drink I decided this might be okay. Mary said it was "foolish." Slim an' Hank came in an' she told them. They agreed with her but Slim said, "I'd go anyway." A bellboy came with another note from Mr Goodnight. He was in the lobby an' would I see him.

I went to the lobby, he was tanned an' stronger lookin'. We shook hands an' looked at each other. "Hell man, I'd never known you were in town but for this front page story an' your picture in the paper."

He came an' had a drink with us. He was on his way to Washington to see his family an' close out some business. He was goin' back to Texas an' be partners with his uncle. He loved the West.

Slim told him about the deal with Tompson an' he said it was a great idea. He had two damn handy men with him who were old fighters from way back.

We would all meet for dinner at seven in the dinin' room an' work out a good plan. Mary an' I went to our room.

We had had the doors opened between her an' my room so we now had four rooms in a row. She went an' changed. I had stripped to the waist an' was havin a cigar an' whiskey. Lucy knocked an' I let her in, gave her wine. She sat lookin' at my chest an' side, at the scars, also there were teeth marks on both shoulders. "Battle scars," she said an' smiled. Mary came back then an' they went to her room.

I dressed an' we went down to dinner. We met Fredricks an' friends. They were enjoyable. A man I'd seen before we went to our room was still havin' coffee. He looked out of place. I mentioned him to Hank an' he said he'd watch him.

We made plans for goin' to Tompson's place. Goodnight an' his friends left. Slim followed a little later. Hank moved over to the man an' sat at his table. The man got nervous right away. Hank walked outside with him an' they got a carriage an' left.

It was nine o'clock, we were ready for the trip to Tompson's. Hank met us in a carriage out front. We went to Twenty-Second street.

"Alright ladies, listen up," I said. "You don't know anyone but us when we get to the saloon. Stay by Hank an' I, play the game. Lucy if Archie is there you know him from last night an' before that but Hank an' I's friends you don't know."

We had the carriage wait for us an' went in. It was a fancy place, a waiter seated us an' took our order. When he returned I told him to tell Mr. Tompson, Will Chase was here to see him. He came back an' said Mr. Tompson would be along shortly.

I thanked him an' looked around. Many people were lookin' at us. Mostly at me. I figured it was part my long hair an' part from the photo in the paper.

Fredrick an' one of his men were at a dice table. Another at a faro table. Slim was at the roulette wheel.

We had finished our drinks when the waiter came with another an' said, "Compliments of Mr Tompson. He will be here shortly." A small man dressed to the teeth came our way. A man flanked him on each side.

He introduced himself an' I asked him to be seated. We talked a short time of little things an' then he came right to the point. Raisin' his voice a bit he said how sorry he was for the incident with his son, he went on tellin' me how I "should not have cut his ear off."

"Mr Tompson, I always do that to back-shootin' cowards an' general scum in this white world."

He nearly choked, when he could talk again he started out. "Well Sir I heard you have a horse that you think can run. I also have one I think can run. Would you care for a horse race, just the two of them?"

We talked of a one mile race on the county race track. I said, Let's run two miles, my horse has never seen a race track. We'll run one mile one way, turn our horses around an' run one mile the other way."

He sat an' thought about this an' then agreed. We'd run the first mile to the left, the second mile to the right. We agreed on ten days from today. That would make it a week from Sunday.

We had everyone's attention, now he said, "Lets agree on the wager. I'm sure you would like to make a bet, let's say a thousand, would that be alright or was that too much." This last was said like maybe I didn't have a thousand dollars.

"Let's make it more interestin' sir, what is this place worth?"

He sat for a while, ordered us another drink, sayin', "It's probably worth fifteen thousand, why?"

"I'll meet you at the Farmer an' Merchants Bank at one o'clock tomarrow in Mr Morecroft's office. You bring the papers on this place an' I'll have cash. Mr Morecroft can hold the bet for us."

Mr Tompson sat lookin' at me. He had been sure of himself at first, now he was leery. "What horse are you goin' to run?"

"Mr Tompson a horse is a horse, I never asked what you were runnin'."

"Okay," he said, "It's a bet. I'll see you In Morecroft's office at one o'clock tomarrow." He got up an' walked away stiffly. We rose an' left also. In the carriage we went straight to the livery. The horses were standin' in stalls when we got there. I woke the night man an' told him about the race.

I gave him twenty dollars an' asked him to stay up an' watch the horses all night. He was excited an' eager. I told him I'd have men to help him tomarrow an' take care of his work so he could catch up on his sleep.

We rode to the hotel then. Hank was smilin' all the way.

Not a word was said about the race until we got to the hotel.

CHAPTER FOURTEEN

War Horse

The hotel was in an uproar when we got there as we walked into the bar, money was changin' hands as bets were bein' placed. Everyone was bettin' on my horse if they could get someone to take the bet.

We had a drink, got some bottles an' returned to our rooms with Slim, Hank an' the two new ladies they had. Goodnight an' his men, Mary, Lucy an' I.

Everyone wanted to know what I had up my sleeve. I lit up a cigar, lit one of the small long ones for Mary an' poured our drinks. The talk was all about horses an' what Tompson wanted to pull.

Hank an' Slim both knew how the Appy colt could turn around but Goodnight an' his men didn't.

"I'm runnin' the gray, he's older an' better I think. We'll try him out tomarrow."

All finally went home. Lucy had sent a message to her paper about the horse race an' the amount of the wager. It would be out in the mornin'. Fred escorted her home that night.

The next day Hank made all the arrangments for feed an' water for the horses. He bought grain an' put a guard on the hay an' grain. Made everything as safe as posible for the safety an' protection of the horses. We all knew Tompson would try something. Guards were hired to guard the barn twenty four hours a day.

I met Tompson at the bank, Dory wrote up the agreement. I counted out the fifteen thousand an' Tompson had his deed. Wrote out: "Lock, stock an' barrel," meanin' everything that was in it. Tompson left us then after he an' I had signed the papers.

Mr Morecroft poured us a drink an' leaned back in his chair. We finished our drinks an' poured again. "Tell me about this race Will. What's your ace in the hole?"

I looked at him an' said, "I have the best horse around this country. I'll win."

"Have you enough money to cover all the bets that will come your way?"

"I think so," I said.

"If you don't you have extended credit here you know."

I thanked him an' started to leave. He said. "I'll see you at supper tonight, I'll send a carriage for you."

We worked both horses at the track that day. The gray looked outstandin'. Everyone had been overlookin' him. We had him under a blanket, on the way back I rode the Appy. There had been over two hundred people there to watch. They all offered to bet different amounts of money.

As we were leavin' Tompson came with three big thoroughbreds, two studs an' a geldin'.

At supper the talk was of the race but Mr. Morecroft got around to the Indian problem in the Black Hills. We talked it for an hour. I tried to answer all the questions as fair as possible.

I told of the cattle ranches I'd started for the Indians, of the two horse ranches, of how my father had opened the post. Brought new thing to the Indians. The evenin' was most enjoyable for both Mary an' I. Lucy had been busy takin' notes. One man, a banker, asked how much money I was worth in cattle, land, horses an' the posts.

"I have no idea." I said, "I'm on my way back to Washington to collect some mortgages I have back there. They were taken for two hundred fifty thousand an' I'm sure if they were liquidated they would be worth far more than that. Half goes into a fund of the Sioux Nation here at the bank. The money is used for lawyers an' lays here drawin' interest for the people back home. Some is used to buy their own land back so when this all ends they still have a place to live an' a land to hunt."

We left an' for the first time returned to the hotel alone. We had a drink at the bar an' the bartender thanked me for all the business I was bringin' him. He gave us a bottle of whiskey an' one of wine. Also he filled me in on the odds on the horse race.

We took the gray to the track again that day. At supper I wore my beaded buckskins an' my knee high moccasins.

Supper was fine but the talk turned rather hard over brandy. The army Generals got purty upset when I mentioned the battle at the Fort.

One jumped to his feet an' shouted at me. "You should be hung for what you did to the General there. He quit the army in shame. Captain Welter was busted to sergeant an' ended up a drunk. He lost his wife an' family, then shot himself."

"General Shellman sent out Welter to talk to me instead of comin' himself. Welter thought just because he had the most men he would win. Welter said I could never take his fort. Hell, we didn't want it anyway it was their prison."

Another General spoke then. He was calm an' polite. "Mr Chase, what do you hope to gain by these constant battles with the soldiers?"

"We are only fightin' for the right to live in peace. We don't bother anyone who stays off our lands. All fights have been on our lands. There would be no battles if the soldiers stayed away.

"We know our end is near but we fight to put it off maybe another year. Each year my people are more ready, each year we gain more knowledge. We will not lose in the next five years but each battle costs us a few braves, if we lose a brave it's eighteen or twenty years before another is there to replace him. If you lose ten in a month you can have a hundred the next month, is this not true?"

"It is true Mr.Chase."

"This is why we must fight you in Wasington, to have things ready for our people when we can fight no more. If we can embarass you in the eyes of your people it is better than killin' you. We have no anger to kill the soldiers. They are just followin' some fool's orders who is followin' another fool's orders who is followin' someone's greed an' gain.

"Look at the slaughter of the buffalo. When it is killed by the Indian it is food, clothes, shelter, tools, weapons, eatin' utinsils, war shields, water bags, nothin' wasted. When it is killed by the whites the hide is taken an' the rest is left to rot.

"In five or ten years you'll be able to ride the plains for days an' never see a buffalo, only bones."

"What will the Indians do then?"

"My people have accepted raisin' cattle to feed an' clothe themselves. We have three ranches now an' hope to get the Indians to the north an' west to do the same.

"It is to late for the Indians to win against the whites. We fight now only to slow it down."

The angry General jumped to his feet again, "We can send in enough men to march across your Black Hills anytime we want to."

I raised my glass an' toasted him, "This is true General an' you will, next May.

"May fifth is when it's set to start."

"You can march across maybe but you will die if you stay."

"How will you stop us?"

"We will not stop you General, but when you're up in the hills afoot an' without food will your men not surrender their guns rather than starve? Will they not ask us to let them walk an' for us to shoot our deer an' elk to feed them?"

"You should be locked up, that would stop all the trouble."

"Again you are wrong General. There are men there better trained, better armed, an' far better mounted than your soldiers will ever be. You will die in great numbers next year whether you shoot me or not. My people are ready for your foolish leaders an' poor soldiers."

The General stormed from the house an' no one else moved.

"I am sorry, Mr. Humes, for upsettin' your guest but it is foolishness an' anger like his that is causin' my people trouble.

"That man couldn't live a month out there, he'd starve to death. If he comes next spring I'll send him back naked an' cryin' out of our world just like he came into this one. He will be given two births, that way maybe he will be smarter the next time."

I turned the talk to other things. It finally got back to the horse race. We moved into the parlor an' talked on. General Gray an' General Hodgegood came an' asked if Mary an' I would have lunch with them the next day. Both promised to bring their wives. We said we would like that. General Gray asked if he could bring his son. I said, "That would be fine."

Mr. Humes was very pleased with himself an' his dinner. He thanked Mary an' I for comin' an' his carriage took us back to the hotel.

The next day the newspaper told of the dinner at Humes' home. It gave a minor rundown of who was there on the society page. The front page had headlines that read, "Outlaw or Saint," Told the whole story of the Generals an' Will Chase.

It told of the simple answer about the horse race. The paper told of the three thorougbreds C. J. Tompson had in trainin' at the race track, of the long lean runnin' lines of my gray horse. The only mention of the War Colt was as the funny colored pony horse.

The bettors were givin' two-to-one odds on the Tompson horse. Some still liked the gray.

That night shots were fired at the livery but nothin' very major happened.

The paper told of this the next day, sayin' it was not known whether the shots had been meant for the gray.

If my gray couldn't make it for the race I'd have to have a replacement or forfeit the bet. We went to lunch with the Generals an' their wives that day. Mary had a fine time talkin' with the ladies. I enjoyed the visit with the Generals. After lunch Mary an' the wives went upstairs to talk more.

They were interested in livin' in the West. They both said they thought they would enjoy roughin' it for awhile. Mary told them not to come. They would definetly not enjoy it at all.

Hodgegood, Gray, myself an' the eleven-year old boy went into the bar. Mr Gray acted as if it were nothin' new to the boy but by the boy's action I could tell he'd never been there before.

When we were seated the bartender was there. He was glad to have us in his place he said an' gave us his excellent service. He brought us a bottle an' glasses an' poured for us. Then returned with a large glass of some fizzie stuff he called sodas.

We talked for almost an' hour. Mary came in an' told us the women were in the lobby. When we had finished the men an' the boy were gettin' up to go. I asked Gray if the boy would "like to go see the race horses work out." He said he was sure he would an' said he an' the boy could "come tomarrow."

This day we let the gray run all out. He made the first mile runnin' beautiful, he slid to a stop an' got the turn in good shape. He ate up the second mile with blazin' speed.

The lookers still never paid attention to the War Colt. After all were gone I ran the Appy colt. He blistered the first mile, slid to a stop, did a perfect rollback, came up in the right lead an' blistered the second mile. When we checked the watch he had finished a full five seconds faster than the gray. He was outrunnin' the gray but not by much. He was gainin' it all on the rollback.

We never took the Appy back with us but put him in a big stall in another barn. We had two guards on it. Hank owned the barn an' land. He moved hay an' grain there. There was a good stream at the back of the barn. We had Slim's saddle horse there for company so he wouldn't go off his feed.

Day eight, the odds were four-to-one in favor of Tompson. I went to the bank an' got twenty thousand as the bank was closin'. Mr Morecroft asked me to wait. He would like a word with me. We had our glass of whiskey an' he straight out asked me. "Will, can your horse win the race?"

I smiled an' said, "Mr Morecroft I'm bettin' fifteen thousand he can."

He filled our glasses again an' said "Hell man, I know you are, you know something I don't."

"Yes."

"What is it?"

I had a sip of whiskey an' said. "I'll let you in on this if you promise not to move until the last hour, is that a promise?"

"Yes Will, I promise."

"You understand there ain't no guaranties. My horse could go lame, he could fall down an' he could get outrun."

"Yes Will I understand, I'm not askin' for a fool proof deal."

"Don't get greedy an' you can make a lot of money. If you get too greedy you'll blow the deal an' no one will make much. Another thing, ten percent of what you win goes into the tribe's fund." He agreed an' we had another drink.

I was nervous, "Mr. Morecroft don't let any of your friends in on this, it's you an' me all the way." We shook on this. He was grinnin' when I left.

I ran into Mr. Gray at the hotel bar or rather he was waitin' for me. We had a drink, there was several officers in there, the bartender had hired two new bartenders an' it was packed, over flowin' into the next room that was for special parties.

Lucy was there in the middle of it all. She grabbed my arm an' kissed my cheek, hung right on. The bartender got us a table. When we were seated an' had ordered I excused myself an' went up stairs. Mary was with a couple women when I got there. She came an' kissed an' gave me a hug. "Sorry Ho, I'm goin' to be tied up for awhile."

I said, "That's okay" I'd just come to tell her the bar was a mad house. "When your finished here I'll come set you for dinner. Don't leave the room alone, keep an eye for me. If something seems wrong I'll let you know." I said to the ladies, "Excuse me for the interuption." They all smiled an' said, "It's okay."

I went back down an' my table was covered up with soldiers an' dandys. They let me have my chair back. The odds were back down to two-to-one. Word was out that the gray horse could run. Mr Tompson came throught the crowd an' stopped at my table.

"Mr Chase, I came to see if you would like to make a side bet on your horse?" I rose an' asked him to join us. Someone gave him a chair an' he sat down. The barman had a drink there at once.

"I have seen your three horses, which one are you goin' to run, the geldin'?"

He just smiled an' said "He's a good one ain't he. He has that turnin' around down purty good. That was a good trick, you almost got me with it but the horses of mine have mastered it rather well."

The other talkers had quit talkin' an' were listenin' to us. "What about another ten thousand? I have the cash right here," he said, pattin' his jacket pocket, "Or would you rather have me put up another saloon."

"I have fifteen thousand at even money now," I said, "An' what are the odds?"

"Three to one."

"It looks like you are awful sure Mr Tompson. Maybe I better keep what little money I have left."

"Tell you what I'll do Mr Chase. I'll give you five to one odds right now, what do you say?"

"Well, I guess I could spare a couple more thousand," I said, "After lookin' at your horses I'm not near so sure of the gray."

He wrote out the bet. I paid up two thousand dollar bills an' he laid out ten. The barman sealed them in an' envelope an' signed across the seal an' put it in his safe.

Tompson left then an' the dandys went wild with their bettin'. The odds were a solid five to one that Tompson would win the race.

I asked Lucy an' Mr. Gray to come upstairs an' have a drink with us. They accepted, on the way up the stairs Lucy was clingin' to my arm. "Will, do you always cause this much excitement where ever you go?"

"Not always Lucy, but sometimes."

"How does Mary keep track of you?"

"This is the first time we have been together. Swan was before, she was always at my side."

"Where is Swan?"

"Is this for the paper or yourself?"

"Myself."

"She is at another place," I said.

We entered the room then an' had our drinks. I told Mary Mr. Gray was here an' we were goin' to visit awhile. When they had all gone Mary an' I sat an' talked. Mary wasn't goin' back until spring. Now that Lester had someone to take care of him she wasn't needed too much.

I sat smokin' a cigar an' sippin' my drink. "I'm leavin the day after the race." I said. "I must hurry back to Washington to help Chester no matter how the race comes out."

Mary came an' sat beside me. "I have helped the Indians here. Lucy has done a good job an' Silas Humes is behind the Indians in their fight. If I can get coverage like this in Washington maybe I can really do some good."

Mary was gettin' mad, I could tell. I'd not meant for the things I said to upset her. I'd noticed she had become colder towards Lucy Morgan. I turned her to me an' we kissed. She kissed with hunger an' passion. Mary an' I went to a late dinner but there were so many people we left an' had our dinner sent up to the room.

The day before the race there were over a thousand people at the livery. We took the gray to the track under his blanket an' gave him a light workout. The horse really looked good. For a minute I thought I may be runnin' the wrong horse. The thought passed, I was sure of the Appy colt.

When we put the gray up I left the final instructions with Slim. He was to do it to the gray at midnight, no sooner.

Hank showed up at the livery. He was smilin'. "The colt is fine, there are four guards with him.

"Goodnight an' his friends put a bundle on the race today, they don't know for sure what's goin' on but they put ten grand an' got four-to-one odds. I told them to go for it, you had something goin." Hank said he was stayin' with the gray an' Slim tonight, there were three other men guardin' him also. Hank didn't know, only Slim did an' he wasn't tellin' anyone. Hank had put a lot of money on the race, maybe more than he should have.

When I got back to the hotel Lucy was in the middle of the excitement. The bar was packed. The barman saw me an' brought me a bottle an' glass to the table. I thanked him an' he went back to work. Lucy came through the door an' straight to my table. He must have told her I was there.

Lucy bounced into a chair. "Will I have some great news for you. I'm sure it's goin' to be a big help to you in the East." She took a drink from my glass, made a face an' poured it full again, took another drink.

"I wired my stories on you back East to one of Mr. Humes' accociates. They have been runnin' them every day.

"The people are buyin' them as fast as they can be printed. The bookmakers are goin' wild with the horse race. An Indian Pony against a Thoroughbred, an' one of the best. The odds are staggerin' back there, as much as twelve-to-one in favor of Mr. Tompson's thoroughbred. One man named Felter made a ten thousand dollar bet on your horse, the paper today called him a fool.

"The Senate an' Congress are holdin' a special session checkin' into all the Indian reservations, the Settlers Act, also they have taken the warrant off of you. They want you back there to talk to them on the fifteenth of April. At the White House, with the President of the United States of America.

"Also this man Felter wired Tompson a short wire, it said 'I know this man, cover your ass.' I wonder what it means, do you know a man named Felter?"

I killed my whiskey, filled it again, killed it again. Damn so close, would Tompson take his advice? Yes he would have his men out right now makin' small bets on my horse. I could only hope he didn't flood it out by mornin'. Maybe my trick with the gray could save it.

Lucy put her hand on my arm. "Will, I'm goin' to Washington on Wednesday, will I see you there? Is Mary goin'?"

"I don't know if she is goin' or not Lucy, she hasn't asked."

"Does she have to ask to go?"

"I don't know about what women do or don't do. I always just said what I was goin' to do an' done it. Swan was there if she wanted to be, or if she thought I needed her."

"You will be a big help to me in Washington. I know the town an' some good people there, I can help you also.

"Here comes Mary," she said. I rose an' pulled out a chair for her. She had two other women with her. They were someone's wives, one of them gave me the "I'm ready look," an' watched me as I drank my drink. The waiter came an' I ordered a bottle of wine for them.

They started yakin' about whatever, I needed to not listen to this crop of relation an' inlaws. I had other things on my mind. I needed to think about them. "Ain't that right Will?" Mary said.

"What?"

"Gladys was tellin' you about the Indians needin' God's teachin's."

"No that ain't right, they have a god of their own, they don't need another." Mary gave me a sharp nudge under the table an' started apologizin' for me. "Mary you hush, if they don't want my honest opinion they don't need to ask."

The good lookin' one laughed with honest laughter, the other one tried to laugh. Mary said. "Will is always kiddin' around."

The good lookin' one looked me dead in the eye an' said, "No, he ain't kiddin'. I'll bet the Indians do believe in their God, probably more so than the Christians believe in theirs.

Have you ever heard the Indians use their god's name in vain Mary?"

Mary looked embarrassed an' stuttered, "No but I haven't met that many Indians."

I said, "Excuse me," an' went to the bar. The bartender found me a table an' brought me another bottle. I should eat before drinkin' any more but I poured myself a drink.

A ladies arm an' hand sat another glass on the table. I fiiled it without lookin' up, it would either be Lucy or the good-lookin' one, either way I was goin' to have her tonight.

It was the good-lookin' one. I knew why she was here an' so did she. "Mary had gone upstairs she said she wanted to see you if you had time, I told her I would tell you."

We had a sip an' some men came an' started talkin' horse race. I said my horse was "ready to run an' by three we'll know who had the best horse."

I capped the bottle an' asked her if she wanted to ride to the stables. I wanted to check on things an' I needed some quiet.

Before she could answer I said "Wait if you want, I'm goin' to see what Mary wants."

I walked into the room, she whirled on me. "How dare you embarass me in front of my friends. That was very rude, you're goin' to have to learn to…"

"Thats enough, Mary," I walked over an' got a drink. By the time I had finished it she had run down.

"Now you listen an' listen good, you had no business bringin' them to my table."

She started in again, "But I thought—"

"No you didn't think, I'm workin' on a two hundred fifty thousand dollar deal that is goin' down tomorrow. It means many things to many people. Lucy had just brought me some damn important information an' you think I give a shit about some prune's idea about givin' religion to the Indians, an' it don't make sense to them."

"Will I didn't know she was doin' anything but chasin' you. I was jealous an' you have no right to talk to me like this, I love you an' get mad."

She was still yappin' as I left. The last thing I heard as I walked away was, "You can't walk out," an' the noise was gone.

CHAPTER FIFTEEN

Flippin' the Coin

I walked down the stairs an' into the bar. Two men sat with the good lookin' woman. When I walked in she rose an' said, "Excuse me gentlemen," picked up the bottle an' came to me. We walked outside an' I hailed a carriage an' we headed off to the livery.

We rode along in the quiet listenin' to the clip-clop of the horses. I had a drink an' handed her the bottle. "What is your name?" I asked, "I never kiss a woman before I know her name."

"Carol," she said as she came into my arms an' we kissed. When we parted she said, "I'm twenty-four an' have been a widow for a year an' a half." We kissed our way to the livery stables. As we pulled up a guard came from each corner. "Ho," I called, to Slim an' Hank inside.

Hank opened the door, "What's the matter Will?"

We stepped down an' walked to the barn. Hank stepped back out of the door an' we went in. Slim was in the door of the office, a gun in his hand. "It's okay but I have some news from back East."

We all had a drink an' I introduced Carol to Hank an' Slim. Hank said, "Let me check on the men first, don't start talkin' until I get back."

Carol set herself in the big chair an' looked around at the office. Slim asked, "What happened to your friend?"

"Hell, she thinks talkin' about preachen' is important."

Hank came back.

"Lucy Morgan's an' Mr Humes' stories are bein' put in the papers back East. The president wants me to meet him on April fifteenth," I said.

"The big shots are goin' to investigate the reservations an' the army. They are checkin' on the crooked army men, also some of the congressmen.

"Now the bad news, Felter placed a ten thousand dollar bet on our horse back there at twelve-to-one odds an' sent Tompson a wire tellin' him to keep his ass covered because he knows me. I don't know what Tompson will do but if I was him I'd have men placin' bets all over town on our horse. The odds are six-to-one on his horse winnin' the race. He could put out ten one thousand dollar bets an' end up not losen much, only his bar. We'll have to play it to the hilt tommarrow I guess. You boys hash this around. Carol and I want to take a little walk out in the woods and listen to the quiet." I picked up a blanket off the bed and we walked out the back door.

"Say there Mr. Guard were goin' out in the woods and listen for a while just to make sure nobody is tryin' to sneak up through the woods, you boys stay on your toes. I'll have a drink for you when I come back, I'll say 'Ho' before I'm too close." I had a fresh bottle in the blanket.

Carol and I walked down the trail a couple hundred yards and turned into the woods. I spread the blanket on the grass and leaves, sat down an' pulled my coat off an' opened the bottle

Carol sat beside me an' we kissed, then had a drink.

"Do you want to talk?" she asked real low.

"No."

We had another drink an' I laid down. She laid across my chest an' started unbuttonin' my shirt, she kissed my chest an' petted it gently with her fingertips. She leaned forward an' kissed me, her lips were gentle and soft. Slowly I undone the buttons at the back of her dress an' slipped it forward over her shoulders. Her breasts were pushed up by her what ever they called them, I kissed them softly an' then her lips again. The birds chirped now an' then, it was cool.

We made love slowly an' gentle at first, it was buildin' to a roar. We went over the edge together and clung to each other, it had been beautiful.

She leaned forward after we had regained our clothes and kissed me an' whispered thank you. We sat together with the blanket pulled around us. We had a couple drinks an' just sat there.

We heard it at the same time. Someone was comin' up the path. They were tryin' to be quiet but were failin'. I pulled her ear to my lips, "Stay here," she nodded her head. I kissed her ear an' slipped my coat on an' pulled my gun.

When they had passed me I counted to seven an' then followed them. They were each carryin' something. I followed along, stoppin' when they stopped. At the edge of the woods they looked at the guards at each corner of the barn. I was close to them now. They were so intent watchin' the first one never heard the blow comin'. it was to late for the other one.

"Ho," I called. One of the guards answered me "Ho." So I walked on up to them. We had some company boys, let me get Slim an' Hank."

Hank brought a lantern an' we walked over to the men. They were comin' around, the things they were carryin' were jars of coal oil. "Take them to the barn, I have to get Carol."

She never said a word when I called her name. I walked up to the blanket an' she stepped from behind a tree. She had a derringer in her hand. "Oh!" she said when she recognised me, the gun was uncocked an' dissapeared.

"Where the hell you get that?" I asked.

"A girl has ways of hidin' things," she said.

I thought I'd searched her rather well.

We walked to the barn, I gave each of the guards a couple sips on the bottle. They said, "Thanks." I told them, "Thanks for bein' on the job." Then just to keep them on their toes I said, "I'd be around now an' then."

I went out front an' gave them guards a drink an' told them what had happened, "So stay on your toes."

Goin' back in the two men were standin' there with their heads hangin' down. I pulled my knife an' grabbed a man an' throwed him to the ground. I sat straddle of him an' asked who had hired him, he never answered. I grabbed his ear an' touched it with my knife. "Who?" Nothin' so I cut a little. He squealed like a pig, I cut a little more, he could feel the blood now, an' the pain.

"Archie Tompson," he said. I let him up an' he clamped his hand to his ear. I tied them up an' had Slim drive Carol an' I to the hotel. She asked to be let off at a house this side of the hotel. I walked her to the door an' kissed her goodnight. "Remember this house," she said, "An' come back when you want," she went in.

I got in the seat with Slim. He never said a word. At the hotel I said,"Thanks Slim, I'll tell her I was at the livery." He nodded. When I got to the room she was still up. Was movin' her stuff back to her rooms. "Where have you been?"

I poured water into a basin an' washed the blood off my hand an' knife. She stood an' looked at me then when I had my hands dried she walked up an' kissed me. I held her in my arms.

"I'm sorry I hollered at you earlier, I didn't know what was goin' on, all I could think about was I was mad because you an' Lucy were settin' there together talkin'. I know there is something goin' on that I don't know about. What was the blood from? Was the…"

"Damn," I said an' got up an' pulled off my shirt. She hadn't even slowed down. I got undressed an' crawled into bed. She was still talkin' when I went to sleep.

I got up an' showered an' shaved, this was the day. Every thing was as ready as I could get it. Now if I could get the bets down an' most of all if the colt could run as good as I thought. Damn there was too many ifs, this had come apart right at the last moment.

I got dressed an' picked up the little derringer an' dropped it into my pocket. The thirty-eight pistol was nestled in its holster on the left side, my knife at my back.

I slipped into my jacket an' picked up my hat, takin' a look at Mary layin' there asleep. She was beautiful. I walked down the stairs for coffee.

There was already a large number of people around.

Mr. Humes an' Mr. Morecroft were havin' coffee, they motioned me to join them.

"Good mornin' Gentlemen," I said an' sat down.

"What's the game plan today?" Mr. Morecroft asked.

I just shrugged my shoulders an' poured some coffee. After a couple sips I looked at them, "Do you men have any bets down," I asked.

They both said they did "at five-to-one."

"Have you heard what the odds are this mornin'?"

Humes said, "the street was three-to-one, a dandy house was two-to-one."

Mr Humes asked if I had gotten "the message from Lucy."

I said I had "an' sure did appreciate the good words spread back East. It would help the Indians a great deal."

I told them of the two men we'd caught last night. They admitted they worked for Archie Tompson. I don't think C. J. even knew about it. "I still don't know what horse Tompson's goin' to run today. It don't matter too much I guess. They all look damn good."

Lucy came in an' joined us, she was eager an' shinin'. "Is Mary up yet?" she asked.

"No, she was up late last night."

Lucy said she would "go up an' see her." She was up an' gone. I was wonderin' what that was all about.

"Gentlemen I must go an' get my money, it's in the bar safe." I excused myself an' walked to the barman who was openin' his door. I looked out on the street, it was sunny an' beautiful. The birds were singin' their songs. I hoped by this time tomarrow I was singin' also.

We went into the bar, he sat me up with a bottle an' glass, poured me a large drink. "Better have it Mr Chase, I have some news."

He turned an' opened the safe an' got my two envelopes of money. He laid them on the bar beside my drink.

"Mr Chase, he brought in a horse last night. The stud from Maple Farms, he's a damn fast horse an' mean as hell. He's won ever race back East, eighteen or twenty I know of. In a dead heat he'll eat up the other horse or jockey, either one he can reach.

"Don't know if your gray can stay away from him, now don't get me wrong but this will sure give him an edge."

I had my whiskey an' walked back to the table. Lucy was back, said Mary would be down soon. I barely heard her.

I told Morecroft an' Humes what I'd just heard. We all sat quiet, thinkin'. I was wonderin' how old this stud was. If he was six or seven, even five, he could scare the hell out of a young stud. But then again the War Colt had his share of fights an' had not been whipped yet.

I got up an' went back to the barman. "How old is this stud?"

"Nine, I think," he said.

Damn, I turned an' went back to the table an' sat down, not noticin' Mary had joined us. This could change things, this could even get the colt beaten. Here I was doubtin' him before he had a chance to show his ability.

"Damn," I said out loud, got up an' went to the desk an' scribbled a note to Slim an' Hank. Walked outside an' hailed a carriage, handed him the note an' paid him to take it to the livery.

When I came back I noticed Mary settin' there. I turned an' went back to the bar an' had another drink.

I got control of my thoughts an' came out smilin' an' returned to the table. I nodded at Mary an' sat down.

She said Mr. Humes told her about the company last night. "Is that the blood you were washin' off?"

I never answered her, excused myself again an' went out the door, hailed a carriage an' went to the livery. Slim met me at the door, a smile on his face. It sure made me feel better.

"Hank has one mare horsein' an' knows of another one that's in heat everytime she's around a stud. He went to get her. The gray is limpin' just a little but enough."

"Okay, we'll leave it on until we get just about to the track, then cut it off an' rub the hair line out."

"How did you know about the stud?"

"The barman told me early this mornin' Slim, we have to take care of him before we leave. Did you decide whether you're goin' East with me or not?"

"If we win Will who's goin' to run the saloon you get? It can't make money if it's closed."

"Let's win it first," I said. Hank came back leadin' a big bay mare. He was smilin'.

"Okay men I'll be back at twelve, can you hold everythig down till then?" They nodded an' said sure they could.

I jumped back into the carriage an' returned to the hotel, There was none of my people in the dinin' room. I looked in the bar, none there. The barman waved me in, he poured another drink for me. We were alone. He leaned toward me over the bar, "Don't know what this means?

"The street has it that the odds are seven-to-one on the stud an' Tompson is three-to-one on him.

I gave him five hundred. "Take this an' bet it on my horse for yourself or just keep the five hundred if your not a bettin' man."

I went up to the room, it was ten thirty an' I wanted to be doin' something but right now it was time to wait.

Lucy an' Mary came into the room, Mary sat down beside me an' Lucy in the chair. Mary put my coffee down an' sat a drink beside it. "Mornin' Mary," I said.

"I'm sorry about last night, Will."

"Okay," I said.

"Do you want to talk about today, I seen the ticket for Washington an' want to know if I should get one?"

"Do you have money to bet with?" I asked.

She said, "Yes."

"Lucy can you be quiet on a deal?"

She said, "Yes."

"Okay girls, here is how it is. Wait until you get to the track, an hour before the race there will be some changes. The odds are goin' to go wild. When they get to about ten-to-one on Tompson's horse bet all you can afford to lose on my horse."

They both nodded. I had the drink an' got up an' walked an' sipped the coffee. If Swan was here she would love this one.

Mary asked again, "What about the ticket?"

"If you change your mind you can always turn it back in," I said. "You know when I'm ready to move, I don't wait."

Mary got her purse an' went out the door.

Lucy looked at me an' smiled. "Will Chase you are rotten." She then came an' kissed me. She tipped her coffee cup an' said, "Washington."

At one o'clock we got to the race track. The big black stud was being led before the grandstand. He was a magnificent animal, dancin' an' turnin' around the pony horse.

Hank an' Slim both ridin' the mares in heat led the limpin' gray horse up to where I was at. The black went past an' got a smell an' went wild. He bucked an' kicked, reared an' pawed the air around the pony boy's head.

Five thousand people rushed to the edge of the stands to watch. I rubbed the gray's left front foot an' had him loped up the track an' back. He was limpin' an' everyone could see it. I rubbed his foot again an' had him loped up the track an' back, it was worse. The black stud came by an' went wild again. This time he knocked the pony boy off his horse. Almost got away. He was bitin' an pawin' the pony horse.

I walked to Tompson an' asked him if he would put off the race for a week. He laughed in my face. I walked away mad as hell, came back an' told him I could "beat him on anything."

"Put your money where your mouth is Indian lover. I'll give you ten-to-one you can't find another horse in this world to beat the black."

I pulled out twenty thousand an' counted it out. He wrote me a marker for two hundred forty thousand, counted my money an' put it into a suit case. He had four guards with the banker who was in his bettin' box.

He picked up a megaphone an' got the crowds attention. Ladies an' Gentlemen there has been a change in the program. Mr Chase's horse is lame an' he has to change horses. The odds are now twelve-to-one my horse wins. No bets refused."

Goodnight came leadin' the War Horse up the track an' I walked to meet him. He handed me the reins an' smilin' said, "He's ready man, he's ready." At that time Slim an' Hank rode past the black stud again an' again. He went wild. All the people were watchin' him. I tightened the cinch an' stepped on. The black stud was swellin' up, he was eager to check this other stud out.

He danced sideways an' started toward the judges, they were flippin' the coin. I got the outside which was good, for at the end of a mile I had to stop, do a rollback an' I needed the room to turn around. I didn't want the black horse runnin' over us.

I was ridin' my stock saddle an' weighted one hundred seventy-five pounds. Tompson's jockey weighed one hundred twenty pounds an' was goin' to ride a flat saddle that only weighed about six pounds.

We were to walk to the line an' start at a pistol shot. The jockey was havin' trouble gettin' mounted. The black stud was buckin' an' kickin'. When he was mounted an' had his stirrups he swung the horse an' went back down the track. He turned an' came back at a lope, the judge said, "Get ready!"

163

I turned my horse an' went the other way. Goodnight eased up by the judge an' said, "This is walk to the line, not one horse came at a run."

The judge looked at him an' nodded his head. "Okay," he said.

We made another try at a walk, Tompson's horse was sideways so the jockey turned him back. He took two or three big jumps. I'll say one thing for him, he was a hand on a horse, an' could ride that little saddle damn good.

The crowd was on their feet, the roar was almost deafnin'. Again we started at a walk, the black horse was rearin' an' lungin', the jockey turned him back again. I turned the War Horse an' we started again. The jockey of Tompson's said, "Get ready for the game, country boy." We were gettin' closer to the line, the black started bouncin' again. He was just startin' to rear. Goodnight hollered, "Go," an' it caused the starter in his excitement to pull the trigger.

War Horse an' I were gone. The Tompson horse had reared an' we were three strides gone before he got started. In the first turn we had him by six lenghts. My colt was runnin' smooth as glass but I could hear him comin' on down the backstretch. I held on to about four lenghts, in the last turn I moved the colt out an' left room for the black. When we hit the straight away we were neck an' neck. The old stud reached out to bite an' we gained on him a little. He came crowdin' then an' pulled back neck an' neck. He bit at the colts neck again an' crowded us out farther. We crossed the line in a dead heat. I asked the War Horse to stop, he slid on his hind quarters. He had to make two tries before he was close enough to stoppin', to make his pivot. He done it perfectly an' we were gone again.

The jockey was fightin' the black stud but got him turned around an' was comin' back fast. Goin' down the backstretch he ate us up. The colt was runnin' all out now an' the old stud was right on our tail. We laid on the rail an' they had to move out to pass. We started down the home stretch, the old stud was bitin' the colts flank. We moved up again.

He was comin' on, his head was past my knee then past the War Colt's shoulders.

I let out a war cry that only the colt could hear an' we crossed the finish line. The War Colt won by a full head.

People were comin' onto the track, jumpin' out of the grandstands an' some were comin' over the fence from the in field.

I got the colt slowed to a lope an' watched the black stud halfway around the track. I pulled the War Colt to a walk an' turned him around, back to the grandstands.

I rode along pattin' his neck an' talkin' to him. The sweat was runnin' off of him. The track ahead was packed with people. We rode into them. They parted all reachin' to touch the colt. Goodnight an' his friends were at the bettin' booths.

Slim an' Hank came on their horses, a smile on their faces. Slim was ridin' the gray an' Hank Slim's horse.

The winners were still cheerin' an' shootin' in the air. The losers were lookin' gloomy as hell. I got down an' handed the colt to Hank but pulled off his saddle first, put the gray's blanket on him. Hank led him on up the track an' turned back with him.

I saw Mary an' Lucy in a box seat with Humes an' Morecroft. They all waved an' looked happy.

I walked over to where C. J. Tompson was payin' off the bettors. Men were bringin' him money an' the banker an' his two helpers were busy countin' out money an' takin' the markers.

Tompson reached out an' shook my hand with a phony smile. He had a large pile of money in front of him. He handed me my twenty one-thousand dollar bills, motioned to the large pile, do you want to count it?

I shook my head no. He put it into a briefcase an' handed it to me, then a set of keys. "There's someone in the East who sure knows you Mr. Chase. I'm glad he sent me the wire. It saved me, he knew what he was talkin' about."

"He had a lesson," I said.

Goodnight an' his friends were waitin' with a carriage.

I stepped to the grandstand an' said to the four waitin', "Hotel, I'm goin' now."

They all nodded an' I stepped into the carriage an' we drove away.

When we turned off the race track I let out a War Whoop an' started laughin'.

Everyone joined in the laughter.

CHAPTER SIXTEEN

Keepin' Order

Fred Goodnight said, "That black stud can run like hell Will, I'd like to breed some mares to him. The Appy can run like hell too. It's a good thing he can turn around like that, you didn't have much to spare at the line."

I just smiled at him, "How'd you guys do?"

"We got enough to buy a lot of cattle, we're thinkin' of comin' up your way."

There it was again, always some one wantin' to come to our country. I even seen the long herds of cattle comin', but wasn't ready to accept it yet. Would I have to fight my friends too?

At the hotel it was a grand celebration. The carriage stopped in the street. People cheered as we got out. They opened a path to the door for us. At the desk I sat the briefcase up on the counter, the desk man smiled as he took it. "How much Mr Chase?"

"Two hundred forty thousand sir, I'm sure the man's word is good."

He wrote out a receipt an' handed it to me. "Your room is ready for you sir." I didn't know what he was talkin' about but I was sure I'd find out.

All four of us went upstairs an' the doors were open to our rooms. People were everywhere. I walked in an' a three-piece band started playin'. The room was full of flowers, drinks in everyones hands. When the music stopped a great cheer went up for me. When it ended I yelled, "Now one for the War Colt."

This one was even bigger an' the band started playin' again. Mary came to my side an' kissed my cheek. People kept slappin' my back, they had all forgotten the bullet hole.

Lucy an' Carol came with a bundle of roses an' handed them to me. A ribbon said, "War Horse." An hour later Mary said, "Your shoulder is bleedin', I better get it wrapped again."

I looked around an' asked, "Where is our stuff?"

"I had it all moved across the hall into another room this mornin'." She told Fredrick, General Gray an' Hodgegood where we were goin' an' asked them to come along, also Mr. Humes an' Morecroft. We got into our other room, there was a knock an' Mary opened it. It was Lucy an' Carol. Another knock, I didn't see who it was but Mary told them I'd "be out in a little bit."

I slipped out of my coat an' shirt. Everyone was lookin' at my scars. Lucy got a lusty look on her face an' ran her tongue over her lips an' smiled. Both Mary an' Carol were lookin' at her. Mary smiled an' started on my shoulder. Fredrick handed me a drink.

Mr Morecroft said, "Well, what are you goin' to do next Will?"

"I have to go to Washington, I have a meetin' with the president an' I better be there. Can you sell the bar for me? Or should I keep it?"

"With a better crowd it could sure make money. If you could find the right person to manage it for you. I could help you get the right person, give it some thought before you sell it," he advised.

Mr. Humes said the story of the race was already in Washington. He had it pre-wrote an' at the telegraph office waitin' to be sent.

"How did you know who would win?" I asked.

He laughed an' said, "I had two stories ready."

Mary finished dressin' my shoulder an' brought me a fresh shirt an' jacket, I'"m goin' an' tell these people to not slap your back." It was "open again an' it's goin' to take a while to heal."

General Gray said he was bein' sent to Scottsbluff an' General Hodgegood was goin' to Denver. "We were wonderin' what you could tell us that might be of help to us?"

I lit my cigar an' sat a moment, then told of what I thought to be the biggest problem around Denver. "Mr. Hodgegood your biggest problem is goin' to be keepin' order with the miners, the riff-raff that follows the gold an' silver. You have a pair of brothers out there, the Parker brothers, they will be your biggest problem as far as the Indians go.

"You have a council of many tribes comin' up next summer There are many whites that don't want any good to come of it.

"Mr. Gray, I like you an' like your family, if there's any way you can not go to Scottsbluff, please don't go there for you an' I will have to fight each other. Scottsbluff is where all my problems come from. They will have you come to my country an' we will have to fight each other, this I don't want. I'm to meet with the president an' I can see maybe get him to change your orders."

Mr. Gray rose an' he thanked me for the offer, he himself would try for a change of orders but not for me to try.

Carol said she had "some experience at runnin' respectable saloons."

I said, "Fine, you can meet with Mr. Morecroft an' work out some deal." If Mr. Morecroft was satisfied we would be at the bank at nine. She could meet us there if she was interested.

We all went back to the party then. It had slowed down an' was much more bearable. The excitement was wearin' off an' the well-wishers were downstairs now. I told Mary about offerin' the bar deal to Carol an' she thought it was okay.

Hank an' Slim came in then an' were a bit drunk. They had their ladies with them. The ladies went an' talked with Mary. We three eased over to the side so we could talk. Hank looked at me an' asked, "How the hell did you two get the gray horse lame an' then sound again so fast?"

"Slim will tell you before we leave."

"No Will, I want to know now, that was a slick trick."

"Here it is then, just tie a string around the ankle ahead of time, quite tight, six or eight hours ahead of when you want him to limp. Cut it off an' rub his ankle. When the blood starts flowin' good again he will start to limp. In an hour he's fine again."

"I'll be damn," Hank said.

We joined the party then. I talked with nearly everyone an' finally most had drifted away. Goodnight's friends had gone to a house of ladies, the rest of us went down to the dinin' room. We ordered champagne an' oysters. The oysters had just been served when a loud voice yelled, "Chase, you son of a bitch!"

I looked up into the hate filled eyes of General Upperton. He was rumpled an' drunk.

"Because of you Will Chase I have lost all my money. First you make a fool of me in the papers an' then again in the horse race. I bet every damn thing I had saved in thirty-five years in this army you call fools. Now I have lost it all an' it's your fault."

"Well Mr Upperton I told you I'd win this horse race. I sure as hell never told you to bet against my horse."

"You cheated, you changed horses, you were goin' to run that damn funny colored horse all the time, you're a crook!" He raised the gun, I ducked down, drawin' my gun as I did.

His first shot went throught the table top an' into my left ribs. It knocked me back onto the floor. I came up an' shot him twice in the chest. He staggered back an' fired again. This shot smashed into the wall behind me. I shot again an' it hit him between the eyes. He flipped over backwards an' smashed to the floor. Half the back of his head was gone.

Women fainted all over the place. I remembered thinkin' I had ruined dinner. I grabbed at the table an' landed with my face in the bowl of oysters. I rose an' slid to the floor, my legs givin' way. Blackness closed over me an' I sank into a great hole.

Mary had Slim an' Hank carry me upstairs. The police an' doctor were notified. They came an' took the body away. Lucy an' Mr Humes went to the paper office an' wrote the story.

The doctor had reached in with his long forceps an' brought out the bullet, decided it hadn't poked a hole in the lung, it had passed between two ribs. He picked the oak splinters out of my side, wrapped it up.

He also doctored the other hole an' was gone, mumblin' about tables, luck an' a damn fool.

When I came to my side was hurtin' like hell. The lamps were turned down low. I could see someone in bed in the other room. It took awhile but I made it up. I was naked as a jay bird. My pants were on the chair. It took awhile but I got them on an' stood up.

I moved into the settin'. room an' turned up the light, lookin' around I found a cigar an' lit it over the chimney.

The first puff made me cough an' the pain was sharp. I then poured me a glass of water for my throat was so dry I could hardly swallow. I had two waters an' then a shot of whiskey.

I was settin' on the couch tryin' to sort out what all had happened. I remembered the oysters clearly, also I remembered shootin' Upperton an' how he had flipped. I was settin' there when the door opened an' Slim came in.

"Howdy Slim," I said.

He jumped a little for he was closin' the door quietly an' had his back to me. He spun around an' looked, "What the hell are you doin' up?"

"Got thirsty," I said. "What time is it?"

He said, "Four o'clock, you been out better than twenty four hours Will. We was gettin' mighty worried about your head."

"My head!"

"Yes you hit it when you fell. Hit it on a chair, you been sleepin' all this time. You ought to see the write-ups in the paper. They sure laid into the army. Guess the investigation is goin' full blast back East. Their diggin' deep this time.

"Carol an' the banker worked out a deal this mornin'. She had the bar open by noon an' it was packed. All the big-shots were there. It's new name is "The 'War Horse." We took the colt down today an' had his picture taken in front of the place. The people love him. There have been two good offers for him."

"Hell, he ain't for sale, never will be."

Slim said, "He's a dandy."

Four days later I ventured down to the bar. The barman shook my hand an' told me how many people had been to see how I was doin'. Some even offered to bet on the day I'd come down. I walked outside an' sat in the sun, it felt good, it felt good to be alive.

About an hour an' I went in. Mary was waitin' at the foot of the stairs. I said I'd like to go up stairs an' asked her to walk with me. She gently took my arm an' helped me climb the stairs. She was now the woman I'd hoped her to be, soft an' gentle.

I laid on the bed an' she sat beside me. She kissed me tenderly on the mouth, stood to put a blanket over me, I dozed off to sleep almost immediately. It was evenin' when I woke. I felt fresh an' stronger for a change.

Mary was settin' in the other room writin' a letter to Lester an' Sherry. She heard me as I came through the door. "How are you feelin' Will?"

"Fine gal, would you like to go over an' see the War Horse? I need to move around a bit an' find out what's goin' on in the world."

She helped me on with my coat an' put on a jacket. We went down the stairs an' out the door. I hailed a carriage. We went to the War Horse. I paid the man an' then paid him to go to the livery an' get Hank an' Slim if they could come, if not, tell them where I was.

We walked in an' Carol rang a bell. Everyone looked our way an' shouted,"Hi." Many came an' shook my hand.

Carol was dressed mighty high-class, looked mighty damn good. My mind gave me a flash of the night in the woods, then it was gone. She came an' kissed my cheek an' hugged Mary, then ushered us to a table that had a big soft chair for me.

We had barely gotten our drinks when Slim an' Hank came in the door. Many men hollered at them. They waved an' sat down with us. We talked awhile about everything an' Slim said, "I'm goin' back to Washington with you if that's okay."

"Sure is Slim, we're glad to have you."

"Lucy is back there with Mr Humes. Their really givin' them hell in the papers. We got a wire today. It was there at the livery just a bit ago."

"We'll leave in a few day I guess. Let's figure on next Tuesday. Has anyone heard what Tompson is up too?"

"The kid, Archie has gone back East a couple days ago. The old man is doin' the same in awhile or so we have heard."

We had another drink an' Mary an' I went back to the hotel. We stopped in the bar an' visited with the barman. He said he had "bet all the five hundred at seven-to-one an' he thanked me an' truly meant it.

Mary an' I made the stairs, it was easier this time. We had a night cap an' went to bed. I was played out again.

The weekend I spent walkin' around the city gettin' my strength back, eatin' like a horse. Monday I went to the bank with the money an' we had a nice talk with Morecroft an' Dory.

Tuesday we boarded the train an' headed East. We were takin' three horses with us. Slim was figurin' on runnin' the gray an' the War Horse. It took four days an' I spent most of the time in the sleepin' car.

We went to the hotel where Lucy an' Humes were stayin' an' had supper with them. Both were surprised with how good I looked an' moved around. The bed in the hotel room felt mighty good an' it was nine o'clock in the mornin' when I got up. Mary had coffee for me by the time I was showered an' dressed.

We went to visit the Browns an' had an enjoyable afternoon with them. The Walters stopped in about four an' we talked for quite awhile. The trees were all bloomin' an' it was warm an' beautiful so we were settin' on the porch. The boys, Billy an' Buster had grown a lot. Were pleased when I told their dad how strong an' healthy they looked. Mrs. Brown was very proud of them also. The boys an' I went for a walk up into the orchard. They asked all kinds of questions about the West, I was surprised at some of their questions but later Walters told me they read the paper every day.

"Would it be okay if we went an' seen the War Horse?" they asked, so I walked to the barn with them. They petted him an' marveled at his color. He was sheddin' his winter hair an' gettin' a shine to his coat.

Chester an' Loraine rode in while we were at the barn so we walked to the house to meet them. Chester shook my hand warmly an' Loraine hugged me tightly an' kissed my mouth like we were at the creek.

We stayed for supper or dinner as these Eastern folks called it. After dinner we men sat in the parlor an' talked of the Indians' problems again. The investigators were really gettin' the people excited. Many inspectors an' a few statesmen had gone West to different reservations but no reports were back yet.

Veldon Brown asked about Swan, how she was doin' an' most of all why "she hadn't come with me?"

I asked Chester about closin' out the deal with the mortgages. He said everything was in order an' we could move into the Morre house tomorrow as soon as we left the bank. He had it all cleaned up an' servants hired already.

An investigator had turned up names on many more people who were in on deals with Morre. He had his fingers in many crooked deals all across the country

The Senate an' the Congress were leavin' no stones unturned. He was surprised at some of the names that were comin' up. The army also was findin' many men takin' early retirement and some were resignin', leavin' the good life of the East and disappearin' into the West.

Archie Thompson was hangin' around with a shady group of men. Mr. Felter had gotten rich on the horse race an' was livin' in style. Messin' around the stock market.

He was formin' a company called, Minin' Investors, Inc. He'd had trouble gettin' investors at first but he had a large bag of gold an' was showin' it to everyone. At first he only got small investors but after the big win he had more rich people lookin' at his sack of gold.

After the brandy we returned to the hotel an' sat figurin' what our plans were. Slim an' Hank were thinkin' on buyin' some good thoroughbred mares an' shippin' them to Kansas City. They wanted to breed as many as possible to the War Horse.

We were settin' in the bar when Goodnight came in. Him an' his partners looked purty ragged. They had done the town last night an' were already talkin' about Texas. This city life was hard on cowboys. We all laughed at this an' had a drink with them before we called it a night.

The next mornin' we presented our papers at the bank an' found the only property we didn't get was Felter's. He had left fifty thousand with the banker an' Chester sorted out the paper work with the banker. Hinkle, Morre an' Lestergoods property was ours free an' clear. Chester took us to the house. Mary was flabbergasted. The house was huge. It had large columns in front an' on both sides. There were fifteen rooms. The parlor alone was as big as most houses. She walked through it twice. She stood lookin' into the bedroom. She had a trunk an' two suit cases an' they looked small settin' in the big bedroom'. She was lost.

Slim an' I went to the barns. They were all painted white as was the corrals an' pens. A large pasture for this country was fenced in with the white boards, the pastures lush an' green.

Slim stood a long time leanin' on the fence. I could imagine his thoughts. He was seein' horses in the pasture.

There was a cook, two maids who were married to the men who worked in the barns. Two other families who worked the farm, their houses were one on each side of the farm in the back. They were painted an' clean, their barns well kept.

"Damn what I wouldn't give to have a place like this to spend the winters at," Slim said.

"What about our ranch in the hills, have you forgotten how good that place is?"

"No Will, I haven't but a man can die so fast out there an' it's so peaceful here."

We went back to the house an' then on to the hotel. Mary was in a whirl about the place. At the hotel Lucy was waitin' for us. Humes was with her.

We went to dinner with them an' four other newspaper big shots. I seemed to do most of the talkin'. Chester told of the papers he had filed to block the Settlers Act again an' hoped for two years. This would give the Indians more time to make adjustments to the times that were to come. Help teach the young the ways they must adjust to. I told of their cattle ranches, one run by Indians an' one run by the Sheppards. How Plenty Arrows had been put into the stockade for sellin' his own cattle. Told what I had heard about their escape.

There were many questions asked about Swan. "What she was doin'? Was she at the Gap gettin' ready for the fights that were to come this spring? Would the men follow her if I didn't go back?"

"Let me tell you gentlemen, I'm goin' back. If we can't get it stopped here I'll try to stop it there. I know we can win again this year but in the end we will lose I'm sure. The Sioux just want to be left alone. They are a happy laughin' people. There are no locks on the doors. My father has run a post there for goin' on thirty years an' there are still no locks on the door. I have herds of horses that have never been bothered. Many times I have talked with men, Indian men,

174

I didn't know an' they would tell me the horse they were ridin' was mine."

The next day it was all in the papers, three different ones. I sat in the dinin' room an' read them. Mary came an' joined me an' said she was goin' to lunch with Mrs. Fairchild, they would spend the afternoon shoppin'. We would have our dinner in the new house if that was okay. She would also see that the rest of our stuff was moved out there. Slim had agreed to stay with us. He was gone with Chester already this mornin' to look at the other two places.

I said I was goin' to the Fairchild Inn an' have lunch there. Mary said, "I wonder if they are related?"

"I'd never thought of this before. I'll ask today," I told her. She kissed my cheek an' was gone.

About eleven I rode the gray up to the Inn, tied him in the shade an' went in. Mr. Fairchild remembered me an' showed me to a table himself. He shook my hand an' said he was glad to have me back again.

We talked of the West after he brought my drink. He was settin' with me drinkin' a cup of rum. No, he wasn't related to the other Fairchild. He had been a sailor many years ago an' built this inn twenty years ago, never went back to sea. He said he liked it here an' had a small farm about three miles down the road.

We were talkin' of the West when Felter came in. He recognized me right away. He had two well-dressed men with him. They looked wealthy.

"If you doubt me," he said, "Right there sets the man who is keepin' us from the gold. Ask him if it's there or not?" Both men turned an' looked at me. "He has killed forty of my men, him an' that heathen called Swan. He's also the one that broke some of us with his gold swindle last year. Beware of him gentlemen for his men are out to keep all the gold in the Black Hills an' that's a lot."

"Keep talkin' Felter an' you will someday hang yourself. The army out there is wonderin' why all your men end up dead an' you always escape. Gentlemen there is one thing to remember, if you don't come out there tryin' to steal the land of the Sioux you have nothin' to fear.

"This man kidnapped Henry Long's daughter, raped her many times, tried to make her tell where the gold was, she had no idea."

"That's a lie!" he yelled, "A damn lie."

"Then when her horse fell on her an' broke her arm an' leg he calmly shot her in the head."

"Don't believe him, he's lyin'."

"I have at the hotel a note in his own hand writin' an' signed by his hand. Now Felter says I am lyin'. I should have killed you two years ago Felter. It would have saved my people, as well as yours, a lot of trouble. If not for your greed the Sioux would still be livin' in peace."

He came out with a one shot pistol an' fired at me. The shot went wide, comin' closer to Fairchild than to me. I had not gotten out of my chair. He was lookin' at the barrel of my pistol over the table. He threw his gun an' turned an' ran out the door screamin' in fear.

Fairchild had not moved. I put my gun away an' said, "Come an' join us gentlemen."

Fairchild got up an' asked what they were drinkin', brought it to our table an' refilled ours. The men came over slowly. Fairchild introduced me an' his self.

They said their names, "George Jimmerman," "William Asher" an' sat down with us.

I had a drink an' said, "What I say gentlemen is true. I can prove it. Alice Long's brother has been with my father an' now me, for over twenty five years. The note was left on the bed she was taken from. I have it in my bag. It's signed by Felter. You saw him run, he's a coward."

We had our drink an' Fairchild got another. They said they had "just agreed to invest a lot of money in the gold in the Black Hills."

"I'll not tell you how to spend your money but the reason I'm here is the president asked me to tell him the Indians' side of things before the Settlers Act goes before Congress.

"Even if they get it past the Senate an' Congress the president can still veto it an' I'm sure he will. If they do pass or reject it there will be so much fightin' you won't have time to look for gold."

They excused themselves an' started to leave. "Wait," I said an' got up an' got Felter's gun an' gave it to them. "Give it back to your partner," I said. "See you in Sioux country gentlemen."

They left an' Fairchild sat back in his chair, "There goes a big chunk of money out of Felter's pocket," he said. I looked around at the other ten or twelve people in the place. There wasn't a soul who would put money with Felter now. Also word would spread fast.

I stopped back at the hotel we had been stayin' in to see if Chester an' Slim were there. They were an' we went into the bar. Slim was his calm self but Chester was wild with excitement. "Tell us what happened?" he said. I did but it never satisfied him. He wanted to hear it word for word. I told him the best I could.

Slim told me how beautiful the other places were. He told about the Lestergood place. He said the house wasn't as big as mine but damn sure plenty big. He had bought ten mares today, would it be okay to put them out there. He brought out the papers on them an' started tellin' me the races each one had won. Three of them already have colts. "Can I breed them to War Horse. My god what colts they'll have." I had never seen him this excited.

Lucy came in an' wanted to here the story of Felter again. She said it was already comin' out in the paper but wanted to know if she had it right. Mr. Fairchild had told her.

"Lucy, I'm sure if that man told you it was exact." She ordered a drink an' started off on a campaign her an' Humes were workin' on. She had my hand in both of hers as she was talkin'.

After we had finished our drinks I asked her if she'd like to come out to the house for a dinner Mary was havin'. She said "Yes of course," where ever I went there was news.

The story was there the next day, on the front page. A demand for a full investigation into the business of Minin' Investors, Inc. This brought a great many questions from the small investors but Felter was out of town on business an' could not be reached.

I went with Slim to get his mares an' colts. They were beautiful, but even more so when we put them into a pasture on his place. He could not believe it belonged to him an' Hank. When we turned the stud out with the mares he was watchin' a dream come true.

He stayed there to watch the horses. He said, "Anyway the cook will have supper for us." Goodnight an' his friends had met some ladies an' they were comin' out for the evenin'.

Chapter 17

Okay Livin'

There were already people at the house when I rode in. One of the men took my gray an' was on his way to the barn with him. Damn, this was okay livin'. I stopped on the porch an' looked at the pastures. They needed stock in them. Guess I'd look around for a few head of cattle. One of the men that worked for me came to the porch. I asked him what he thought.

He was all for it he said. He'd had a milk cow once. "She died last winter, just got old. We been savin' for a mule an' milk cow but had to do the garden by hand last year."

I told him to get the other man an' meet me here in the mornin'. We'd work out some kind of a deal on stock. "Every family needs a milk cow." I asked how many children there were. He had three an' the other man had two.

"Would it be okay if I came down an' met your family in the mornin'." He smiled from ear to ear, nodded his head an' said it would be his pleasure to have me come down.

I walked into the house an' a man took my hat an' coat, called me "Mr.Chase" an' said, the guests were in the parlor. Dinner would be served in one hour.

As I came into the room all heads turned my way, conversation almost stopped. Mary came to my side lookin' beautiful in a new dress, anyway I'd not seen it before.

She introduced me to all our guests. I shook hands with the new as well as the ones I already knew. A maid brought me a drink, it had ice in it. I was talkin' with four men I had just met, the youngest one kept lookin' at my gun so I decided I'd better get my coat.

I excused myself an' started to go back an' get it, Mary came an' took my arm, said my clothes were laid out on the bed. I went an' washed up an changed. Then hurried back down the stairs. I had time to finish my drink before dinner was served.

We had twenty-five guests but I had no idea where they had come from, only that they were all there.

Mary had a beautiful meal an' we men moved to the parlor with our brandy. Mr Humes more or less took over the conversation, steered it to the Indians back home.

"Did they need school teachers, preachers or agriculture directors?"

"Maybe a couple of teachers but they didn't need agriculture men up there an' most of all no religion people. Now more than ever they needed to cling to the old religion. This would be too much of a change. Besides if the whites' religion was so great why did the whites have so much crime an corruption."

We talked of the gold quote, "swindle." I said, there were gold pockets everywhere, in almost every stream. I'd bet I could find more gold in them streams but that didn't mean it was worth minin'.

We talked of the horse race an the War Horse. I told about Petey trainin' him an' how Petey had come to be with us at the Gap.

Someone asked of Swan. I said she would be there when needed. A newsman came up with the theory she had been hurt in a battle an' was either dead or holed up somewhere gettin' well.

I told of the other Appy stud with the band of mares an' geldin's up West. Told of the mares Slim had bought an' now had with the War Horse.

When the evenin' was over Mary an' I sat in the empty parlor an' watched the fire burn, we finished our drinks an' retired. We made love an' then lay talkin'. Mary said she'd "never been happier" or had "more to be happy about." We went to sleep with these words.

I rose earlier than usual an' had coffee with the black man who was the butler an' ran the house. All that worked in the big house an' barns up here were satisfied with their wages an' every thing as it was but said the farm hands were short.

I told him that everyone here was to have a ten dollar a month raise an' I'd see Mary talked with him of new clothes an' whatever they needed. He was surprised an' very pleased when I left for the farmer's house below.

My horse was saddled an' waitin' at the porch. I asked the young man's names, it was Tye. I rode up to the house an' the man came out, his wife an' three children, the little one in his mothers arms.

"Bo is my name Mr. Chase, my wife Letty an' the chillin's. We are free men an' have papers . We is legal man an' wife."

I stepped down an' the oldest boy, perhaps five, came an' held my horse. He was very business-like about it. Letty asked if I'd "like a glass of water?" I said, "No," an' asked Letty if there was anything they needed for the house. She hesitated just a second an' then said, "No, Mr. Chase."

I told her what a nice lookin' family she had. She flashed me a big smile an' said, "Thank you sir," an' did a little curt-sy. I took the horse an' Bo an' we walked together a hundred yards to the other house. It's barn was good an' well kept.

At the door Bo introduced me to Mister an' Sue. They were light colored an' also very clean as was the porch. There were two kids, one crawlin' an' one walkin'. Another woman came out, her name was Kay. She was beautiful an' moved like a cat. Her young breasts strained at the old dress she wore an' she had long legs, they were something to think about.

Mister also said they were free men an' he an' Sue were legal married. Kay was Sue's sister an' lived with them.

I started to tie my horse but Kay was there an' took the reins. I thanked her an' she gave me a nod an' flashed a slow smile that would make any man think of things.

The men an' I walked out to the garden. It was bein' turned with a shovel an' it was a big garden, about two acres. I asked about the horses or mules to plow it with. Bo said there was a plow an' harness but no horses. They had been doin' it by hand for five years.

I asked to see the barn an' we walked there. I looked it over, the barn was in good shape but looked bare like all empty barns. The pig pens were also empty as were the corn cribs. I looked back at a ten acre field that was unplowed.

I walked back to the house with the men an' we sat on Mister's porch. Kay was brushin' the gray horse with a hand-full of grass. Sue brought cups of water an' we sat there sippin' it.

"Would you men like to work an' have stock here?" I asked. They both said, "Yes," they'd love to have stock an' "Yes" they'd work hard for me.

"Not for me but for us, I'm goin' back to the house an' have breakfast. You make up a list of what you need an' come up there in an hour or so. Do you have stoves in your houses?" I asked. They both said, "No."

"Mister, may I look in your house?" I asked.

"Yes sir, Mr Chase, it's clean."

We went in an' it was clean but I lived in teepees an' caves that were better furnished. I thanked Sue an' told her she would have a stove when the sun went down. "Is your house like this?" I asked Bo. He nodded his head.

"Do we have a wagon?" I asked.

"We did but it wasn't too good."

"Meet me at the house in awhile," I said.

I had more coffee with Mary an' told her I was goin' in to town an' go through the warehouse we had gotten' from Lestergood. Also I told her of the poor conditions of the families an' that I was goin' to get them a milk cow.

I met Slim on the way to town. He was comin' along to show me the team that he'd just bought. I bought them from him an' we went back an' harnessed them up an' hooked up the old wagon. Mister, Bo an' I went to the old warehouse. We took Letty an' Sue along. Kay stayed home to watch the children.

Slim said he could find another team an' wagon. I told him to "find some milk cows that were fresh." He said he knew where there was one for sale.

"Look around for some hogs, a couple sows, a couple to butcher, Slim, anything they can use." He rode away smilin', he liked to trade.

We opened up the warehouse, it was a store also. I told the women to get what ever they needed. They just looked at me. Never in their wildest dreams had they ever thought of goin' into a store an gettin' what they needed.

Bo an' Mister went into the back with me. We found stoves, sat them out. "Wait," I said an' opened the big doors. "Bring the wagon in here." Bo did. We loaded the stoves an' stove pipe, tables, chairs. I found beds with mattresses, blankets, two rugs, the wagon was full, to overflowin'. Just as it pulled out a young black man came with another team an' wagon. I gave him a dollar an' he went away whistlin'.

We pulled this wagon into the warehouse an' filled it. The two women stood an' looked in wonder at all the stuff. I looked at them an' laughed. They had a fryin' pan, a couple new cups apiece an' each had a ladle. I put my arms around each woman an' walked them back into the store part, took them to the clothes rack, held up dresses to them. "Now ladies I want each of you to pick three dresses to take home an' one to wear now." They just looked at me. "Also get four for Kay. Then clothes for your men an' children."

It took three trips with the wagons. The women went home with the second load an' Kay came back, her dresses had been too small. She asked if she could change them. "Of course girl." I said. "Help yourself!" She gave me that smile an' went to the dress rack.

While they had been loadin' I had Kay in her new dress. It fit like a glove. "Walk across the street with me to a grocery store, get anything they need for food." She looked at me an' said, "Anything." I nodded. She got a pound of candy for the kids first then beans, peas, coffee, sugar, she looked at me when she had two scoops of sugar. I nodded so she put two more in another bag. Salt, flour, cornmeal, she looked at me again, I nodded. She was gettin' two of everything, cheese an' finished up with tea. I added four of whiskey an' five of soda-pop.

At first the grocery couple had been cold towards me but when he learned she was buyin' for two families that worked for me they warmed right up a little. By the time we finished the woman was helpin' Kay an' the man was talkin' a blue streak.

I walked across the street an' closed up the warehouse an' store. I had Bo an' Mister pull the wagons over to the store an' start loadin' the food into them. I went to the woman an' told her that I wanted "six bars of white soap, three bottles of perfume an' some towels, twelve of them."

She jumped right to it. I told her to "put these in a separate bag."

When I paid the bill the man was smilin'. I got the men each a shotgun an' box of shells. "Now sir," I said, "I'm goin' to leave a hundred dollars on an' account here. If they need anything you let them have it on there mark." I had Bo an' Mister each make W.C. an' then their initials behind it, after I showed them how. If it went over I'd have, someone come in each month an' keep it paid.

I got them started home an' swung into the Fairchild Inn. The place was packed. I had trouble findin' a place to tie my horse. When I walked in Fairchild found a table an' brought him an' I a drink an' joined me.

When we got seated he started right in on me. "Damn you Will Chase, I use to run a nice quiet place here, you come along an' start trouble, one shot is fired, the newspapers hear of it an' now my nice quiet place is shot to hell." He laughed an' said, "I love it."

We talked of Felter a little. I told him the story of how I had blocked him from goin' through the Gap an' then rode like hell to beat him by half a day an' more to the fort.

Fairchild laughed an' so did the other people who had listened. I finished my drink an' started to leave. Fairchild stopped me an' said, "Watch out, Archie Tompson has been talkin' big." I thanked him an' went home.

Tye took my horse an' had an extra big smile. "Mr Chase, Mr Slim is waitin' for you."

Slim an' Mary were in the parlor. Mary kissed me an' handed me my drink, asked how the day was goin'. "Fine," I said. "We been to the warehouse in town. Did you know these people who work for us didn't even have stoves?"

"I seen some go there today," she said with a smile, "Good old Will," she laughed an' gave me a hug. "I gave the people an extra ten apiece as you told Edward they were to have, put an extra hundred in the kitty for the house. If you have a warehouse full maybe you can bring some clothes for the outside men. I sent a message to a tailor Mrs Fairchild suggested for the help here at the house."

Slim started tellin' me about the stock he had bought for me, eight hogs, ten cows, four of them milked, two were already fresh. One bull, a herford, two teams, two sets of harness, two wagons, one mower an' a rake. Four ridin' horses. Two were broke to work to the carriage he had gotten.

"There was a auction at a farm today," he said. "It's only one farm away from mine so I bought it also. Lets go look at the stuff," he said. He was excited, "Do you know my workers don't have much either?"

It was beautiful out, evenin' was comin' an' the birds were gettin' in their song before the sun set. We walked to the barn an' looked at the horses. Tye an' Broom were proud as hell to have horses in the barn. Their white teeth shinin' in their black faces.

We brought over a half a load of corn an' some oats for the horses. "We can get more moved tomarrow. I got a lot with the place," Slim said.

We walked down to the house of Bo's an' Mister's. There were hogs in the pens an' horses an' cows in the barn. Everyone was at Mister's so we walked over there. A wagon was by the house an' I seen my two bags in it, also the shot guns an' shells. Slim an' I picked it all up an' walked up on the porch.

I called "Ho" to the house, an' everyone came tumblin' out. The kids eatin' a stick of candy. Sue took my hand an' led me into the house. It looked good now, everything had a place an' the cupboard was full. She kept my hand an' showed me the bedroom an' then Kay's room, then the childrens'.

She kept squeezin' my hand. I looked at her in her new dress, she looked good. When I looked at her face big tears were rollin' down her cheeks. She just grabbed me an' gave me a big hug.

Slim was lookin' Kay over an' she was likin' it as Sue an' I came out. I dug into the sack an' gave the ladies the towels, then the good smellin' soap an' then each a bottle of perfume. Each man I gave a double barrelled shotgun an' a box of shells. The women went into the house an' put their towels an' stuff away. Letty took hers home.

After they were gone us men talked of the quail that were on the place an' up in the woods. Bo said, "Sometimes there are turkeys up there too."

I opened a bottle an' had a drink, handed it to Slim. He had one an' gave it to Bo. He looked at me, I smiled an' he drank an' passed it to Mister, he drank an' passed it to me. I drank again an' sat the bottle on the porch between us. They had never drank with a white man before, lookin' at each other an' then back to Slim an' I.

We talked of plowin' an' plantin'. How soon I wanted them to butcher hogs. "That's up to you men, butcher an' cure one tomarrow if you like. Is there a grinder at the big house?" I asked. They both nodded.

"We need the garden planted first. Get the seeds at the store, keep the big house supplied with vegetables, yourself, an' sell the rest, the money is yours."

All three women came back about then. All smellin' of perfume.

We men had another drink, then Mister had Sue bring some glasses. She came back an' I poured each woman a glass, had another drink an' passed it around. Each woman sat by her man an' sipped their drinks.

"Is everything alright with you women, do you have everything you need?"

"Oh yes," they said. They'd never had so much. I reached in my pocket an' pulled out some money.

"How much wages do you get?" I asked.

Mister an' Bo looked at each other an' at me, then at their wives. Mister said, "Mr Will we get to live here, you have bought us food an' all those things, tools to work with, this is more than we ever had before. Sometimes we work for others they pay us twenty-five cents a day."

"Now you work for me all the time, you are also workin' for yourself now. Half the hogs an' cows are yours an' half are mine. It'll give you ten dollars a month each if that's okay with you. You keep the place like it is, clean an' nice. I'll gave each man twenty an' each woman ten, next month the men each get ten an' the women each five. Kay ten if she helps in the garden an' with the chores.

"If Mary needs help up in the house she can help there also. Okay?"

They nodded their heads. I opened another bottle an' we all had a drink. We sat an' talked of the old times when their fathers were slaves.

I told them where I lived in the West, of our fights with the soldiers, how I was here to talk with the President of the United States.

They couldn't believe he had sent for me to talk with me but never doubted what I said, just that they had never heard of the Sioux Indians, There were Indians here but they didn't fight the whites.

It was nearly dark an' Slim said he needed to "head down the road." Everyone stood up, Kay reached an' took my arm, gave it a squeeze. We walked to the big house.

Slim said, "That's what I'm goin' to do tomarrow. Will, can I buy the stuff from you?"

"Hell Slim you can have it, don't you remember you an' Hank, Swan were in on the deal too."

"Yea Will, but you are the one who made it work. Hank an' I'd still be in the big country. I'd still be holed up in that draw or dead if not for you."

"What do you think of these people Slim, will they stay an' work?"

"Till hell freezes over Will, an' that Kay, damn I'll bet a man better take his lunch when he starts lovin' her."

CHAPTER EIGHTEEN

I Need to Fight

Slim spent the night with us, after eatin' he, Mary an' I sat on the porch an' had brandy. We talked of what was to come. Mary said we were havin' dinner with Mr Humes the next evenin'. He was goin' back to Kansas City the followin' day.

"Are you goin' back West with us Slim?" I asked.

After awhile he said, "No, guess not this year. There's goin' to be a hell of a lot of trouble. You'll go back to the Gap an' fight all summer an' fall. The boy Chester can run the ranch. He can get supplies from Lee an' he has Goodhorse. I know you left him plenty of money an' word with Lee to get him all he needs.

"Hank is stayin' in Kansas City, he don't need me. Why don't you stay here Will, you're a rich man now?"

Mary said, "I'm stayin' here Will."

This gave me a start, I'd not thought about her not goin' back to Laramie with me. I sat awhile thinkin' how good it would be to stay here. I could run the warehouse an' trade, this was a nice place.

"I must go back," I said.

We all sat still an' sipped our drink.

"Why?" Slim asked.

"The people need me," I said.

"And Swan?" Mary said.

"She is part of the people an' they need me more this year."

Was I imaginin' it or was there someone out there movin' towards the house. Here we sat like settin' ducks. I had my knife but Slim an' I had both left our guns inside.

"Mary," I said very quietly, "Go into the house an' get our guns an' bring out the bottle of whiskey. Give us each our gun an' pour our drink. Go back into the house after pourin'. Do it when I say." Slim had heard me.

Raisin' my voice I said, "Mary, I'm out of whiskey."

She stood an said. "I'll get more," an' she was gone. She came right back an' for a second I thought she'd not brought the guns. She poured Slims first an' I saw his gun dropped into his lap, then mine was in my lap an' my glass full. "There's one behind the bush by the edge of the porch," she said, turned an' went into the house.

"Say Slim, remember the time I shot that turkey hidin' in the bushes. We each have one this time, yours out a ways, mine is close."

I whirled an' fired three times. I heard Slim shootin' as I vaulted over the rail into the bushes. I landed on a man an' crushed him to the ground. He shot twice before my gun clubbed him senseless.

I looked an' Slim was gone from the porch. I heard him cussin' out in the yard. He came back draggin' a man by the hair.

I stuck my pistol in my belt an' throwed the turkey on the porch, drug him around to the porch steps where Slim had his flat on the ground.

Tye an' Broom came from their houses at the back of the big house. They looked at the men on the ground. Mary came out with a lamp. I heard Bo an' Mister comin' up the road from their houses. Kay got there first, she had a butcher knife in her hand. Slim looked at her an' said, "That one will do."

Bo an' Mister had their new shotguns in their hands. Slim had shot his stranger clear through the right shoulder.

He wasn't bleedin' too bad but he was cussin' us.

"Where are your horses?" I asked.

"Go to hell!" was his answer.

I pulled out my knife an' cut off his ear. He sounded like a pig squealin'. I grabbed his other ear, "Where are the horses?"

"Down the lane at the end," he said. He was very polite.

"Anybody with them?" I asked.

"No sir," he said.

"Would a couple of you men go get them?" I asked, as I looked around all the people were starin' at me. Tye an' Broom left for them. I shook the other man an' he sat up, looked at me then at everyone else.

"Can you see your friend over there?"

He looked around an' said "Yes."

"Did you notice he only has one ear?" He looked again, fear came to his face. "I asked him a question an' he didn't give the right answer, he did the second time. Now who sent you?"

"I can't tell," he said.

I cut off his ear but got some scalp with it. I grabbed the other ear, "Archie Tompson!" he yelled.

We put them on their horses an' sent them home. The black people were lookin' at me an' then the ears.

Kay was breathin' heavily, her breasts risin' an' fallin'. She was lookin' at me with an' expression on her face just like Swan got. She was excited by the action. A faint smile on her face.

Mary had sat the lamp down an' went into the house. I walked up on the steps an' got my drink an' finished it. Mary was standin there in the door. She looked at me blankly. "Will Chase, you're a savage, them poor men have to go through life with one ear."

"If they had their way I'd be dead, now bring out a bottle." She then turned around an' went back in. I poured whiskey on my hands an' washed them, a little more an' washed them again, then had a drink an' passed the bottle to Slim, he drank an' passed it on.

"You better go talk to her Will."

"She's not ready now," I said, "It'll just end in a fight. I'll talk to her in the mornin'."

Slim handed me the bottle an' I drank again. He went into the house. Tye an' Broom went around to their houses. I walked to Bo an' Mister's house with them. Kay walked beside me.

We sat on Mister's porch. Sue came an' sat also. "Fellows, in a week or so I'm goin' to have to go back to my people an' fight the soldiers. No matter what I tell the president he can't stop the fightin' that will come this year. Maybe it has already started. As you seen tonight there are people here that would have me killed. I should have killed these two tonight, but by markin' them others may not come.

"Mary is stayin' here for the summer an' I ask you to watch out for her. You don't have to guard her but just kinda watch. Slim is stayin' also. He will watch also.

"Sue is there a drink left?" She jumped up an' got the bottle from the house. I had two long drinks an' then passed it on. Kay was by my side so she was next. It made the rounds an' came back to me. I finished it an' sat it down. Sue went an' got another.

"I would like to stay here but I can't, my people need me. Swan needs me. I need to fight, I like it."

I had another drink an' passed the bottle. "I'll see you good people in the mornin'." I walked up the road slowly. I heard her comin' but walked on. When she touched my hand I stopped an' turned to her. She came into my arms an' we kissed. She had the same wild passion that Swan had. Her arms went around my neck an' the kiss lasted a long time. When we parted her hands went to my belt but I stopped her.

I took her hands in mine an' held them. She looked up at me in the dark. I kissed her again more gently this time still holdin' her hands. I took both hers in one of mine an' touched her breasts with the other. They were firm an' the nipples hard. I kissed her cheek an' said "Thank you Kay, when I come back next winter." I walked back to the house, the lamp was gone from the porch.

When I crawled into bed with Mary she asked, "Was she good?"

I put my arm around her an' pulled her to me, "I wouldn't know," I said. Mary came into my arms then an' gave me what I needed.

In the mornin' on the way to the barn I picked up the ears an' walked to the fence, throwed them into the pasture. The men brought our horses to us an' Slim an' I told them to bring both wagons to the warehouse as yesterday. I gave Slim the keys an' rode on to the Browns, to see Chester.

I had coffee with them an' told Chester an' Veldon of the night before.

"Hot damn Will, do you have to cut their ears off! If this keeps up people are goin' to get upset with you."

"At this time I don't really care, they quit comin', I'll quit cuttin' ears off."

Chester said I could "talk with the Senate today, this mornin' an' the Congress this afternoon."

Good, then the president, an' I can go home."

I answered questions for the Senate an' we quit for lunch. They wanted to talk more the next day.

After lunch I talked with the members of Congress. They asked many questions of my action in the West against the army.

"Mr. Fairchild if someone came to your house an' tried to take your wife would you fight?"

He said "Yes."

I turned to another man, "Sir are you married?"

He said, "Yes."

"Do you have small children?"

Again he said, "Yes."

"And the men killed you an' raped your wife, then burned down your house, left the children to starve in the hills, would you not expect some of your relations to go find the children an' save your wife?"

He said, "Yes," he would expect this to happen.

"They have done all this an' keep tryin'. We fed the trappers an' furnished horses for the soldiers, helped white women who the Pawnee had taken, gave back all the horses to the army that was not ours an' had any marks. What do we get? More soldiers even after right here you told me the Settlers Act was dead for two years. By the time I got home there were soldiers there. I sent them away an' they came back with surveyors an' more soldiers.

"They chased, an' killed us, we killed back an' let them live again. Let them walk home. Now there is to be a great number the fifh of May. You have great piles of supplies at Scottsbluff. You have scouts up in our country actin' as trappers, I know all of this for the General who shot me told me these things. He was angry over a horse race."

I stopped an' calmed down. "I'm sorry gettin' carried away but what I say is true. You send good men led by fools, they let their hatred rule their judgement. I am done now, do you have any more questions?"

An older man with white hair said, "Yes. Mr. Chase, is there gold?"

"Sir, there is gold in most streams if you know where to look."

"Could you find gold in the stream that was sold to the man Felter?"

"I'm not sure, it has been worked out mighty well hasn't it?"

"Yes, it has Mr Chase. Do you have any gold with you now?"

"No sir."

Mr Chase if you can come in here with gold by this time tomorrow all the doubt about that land sale last year could be cleared up an' I'm sure your case would be very strong with the rest of the Congress."

"Very well sir but who owns that property?"

He looked around very embarrassed, "I do," he said.

"Well sir but how much land is there in your name?"

"Twelve hundred acres," he said.

"Is it the piece of land the first gold was found on? If you'll put the land up for twenty dollars an' acre right now I'll buy it for twenty four thousand dollars whether I find gold on it or not."

Now he was sure there wasn't any gold in that stream but just in case there was that wasn't enough money for it. He was thinkin' of what it would be worth if I did find gold.

"If you do find gold will you sell it back to me? At what price?"

"Sir, if I find gold you can have it back for thirty-six thousand."

All the Congressmen were on the edge of their seats. Greed had him again. His mind was sayin', that was a big profit for me, but damn.

"Okay," he said, "It's a deal. If you find gold I'll sure give you twelve thousand profit on the land."

"Gentlemen, I must go an' change clothes an' get a few things. What time is it now?"

Mr Fairchild looked at his watch an' said "Four twenty-five. If you're back here at four thirty tomorrow that will be fine." He asked the other if that was "Okay."

They all said, "I'll give two-to-one odds on Chase."

I asked, "One more thing, I want the man Slim Turner to go with me so he can show me where he found the big nugget. That way I have an idea where to start. This is not too much to ask I hope, I have never been there an' he has."

They all agreed, "Another thing gentlemen, who's goin' with me?" There was ten or fifteen men who volunteered. "I need two men to go with me while I change an' two to go get Mister Turner."

I seen Lucy Morgan leavin' an' knew the paper would have a story tomarrow.

We all left the hall an' two men sent messenger boys to get them other clothes, food an' blankets. We arrived at my house an' Mary was on the porch. I explained what was goin' on. "These men are goin' upstairs with me, would you put together a bit of food for us, plenty of whiskey an' a couple blankets."

The men came upstairs with me. I pulled off my coat an' shirt, got out my buckskins. Both men were starin' at my upper body. It was scarred an' muscular. The hole in my left shoulder was about healed. The one in my left side was still quite fresh lookin'. I turned to them an' said,"It's a hard world out there men."

I slipped out of my pants an' drew on my tight buckskins, then the huntin' shirt with the fringe an' beads. It was beautiful an' felt good on my skin. Next came the knee high beaded moccasins an' the head band. I looked in the mirror an' straitened out my long hair. Buckled on my pistol an' knife. Came out with the derringer, checked it's load an' put it in my moccasin.

I picket up my shoulder bag, dumped it on the bed so they could see what it contained. Matches, steel an' flint, a small knife with a two inch curved blade. I was ready.

We went back downstairs into the parlor. Mary had us whiskey poured an' we drank. I went to the buffet an' opened a drawer, pulled out my big watch, holdin' the nugget in my hand I showed it to them an' dropped it into my bag. This large nugget I had found when Swan an' I were camped high in the hills, when I bent to wash a fryin' pan. This nugget was finally goin' to help the Indians.

Mary said she had Tye get my pick, shovel an' gold pan from the barn an' the bedroll was by the door.

We had another drink when Slim came ridin' in with his two men an' war bag. He was leadin' War Horse an' a pack horse. Slim was wearin' his buckskins also. I picked up everything an' loaded it. We smiled at each other an' rode away. I waved at Mary as we left at a lope. My rifle hangin' by it's thong from my saddle horn.

Lucy an' a hundred people were at the creek when we got there. It was only a couple hours before sundown. Lucy had three pictures taken of us in our western outfits. Two other papers took our pictures also. They wanted an' interview but we didn't have time.

The place was a mess, it had been dug, blasted, shoveled an' the stream had been changed in many places. Slim led us up about a mile, looked around, pointed at a large dead tree an' nodded. It sure looked different he said.

We unpacked an' picketed the horse. Slim took his pan, went to the stream an' started to work. He worked his way up stream. I set up camp. Everyone was watchin' him. He would dig a pan of gravel an' rock an' slowly swirl it around, back an' forth, then go through what he had left, then do it again.

I never went near the stream except to get a coffee pot an' stew pot of water. I put the coffee in the coffee pot an' set it on the fire. Then set the stew pot on an' dropped some meat an' beans in it.

I then walked the rocks lookin'. I got behind a big rock an' picked with the big clumsy pick, came around an' looked again an' went back behind it an' picked again. I brought out the watch an' smashed the nugget off the chain. It broke loose in three different pieces. I ground out the drill holes on a rock in the two that had them, dropped all three back into my bag an' walked back to the fire.

Lucy an' about fifteen men were still there. It was nearly dark an' Slim was comin' from the stream. I poured him an' I coffee an' put a couple sticks into the fire. As he sat down by the fire I handed him a bottle. He drank as I did. He asked how much gold we got to find. Everyone was listening. "They didn't say Slim, you have any luck?"

He opened his hand, there were three small nuggets an' a few flakes. We nearly got trampled by the reporters as they crowded in to see. Half of them went stumblin' down the stream to spread the word. Finally all were gone but Lucy an' the four men who were sent to watch us.

We drank some more from the bottle, got to feelin' good. The moon came up full an' the valley turned bright an' beautiful. We drank some more. I gave the young Congressman the rest of the bottle an' got out another. Lucy asked if she could have some coffee. I poured her half a cup an' laced it good with whiskey. She smiled warmly an' drank about half of it.

Slim an' I started talkin' of all the campfires we had sat around. He told of a time in Texas when he had went four days without food or a fire.

Some Apaches had him holed up. They knew he was there but couldn't find him. All the time he had been in a hole within a hundred yards above them. We drank again an' he went on. They cooked a whole beef right below him an' he could smell it. He said he'd got so weak he couldn't hardly crawl out of the hole.

The Congressmen moved close to the fire an' were lookin' at the stew pot. I offered them coffee, they had some. Lucy got another half cup of coffee an' I filled it the rest of the way with whiskey. She moved closer.

One of them asked if the stew was "about done."

I said, "I reckon, let me add some more water an' cook it a bit more. You boys been livin' too close to your table." They all laughed an' when I didn't do anything to the stew they looked at me then back to the stew.

"Do you men know why the cavalry can't beat the Indians?"

They all said "No."

"You're feelin' it right now, hunger. An Indian can eat a few bites every other day an' keep goin'. The soldiers have to rest every other night an' eat twice a day."

I drank an' passed the bottle around again, had my drink an' poured all the coffee into their cups. I went to the stream, washed out the pot, came back, added water to the stew, stired it an' put more wood on the fire.

We talked of many times an' many fires. "Well Slim, too bad you 'ain't goin' back this year. I'll get drunk with Hank for you before I go on."

He laughed an' said, "I guess you'll have to stop an' check out things at the War Horse. Mary will set here all summer an' think about Carol an' Swan.

"You be sure an' tell that tough gal I send her the best. She's the toughest I ever seen."

"Well Congressmen, finish your coffee an' put some stew in your stomachs." I lit a cigar an' walked away from the fire.

Settin' on a rock, I heard Lucy comin'. She stopped in front of me. The moon was lightin' up her face. She pulled me to my feet an' said, "Kiss me." I took her in my arms an' when I finished kissin' her she sagged at the knees. I had to hold her up. "Let's go further away," she said. She was breathin' hard.

I could hear Slim tellin' another story. They looked good settin' at the fire. "No Lucy, not while I'm here with Mary. She ain't goin' back West with me an' will probably find someone else while I'm gone."

"Will you find someone else?"

"I have Swan out West."

"What about Kansas City?"

"Carol is there."

"Damn you Will Chase, when!"

"We have four days an' four nights on the train." We walked back to the fire.

They had saved a cup of stew. I poured it into a cup for Lucy. She gulped it down an' went to bed.

Slim an' I were workin' the stream when everyone got up. I had the three nuggets an' a quarter ounce of flakes. Slim had some small nuggets an' about the same in flakes as I had.

We went to the fire an' had coffee. The Congressmen looked like hell. Lucy didn't look all that good either. "Will, do you have enough gold to satisfy the Congressmen?"

"I'm sure we do, so if you folks will drink your coffee, we can go back to town."

As we were ridin' back towards the road we passed eleven men pannin' for gold. We rode to the hotel for breakfast. After we ordered Slim asked for a plate, when it came he pulled out his bag an' emptied it into the plate. I did the same. There was probably an ounce or a little more. It sat in the middle of the table. Lucy looked at Slim an' I. I shrugged my shoulders an' nodded at the men. They watched me all the way from naked until now. Slim said, "The same here."

She left with out eatin'. Many people looked at the gold. The Congressmen confirmed it had come from the stream.

We put the gold back into one bag an' gave it to the Congressmen .

Slim said his people had been happy as hell with their stuff but he had better go see how things were goin'. I thanked him an' said, I'd stop by in the evenin' for the gray. Last night had almost changed his mind about stayin' here.

The Senate had heard of the gold deal with the Congress, that I'd found gold in the stream here. They voted on the Settlers Act an' voted it down. Lester Walters went to the Fairchild Inn with me an' we had lunch. He asked Mary an' I to dinner with he an' his wife that evenin'. I'd check with Mary an' sent a message right away. We were havin' a brandy when a messenger came to me an' handed me a telegram.

"Trouble At The Gap. Hurry, Henry."

I handed it to Lester an' paid the boy an' thanked him. He handed it back. "When will you leave?" he asked.

"Tomarrow, as soon as I see the president. Now if you'll excuse me I must go to Congress."

At the door I went back an' shook his hand, "Tell the boys good-by an' your wife also. Now Lester do you see why I fight. Here they say one thing, out there they do another."

The gold was the first thing for Congress. The four Congressmen were now cleaned up but looked tired. They told of watchin' Slim an' I change clothes, checkin' our bags an' everything. They were satisfied, the gold had came from the stream.

I asked if the man wanted his land back. He said yes an' wrote me a draft for twelve thousand dollars. I then asked to be heard an' got the floor. I pulled out the telegram an' read it to them. "Henry Long would not ride three hundred miles to send this to me if I was not needed. What you say here today cannot stop a bloody summer. This is the beginnin' of the end of the Sioux. They will never be the same again. All because of the greed of the white man.

"You have gold right here but because it must be worked for, everyone looks for gold in big boulders. I now ask for a vote, not that it can stop the soldiers but because I will have done all I can except die for my people."

They voted, the bill was killed again. I thanked them, told them all good-by. I was leavin' first thing in the mornin' after I talked with their president.

"If you would like to see War Horse look out the window."

I shook hands with Fairchild. He looked into my eyes an' said, "Good Luck Son."

CHAPTER NINETEEN

Mr. President

I stopped at Slim's an' got my gray horse. We had a drink an' shook hands. He looked at me a long time then said. "Ride slow." I steped up on the Appy an' sat lookin' at Slim, in two years we had rode a long way.

At his gate I looked back. He was still there an' I think he knew inside himself that I would never be the same. He never waved.

Mary was settin' on the porch waitin' for me. Tye an' Broom took the horses. They had smiles but were not the same. I took Mary in my arms an' held her a long time. I started to tell her, but she stopped me, "I know Will, I know."

We walked down to the two colored families' houses, some how they knew also. I shook hands with them all an' said, "I'll try an' be back."

We turned an' walked toward the house. Kay was standin' at the edge of the woods. She waved her hand. I waved back an' we went through the gate. At the house my rifle, bedroll an' duffle bag were by the door. I pulled off the moccasins, britches an' huntin' shirt, put them in the duffle bag. I walked into the parlor, got a bottle an' went up stairs.

After I had my pants an' boots on I sat on the bed an' had several drinks. I wrote out a paper sayin' in the event anything happened to me this place was Mary's, the War Horse saloon Carol's, the new ranch was Slim's an' if Slim was dead it went to Chester Marrow. The post to Lee Henderson, the Gap to Henry Long. All my money to Mary an' the Sioux Nation, fifty-fifty. The War Horse to Petey.

I read this an' then signed it, had a couple of drinks an' went downstairs. There were voices in the parlor as I walked in. Chester an' Loraine were there. I said, "Good evenin'," an' excused myself for not havin' a shirt on. I really didn't give a shit.

I handed the paper to Chester an' went back up stairs for my shirt an' coat. Comin' back Mary had a drink poured for me. When I finished makin' out a check to Chester or rather two checks, each for fifteen thousand. These I gave to Chester, also I handed the one from the Congressman to him, told him to put this in Mary's account.

I sat back an' we had our drinks. Chester pointed to the papers an' said, "You're actin' like your not comin' back."

"Chester, where I'm goin' who knows? If I'm alive I'll be back but when there's hundreds of bullets an' arrows in the air all the time who can tell? This is goin' to be a mighty tough summer. I have made many enemies, even here in Washington."

Mary got up an' poured more drinks. She looked beautiful in a light blue dress. It was molded to her luscious body. As she moved around the room I watched her an' wanted her.

"When are you leavin' Will? There are things we should talk over before you leave."

"Chester, just do what you think is right. I'll be behind all you do, if it's for the better of the Indians. Come West when you can, put out word to me up there if you need me."

Finally he couldn't stand it no longer. Chester jumped to his feet. "Will, is there gold in that stream?" He looked embarassed at the loudness of his voice. He was standin' there lookin' at me.

"Chester, they watched me dress an' looked at everything I took. The same as Slim. They were there when we came out of the stream with gold. I wouldn't invest money with anyone on it if I was you, an' damn sure don't put any of mine there."

We talked of many things an' then they left. Mary an' I sat together awhile in the parlor. Finally I said, "Mary I wish I could stay, it's so beautiful here. In awhile things would quiet down an' we could lead a normal life. For awhile it would be great, then without the danger and excitement it would turn to boredom an' soon I'd be like all the rest of the people back here, bored, unhappy to watch the world go by. The Sioux would lose their land a little sooner. People would forget I had ever been among them. I'd lose the want to look over the danger edge an' I'd just be another man goin' along waitin' to die. You'd grow tired of me settin' here on the porch waitin' for something to happen."

We were quiet for awhile an' then she said, "I know Will, I know. I'll be here when you come back."

I walked upstairs with my arm around her an' we made love like it had to last forever.

I rode to the Capitol buildin' on the War Horse. The gray carried everything I needed.

Funny thing was that all the wealth an' things I had in this world, it was all I needed or wanted right here on myself an' these two horses, three guns, my knife.

Mary an' I clung together for a final kiss, when I left. I knew I'd see her again but things would be different. I went past the Fairchild Inn an' had a glass of brandy with the big man. When I left he walked to the door with me. He said, "Tell the president 'Hi' for me," an' smiled.

I walked into the President's outer lobby, two soldiers stepped up beside me. "We must have your gun Mr. Chase." Damn this was just like Scottsbluff, was this a trap again? I looked back at the door. It was open but two more soldiers were out there. I'd give anything to have Swan here by my side. Should I hand over my gun?

"Mr. Chase, the President is waitin'." Captain Bush an' Lucy came into the room. Bush right away reckonized the situation. He unbuckled his gun an' laid it on a desk, made a motion with his hand to me. I again looked at the soldiers. They had backed away an' were standin' at attention. Captain Bush saluted them an' they moved to ease.

Bush waited as I unbuckled the belt an' laid it beside his. He looked at the gun an' knife, "Heard you been usin' that knife." I nodded my head. We shook hands. "I seen the horse out there," he said. "He's all an' more than I expected."

Lucy smiled at me then an' we walked into an' office an' sat down. Bush an' I talked awhile of how he liked the East.

He asked about different people out West an' seemed to miss it. The president came in then an' we stood up. Captain Bush saluted him an' stood at attention. "At ease Captain, please be seated," he said.

He came around his desk an' I stood, he put out his hand an' I shook it. The hand was strong, the hand shake honest. "Mr Chase, I have been lookin' forward to this meetin'. I have read so much about you an' heard more. Please he said, 'be seated.'" He pulled up a chair an' sat. We were in a circle.

"Tell me Mr Chase, how much gold is in the stream outside of town?" He had my bag in his hand an' shook out some into his palm.

"I'm not sure sir, but that much came out yesterday."

"Tell me how much gold is in the Black Hills?"

"I don't know sir. I'm sure there is gold there. The rocks an' streams are right."

"Why not open it up an' let the people find it?"

"Because they must kill another people to get it, they even kill each other."

He sat lookin at me for awhile, I was nervous as hell. Captain Bush was also but Lucy was busy writin'.

"What do you hope to gain by keepin' it all to yourself?"

"I don't want the gold sir. I just want the Indians to stay like they are, free an' happy."

"Yes," he said, "We are checkin' into the reservation situation an' find many of the things you say to be true. It does start here in Washington an' goes all the way down the line."

I added, "And ends with the Indians starvin' an' dyin' so some white man can buy better things for himself. What is money to the Indians, Sir? If you took it out there by the train loads they wouldn't want it. They can't sleep under it, eat it, shoot meat or cook it. They fight, Sir, not for wealth but for a way of livin'."

"How come you didn't kill all the soldiers you let walk home?"

"I though it better for them to live an' tell others the Indian was fair an' only wanted to be left alone."

He called out an' a soldier came into the room. I looked at Bush, he nodded, the president said, "Cigars an' brandy." The soldier had it for us immediatly. He killed his an' held out the glass an' said, "Now pour us a drink." I killed mine an' it was filled again.

"What are we goin to do with you Will Chase? You have made fools of us, defeated us, an' in general, raised hell here in Washington." I sat an' sipped my drink.

"I can appoint you over all the reservations in the United States, you can deal with the problems yourself."

"Will it stop the soldiers who are invadin' our lands?"

"No."

"Then I can't be of service to the reservations," I said.

"You could name your own price," he said.

"I'll take the job then."

"How much money do you want a year an' when can you start?"

"I want no money sir. My price is the total an' complete isolation of the Sioux Nation. Whites can't come on the land before they come before a tribal coucil."

He sat an' smiled. "Mr Chase, I can't do that."

"Then I can't see to the reservations."

"What are your plans then, Mr.Chase?"

"I'm leavin' today for my country."

"What will you do there?"

"First I'll ask the soldiers to stay out of the Sioux land."

"And if they come anyway?"

"We will fight sir."

"Like before, hit an' run, send them back walkin'?

"There is only one man who will get a chance to walk, but he won't. He'd not leave his men."

"Who would that be Mr Chase?"

"General Gray, he's at Scottsbluff."

A man came in an' said "Sir you are to speak to the Senate."

"Mr. Chase, can we talk tomarrow?"

"No sir I'm leavin' within the next couple hours."

"But are you packed an' everything, can't you wait a couple more days?"

"What I need is on my horse, Sir." I pulled out the telegram an' handed it to him.

"Trouble at the Gap. Hurry, Henry."

"Your soldiers are already movin' Sir or gettin' ready to move. It was goin' to happen May fifth but must have been moved up. I'm needed back there."

He shook my hand an' said, "We will talk again Mr. Chase. In Denver when you come out this fall for the big meetin' with all the tribes an' bring your great gifts of beads an' trader knives."

"No Mr. President, you will not come an' if you did the Sioux will not be there anyway.

"They don't need beads an' they already have good knives, not the trader's junk. They have repeatin' rifles, gattlin' guns an' in a month will have cannons an' powder. They have dynamite, know how best to us it, ask about The Battle of the Fort, ask General Shellman.

"No Mr. President, what you allow to happen for greed will cause you much grief. Cost many lives. We will lose in the end but you will not win. For a hundred years from now you whites will still be fightin' for the Black Hills."

I turned an' walked out then. In the outer office I put my gun back on an' checked the loads in it, walked out to the horses. I stepped on an' rode down the street. I looked up at his window. He was standin' there watchin' me. I waved an' he waved back.

When I got to the depot my box car was waitin'. I put my saddle an' packs aboard. There was hay an' grain, two large barrels of water.

I kept two shirts, another suit, my razor, two bottles of whiskey an' two decks of cards in the smaller bag. Some day I would learn to play poker like everyone else did. Dice had been easy for me. I'd rolled bones with the Indians all my life.

I turned the horses loose in the corral so they could roll an' move around before the long ride.

I walked up on the depot platform an' sat on the bench lookin' at the new leaves an' all the green on the distant hills. This was nice country.

My mind turned to the Gap. There would still be snow there at this time of year but if it was an early spring there would be a little grass tryin' to sprout.

It was gettin' time for the train to come in, well maybe I was just in a hurry to be on the move. I saw Felter at the corral before it came to me that he was there. He an' another man were facin' me, they had tied their horses an' were comin' my way.

"Will Chase, you have ruined me for the last time," he said. "That deal at Fairchilds should have ended it. Then you find more gold after I had spent all my money an' sold the land. Damn you! You bought it back, showed them more gold an' sold it again. Damn you, Will Chase, your luck has run out."

He was workin' himself up to kill me. He wanted to, so bad. The man with him was ready but Felter was stallin'. What did he have that I couldn't see?

I heard a boot scrape behind me then. The ticket man was lookin' out his window past me. Someone was back there, was it another passenger or another gun!

I drew an' shot the hired gun. He was fast an' had his gun out, as I shot I dived. Right at the same time there was the roar of a shotgun, the shots whistled passed. I turned as I dived at the plank floor. Archie was bringin' the shotgun to line on me. I shot him twice, the other barrel went off an' hit the planks at my feet. Archie spun around an' went down. Some of the BBs hit the calf of my leg. Felter was shootin' now an' wood splinters were flyin'.

I was still rollin' but couldn't get a shot at Felter. He had fired four times so far. When I rolled away from him I couldn't shoot, I was either on my back or on my shootin arm.

I came to my knees an' a bullet hit my head above the ear, knockin' me down again. His next shot I don't know where it went. I was back on my knees, I shot him in the belly. He staggered backwards an' dropped his gun. I came to my feet, he was holdin' his stomack with the other hand stuck out in front of him. I shot him again, the bullet went through his hand an' hit him in the face, takin' away one side of it.

I walked toward him hatin' everything he stood for. He dropped to his knees an' put out his hand again. He tried to speak, to beg, to plead for mercy, there was none in me.

I heard horses comin' as I shot him again in the head. It flipped him over backwards. My head was buzzin' but my hands were reloadin' the gun. I was stuffin' in the third shell when I heard voices yell, "Drop it." I looked up into the faces of many soldiers, all had their guns on me.

Lucy was runnin' down the platform, flung her arms around my neck an' put her back to the guns. I stuck the pistol between us into it's holster, went to the bench an' sat down. My head was about to explode.

Things got confusin', someone was wipin' my face. When I looked up it was into the face of the President of the United States.

"Are you feelin' well enough to talk?" he asked.

"Yes Sir."

"You are a brave man Will Chase, as well as tough. The soldiers will catch hell when you get to the Gap. I just want you to know Mr Chase I'll do everything I can to stop the soldiers from movin' on you, I'll sign the stoppin' of the Settlers Act, stop them from movin' up onto your Sioux land."

"Lucy," I said, "Get some whiskey out of that bag there an' put it on my head." She did, it burned like hell. The President sat down beside of me. I had a long drink an' handed him the bottle, "Sorry I don't have a glass Sir."

"Well son, we're out West," he said an' drank. Handed back the bottle. I poured more on my head an' drank again.

The train was pullin' in. I looked up an' there was stood Mary. I looked into her beautiful eyes, pushed my hair back, an' said, "Hell of a mess to look at ain't I!"

She raised her dress, ripped up some pettycoat an' wrapped my head up tight.

They were hookin' up the boxcar, the horses were loaded. I stood an' shook the President's hand, kissed Mary an' held her tight. I turned an' walked to the edge of the platform, slid open the door, set my bag in, came back an' got my bottle. I looked the President in the eye an' said, "I hope you hurry."

I kissed Mary again, walked into the boxcar an' shut the door. Both horses came to me. I petted their necks an' looked out the crack in the boxcar. The train started an' I laid down in the hay.

The President turned to Mary an' said, "I hope he makes it."

She looked at him an' said, "He'll be back, there will be a lot of dyin' first."